"CAMILLE, DON'T BE MAD AT ME. YOU DON'T UNDERSTAND."

"Did you already know that shit was gonna happen?" I shouted, crossing my arms.

Peaches looked like every ounce of her soul was drying up. I saw her shudder, and then clench and unclench her fists.

She stared at the floor for a long time, and then she looked up. "Camille, I'm here to convince you to stay and work for Nut."

"What?" I asked, shocked. "What you mean? What kind of chick are you? I swear I thought more of you than that . . . all this time, I had no idea." Here I was thinking she was in night school, and really and truly, she was out tricking.

"You think you better than me, Camille? You used up. Just like me," she yelled. "Bitch, you been f—ing for money. Don't get it twisted!"

I took a step back.

"Yeah, you was f—ing Chu for money. For clothes, for nice dinners, for jewelry and for whatever else he was doing for you! So what's the big difference? You need to wake up, sweetie!"

DAMAGED

a novel

KIA DuPREE

GRAND CENTRAL
PUBLISHING

NEW YORK BOSTON

This book is a work of fiction. Names, characters, places, and incidents are the product of the author's imagination or are used fictitiously. Any resemblance to actual events, locales, or persons, living or dead, is coincidental.

Grand Central Publishing
Hachette Book Group
237 Park Avenue
New York, NY 10017

Printed in the United States of America

Grand Central Publishing is a division of Hachette Book Group, Inc.
The Grand Central Publishing name and logo is a trademark of
Hachette Book Group, Inc.

ISBN-13: 978-1-61523-957-3

To my sister DeAnna Dawkins.
Keep making me proud of you, and don't ever give up on your dreams,
despite the many obstacles
that come your way.

ACKNOWLEDGMENTS

The road has been long, but oh, so worth it. Without the encouragement, love, and support of my mother, Cynthia Dawkins, and my father, John Dupree, none of this would have been possible. I have to thank my brothers, John Antwan, Jonathan, Douglas, Doug, Michael, and Timothy, and my sisters, DeAnna and Janai. For my family and friends, like my aunt Angel Abraham, Earl Milligan, and Melvina Buchanan-Jones, who sold my self-published novel, *Robbing Peter,* out the back of their trunks or store shops. My constant support team: my best friend, Sherry Oden (definitely for a place to stay and all our shared secrets), my college roomie, Wilfrance Lominy (who stayed on me to finish), and my Brooklyn ace Dionne Victor (thanks for your early critiques); Nikoshia Williams (for always being positive when I'm not) and your mom, Patricia Smith (for that bug you put in my ear years ago—thanks for sharing); Darlene Backstrom (for everything you do for me). Thanks also to my mentor Victoria L. Jones and Yuri Milligan, Towanna Sebrell, Sarita Scott, Tomeka Winborne, Ivan Shaun Gholston, Shonda Buchanan, Ronald Cope, Aaron

Lomax, Gladys Smiley-Bell, Angela Gray, Jerome Davis, Verna Shamblee, Michelle Richter, Liz Curione, Lisa Goris, Khia Jackson, Sanura Weathers, Julie Ritchie, Chris Sanders, Chris Brown, Wesley Peterson, Paul Saunders, and the Fuzz Band. Thanks to my peeps, Ashura Kenji, Aisha, Yani, and Darlene. Thanks to all of my sister friends from Hampton University: Natalie Graham, Anne P. Land, Ivy Carter, Kisha Roy Reaves, Marneisha Freeland, Lynnea Cornish, and Christina McDowelle.

Thank you so much to my agent, Victoria Sanders, for not giving up on me, and to her staff, Benee Knauer and Chris Kepner. I'd like to also say thanks to my editor, Karen Thomas, for believing in this novel, her assistant, Latoya Smith, for all you do, and to all the good people at Grand Central Publishing. I have to also give a big thank-you to Monique Patterson for teaching me some of the most important secrets to writing and the book business.

And last, thank you to my husband, Donnell Joppy, for listening to me read every single line of this book over the phone, for dancing with me in the middle of the grocery store aisle just because, and for our beautiful son, Izaiah.

DAMAGED

LIKE DOG SHIT

ON A FRESH BED OF SNOW,

BEAUTY CAN BE RUINED

SIMPLY FOR THE NEED TO SURVIVE.

WASHINGTON, D.C.

JUNE 2007

In walk these dudes wearing raggedy wife-beaters, and all three of them got dark yellow sweat stains underneath their armpits, looking dusty and hot like they just got off from working construction all day. The little one keeps scratching his neck and licking his lips like he dehydrated. He can't take his eyes off me. I swear I can smell the bullshit before he even thinks about cracking open his mouth.

No, not today. I'm just here to get this money Tep wired me and I'm walking right out the door. I cross my arms and rock on one heel just to let him know he better not even try it.

"Damn, Ma," the little one says as he steps closer. "You wearing the fuck outta dem jeans."

"No bull," says the one with the Redskins cap pulled low over his eyes.

The little one leans over my shoulder and whispers, "When you gonna let a nigga hit?"

I roll my eyes, not only at Shorty B. Bop or his hot alcohol-smelling breath but at the fat lady behind the counter taking her sweet precious time counting people's money. Each bill hits the counter, as slow as the ticking second hand of the clock behind her big-ass head. I feel like leaving since I'm the one, two, three . . . fourth fucking person in line, and Fat Girl is the only one working the damn front.

I suck my teeth and turn to look past the sweaty men, through the scarred-up front door. Rob gonna be pissed I'm taking so long, but I really need the money now. I hate coming to check-cashing places. They charge too damn much and they act like you a thief or something right from the gate. Taking your picture on a sneak, making you sign I don't know how many papers, asking for two types of ID.

"Nectar? You gonna act like you ain't hear me and shit?" the little one say, taking another step closer. "I'm 'bout to get some money right now. What's up?"

Shit. I flinch when he say my name—or at least the name I been using for some time now. I shake my head and turn around to face him. "I ain't working."

"What?!" he say, laughing. "How a ho gonna be off duty?" His two friends laugh with him. "Bitch, you want this money or what?"

I roll my eyes and take a step forward in line. Two people in front of me hear our conversation and turn around to sneak a peek. I cock my head and grint on both of them. *What the fuck are they looking at?*

"Nectar, the answer no?" The filthy guy repeats my name.

I nod and continue waiting my turn. I ain't choose the name Nectar. My daddy gave it to me. He said I was sweet and juicy like fruit and that he never ever fucked someone who got as wet as me. For a long time, I believed him.

I'm calling it divine intervention—the day Rob pulled up in front of that rundown pawnshop on Fourteenth Street. I was trying to clean my pussy underneath my miniskirt with the last baby wipe I could find in my knockoff Prada bag, when I heard a familiar voice call my name out.

"Camille?" he asked.

I dropped the used wipe on the ground and turned to see who it was, hoping it wasn't somebody who remembered me from middle school. Rob's face sitting in the big green truck brought back memories of a different time and of a different place and of a person who I had been trying to forget. I lit a cigarette and walked over to his truck.

"Camille?" he asked, confused.

"Hey, stranger," I said. "You wanna date?"

IN THE BEGINNING . . .

I

WASHINGTON, D.C.

OCTOBER 2000

Before I showed up at their door, the Brinkleys was already a big, old happy family. Their light blue house was just off of Rhode Island Avenue, and they had three big football-playing teenaged sons—Jamal, Ja'qui, and Jayson. There was another foster child named Danica, too. She had the biggest smile on her face when Ms. Lewis introduced me to everybody and grabbed my hand as soon as I walked inside.

"What's your name?" she asked, smiling and twirling one of her braids between her fingers. She had chubby cheeks and a belly that poked out a little.

"Camille," I said as I looked around the living room. Their house was just like *The Cosby Show* and nothing like mine. Family pictures was hanging on the wall, and there was a big-screen TV in the middle of the floor. A picture of white Jesus sat on a large bookcase with plastic flowers and tons of books. Mr. Brinkley was a tall, big man with shoulders that filled the whole doorway. He had a belly, but not as big as Santa Claus. When he smiled at me, the first thing I noticed was his chipped front tooth. Mrs. Brinkley smiled but turned away before I could smile back. She was tall and had frizzy golden brown hair. Mr. Brinkley took my suitcase, then him and his wife started talking with Ms. Lewis in the kitchen.

"How old are you?" Danica asked.

"Ten."

"Oh, I'm eleven," she said, smiling. "You like magazines? I got some in our room upstairs."

I shrugged my shoulders, not really caring one way or the other. "A little bit," I mumbled. This was gonna be my second foster family in a year, and even though Danica was being friendly, after my last family, I knew not to have high hopes.

"It's okay if you want to call me Mama," Mrs. Brinkley said after she saw me in the room with Danica. Mrs. Brinkley had real long fingers, and she kind of reminded me of Sideshow Bob from my favorite TV show, *The Simpsons*, with her frizzy, wild hair. Plus she was tall and slim except in the middle, just like him. I wondered if she was a little sneaky, too. Her eyes shifted around a lot, just like his did. She rubbed her hands and then combed her fingers through her hair as she looked around the bedroom. I watched her hand move jittery across the pink and purple bedspread on the top bunk bed. She said, "I hope you like it here. God blessed this home and this family."

I hadn't seen my real mama in two years, and I ain't have no plans on making this strange lady my mama. The last time I saw Mama, she was going through Nana's drawers searching for something. Tossing papers, family pictures, and clothes all around Nana's bedroom. Mama left out the house with a glass jar full of pennies, and I ain't seen her since. When Nana came home, she cried and fussed about the mess Mama left behind. It was the first time I ever seen her crying. She sat me down and told me she was tired and she couldn't do it anymore. Mama had to leave. My heart ain't stop hurting for months after that.

"Well, I'll leave you two alone," Mrs. Brinkley said before heading out the door. "I need to get dinner ready. Oh, Danica, don't forget to show Camille where to put her things."

"Yes, ma'am."

I stared at the magazine in my lap with Lil' Bow Wow on the cover, but I really just wanted to take a nap. I ain't wanna go through this again. The introductions, the new routines and chores, the new school. I just wanted to sleep and wake up back home with Mama and Nana.

"You like this skirt?" Danica asked, holding up her magazine.

I nodded. "It's pretty."

"Yeah, I'm gonna ask Ja'qui if he can get it for me."

My eyebrows rose up. "What you mean?"

"He my boyfriend, but don't tell nobody, though."

I ain't know what to say to that so I looked back at my magazine.

"Ain't he cute?"

"Who?"

"Ja'qui?" she asked, all excited.

"Yeah, but . . ."

"But what? But nothing! He's a cutie!" she said, rolling

over on her bed and kicking her feet up to tap the bottom of the mattress on top of her.

"How long you been here?" I asked.

"Since the beginning of last school year," she said. Her mood changed and she sat up. "I came after our house caught on fire. We all got split up—my mother, my sister, and my little brother."

"Oh."

"I see my mother sometimes, but she live in a shelter, and she don't want me living with her."

I turned back to my magazine. I hoped she wasn't gonna ask about me, cuz I ain't wanna talk about it.

"What about you?"

I thought about telling her a lie, that my mother was in the army and that she got killed overseas or that we had a house fire, too, but the words ain't come out. So I told her half of the story. "I used to live with my grandmother, but she died last year."

"Oh, sorry," she said touching my knee. "I know you miss her."

I nodded, surprised by the tears in my eyes. I blinked and one dropped. My grandmother was the only person who knew everything about me. The way I felt inside and how I felt about Mama. She was the only person I told when I saw Mama sucking smoke from out of a pipe in the bathroom and when her ex-boyfriend Tony smacked her three times in the living room. She was the one I told about Lil' Damien teasing me about my boney legs, and how he called them crooked and retarded looking. I never told her that I caught him by the big trash can

beside the building and beat him up, even though he was
bigger than me.

I loved Nana so much. She used to say, "God is in the
rain, don't be afraid," every time a thunderstorm scared
me into her lap. The words always made me feel better,
cuz Nana never lied. When she could only get around
the house in her wheelchair, I was the only person who
she asked to get her medicine. Mama always fussed about
doing stuff for Nana. "Mama, why you always calling my
name?" she used to yell. "I get so sick of hearing you
yelling 'Shelly' all over the damn house like I'ma slave or
something."

But Nana wasn't the only person I missed. I missed my
old neighborhood on Stanton Road, I missed the hills and
the buses and going to Wilkerson with my friends. Sometimes, I missed Mama, too. Even though she sometimes
acted like I got on her nerves and that she wished she never
had me. Sometimes she let me lay my head in her lap and she
would brush my hair, or sometimes she would even braid it
up with zig-zags like everybody else wore them at school.
Sometimes Mama pushed me away from her. She said I
wanted to be a baby, even though I was a big girl. "You
always up under me," she used to say. But I wanted to be up
under her. Her skin used to smell like vanilla and cocoa butter until after I started seeing her staying in the bathroom
all the time. Then I noticed her skin ain't smell like that
no more and I ain't care no more that she ain't want me up
under her, either. Nana let me cuddle up to her whenever I
felt like it, and she always smelled like cakes and pies. So that
was good, too.

"Well, don't feel so sad," Danica said, looking me in my eyes. "You got me now. I'll be your best friend."

I wiped my face and smiled.

My first week with the Brinkleys turned out to be okay. They told me I had to help with some of the chores. The bathroom was my responsibility, and I always had to clean the stovetop after dinner. I ain't care. I helped with chores at Nana's and even at my last foster house. I always used to help Nana in the kitchen. She even let me help her make pancakes once. It was so easy.

The brothers spent most of the day teasing Danica and me. I walked in the room once just when Ja'qui was about to kiss her, but when he saw me, he walked out the room. He was fifteen, and I just couldn't believe that she and him was messing around.

"Girl, you gonna get in trouble," I whispered after he left.

"Not if you don't tell," she said, smiling.

"But what if I was Mrs. Brinkley? She would've seen y'all!"

"That lady walks around here sleepwalking. I'm not worried about her. All she wants is for me to call her Mama and help her do the damn dishes. I ain't thinking about her."

I ain't know what Danica meant by that, but I started paying more attention to Mrs. Brinkley whenever we was in the same room. She spent most of her time cleaning this and wiping down that, spraying bleach or Windex, or reading her Bible. Besides seeming nervous all the time, I can't say that Mrs. Brinkley was sleepwalking. I thought she noticed every single thing that happened under her roof, even like whenever somebody moved the seasonings around in the cabinets.

One day I was in the living room watching TV when Mr. Brinkley walked in from work. He had hands so big that looked like they could pull trees up from the roots. Danica told me he used to play football for a minor league before he messed up his back, and that's why he wanted Jamal, Ja'qui, and Jayson to play so bad. But now Mr. Brinkley worked at an insurance company out in Maryland and spent most of his time trying to coach from the bleachers with the rest of the fathers who wished they could still play.

Mrs. Brinkley seemed nervous as usual when he walked in and she headed straight to the kitchen. I can't figure her out yet, but she never said nothing unless she was saying something about the Bible or church or chores. I can hear her opening and slamming cabinets shut and metal pots clanging together.

"How you doing, young lady?" he asked me as he stood in the hallway with his hand lying on his stomach, holding his work bag with the other.

"Good," I said before turning back to the TV.

"You don't have any homework?"

"No."

"No, what?"

"No, I don't have no homework."

"Sir?"

"Sir?" I asked, confused.

"Yes, in this house, you call me sir, and Mrs. Brinkley ma'am."

I can't help but roll my eyes.

"Is there something wrong with your eyes?" he asked as he leaned forward, his forehead crinkling up into lines.

I shook my head.

"Is that supposed to be an answer, young lady?" Mr. Brinkley asked.

"No."

"No what?"

"No, sir?"

"That's it."

I sat staring at the TV, but I wanted to get up and leave. His presence made me feel funny, like I was doing something wrong by just breathing. I ain't like Mr. Brinkley, and it was clear that Mrs. Brinkley had issues with him, too. I tried to breathe soft whenever he was in the room.

A few weeks later, I woke up in the middle of the night because I heard strange sounds coming from Danica's bed. I rolled over and looked down, straining my eyes to see, since it was so dark. But even in the pitch-black room, I can see a large figure sitting on her bed. I covered my mouth with my hand, to keep me from making any noise, and then I listened close. I can tell Danica wasn't screaming, either. She was moaning, and I can hear another voice whispering something I can't understand.

I rolled over on my back and stared at the ceiling. I ain't know what to do. I closed my eyes real tight when I heard the person standing up and the shrill sound of his zipper closing. I ain't wanna hear. I ain't wanna know. I ain't wanna see, but my eyes opened just as Mr. Brinkley closed the door.

I stared up at the ceiling for what felt like hours listening to cars driving down the street. I must've finally fell asleep, cuz Danica pushed me awake the next morning yelling, "Get up, girl! You overslept! We goin' be late!"

"Huh?" I said, wiping my eyes.

"It's Friday, and I can't wait to get home from school. We're gonna see Ja'qui's football game," she said, smiling and running to her closet. "What am I gonna wear?"

I hurried to the shower and washed up. It wasn't gonna take us long to get to school since it wasn't that far of a walk. On the way, I looked over at Danica to see if she'd act different or if she'd say something about what happened last night, but she didn't. She was the same as always, talking a mile a minute, this time about the tennis shoes Ja'qui was gonna buy her. That's when I knew whatever happened last night had been happening for a long time.

2

TWO WEEKS LATER

That stupid wench skinned me with the rope on purpose. She ain't like me since the first day I stepped foot in class. I knew it cuz I heard her and her friends talking about my clothes and my skinny legs when I walked to my seat. The dark-skin one with long hair was the ringleader. She was the one who tapped me on my shoulder asking me who did my hair. When I told her I did, she said, "It looks like it." Then she cracked up laughing and so did her hyena-sounding girlfriends behind her. Then she said, "Why her ponytail look like a baby fist, y'all?" The girls laughed some more. I ran my hand across my ponytail and turned back toward the teacher and rolled my eyes. So what, my hair was short. I can't help it.

The same dark-skin girl, who everybody called Nissa, asked me a few days later if I knew how to jump double Dutch. I told her I did.

"Okay, you can play with us at recess," she said.

I ain't know if I should at first, but since I ain't have no friends and Danica had lunch at another period, I said okay. Shoot, nobody else was talking to me anyway.

For a long while, I turned the raggedy telephone cord they was using as rope for everybody else. When it was finally my go, Nissa took the rope from me, and she and Lauren started turning. The rope went up a few times, and I tried to jump in, but it seemed like they was turning faster and faster. I finally caught the rhythm and jumped in. I was jumping for a few seconds before I did my favorite double-jump pop-up, where I skipped a beat and turned around on one foot. As soon as I went to touch my toe, I felt the rope speed up a notch, but I was still good. I been jumping double Dutch since I was in the second grade. My friends around Stanton Road always had contests, and the winner always got something from the ice cream truck for a dollar from Ms. Penny. I got real good, cuz Mama never had money to give me for the truck. So when I turned around and did the double-jump pop-up again, I went down and touched the ground, before jumping the double again. I wanted to show these Northeast girls how we did it in Southeast.

A small crowd started coming around and some kids was saying how good I was, just when the rope was speeding up even faster. The swishing sound of air being sliced up reminded me of helicopter blades. Nissa and Lauren was definitely trying to make me mess up. Just when I was gonna stop the rope on my own with my foot, they stopped it for me and the telephone cord whipped the skin on my legs.

"Ow!" I screamed.

"My bad. Did that hurt?" Nissa asked, snickering to her Hot Girl clan standing behind her. She put her hand on her hip and turned to walk away.

Without thinking, I rubbed my leg and then charged

right for her. My hands swung like a windmill, my fingers clawed at hair, scraped at flesh. I heard the voices around me getting louder. People yelled, "Fight! Fight!" Nissa squeezed my arms and kneed my stomach. But my legs was strong enough to thrust me forward and knock Nissa flat on her back. I sat on top of her and punched Nissa over and over in her face until someone pulled me off.

"Camille Logan. Now, this we cannot have!" Mr. Polk yelled, grabbing my shirt. I cracked my knuckles and rolled my eyes at the Hot Girl clan before Mr. Polk took me in the building.

I sat in the principal's office until Mrs. Brinkley came to get me, and now I was being suspended for three whole days. Nissa ain't hurt me at all, but I had scratches on my arms. The school nurse gave me alcohol packs to wipe them down. On the walk home, Mrs. Brinkley kept holding on to the tiny cross on her necklace and mumbling prayers. I thought she was at least gonna tell me off about what I did, but her mind seemed to be on something else.

As soon as we walked in the door, she told me to go to my room and wait until *my father* came home. *My father?* Now I never met my father, but I guess she talking about Mr. Big—I mean Mr. Brinkley. I had been trying my best to stay away from him since the night I saw him on Danica's bed. He came by the room twice since that first time.

I lied on my bed and closed my eyes listening to all the sounds of the house: Mrs. Brinkley vacuuming, *As the World Turns* on full blast from the big-screen TV, followed by *The Montel Williams Show*. Later, the smells of meatloaf and maca-roni and cheese eased under my door. My stomach grumbled. I tried to take a nap while I waited for her to call me down for dinner. Was I gonna be allowed to eat?

Danica's harsh footsteps walking up the stairs woke me up later.

"Girl, I heard about you whipping Nissa's ass at lunch! You know how many times that girl been stepped back?"

"Am I gonna get in trouble when he get home?" I asked, wiping the sleep out of my eyes.

"Girl . . . don't worry about him," Danica said, looking away.

"Is he . . . is he gonna try something with me, too?" I sat up and swung my legs out of bed, letting them hang in midair.

Danica looked at me like she'd seen a ghost, and then she shrugged her shoulders. "I don't know what you're talking about. And anyway, it wasn't your fault. She hit you first, right?"

"Yeah, she hit me with the rope," I said, jumping down. I wanted Danica to tell me what was going on, to warn me about how Mr. Big would act. But she wasn't even trying to look me in my eyes.

She hooked her book bag on the back of the chair by the desk and hung her jacket up in the closet. Then after a minute, Danica said, "Everybody been talking about it at school. Especially since you so little. They said she was bleeding and everything! Man, I wish I was there. I heard you beat the shit out of her boney black ass!"

I sighed. "Should I be scared when Mr. Brinkley comes home? Have you been in trouble since you been here?"

"No, not really. He never spanked me, if that's what you're asking."

"What about with Jamal, Ja'qui, and Jayson?"

"Man, he spoils them boys," she said, shaking her head. "They can never do anything wrong in his eyes. As long as they doing good on the team or whatever, he never has anything to say about anything they do."

"Hmm," I said, sitting down at the desk. I held my head up with my hand and flipped through a *Seventeen* magazine.

"I'm going downstairs to get a snack. You want me to sneak you something?"

I shook my head. She was always snacking. No wonder she was so chubby. I can't think about eating. My stomach felt funny like there was butterflies with wings on fire.

"All right then. I'll see you later," she said, walking out.

I stayed in the room flipping through a couple of the magazines that was on the desk until I heard the boys come in from football practice. Jayson poked his head in the door before he went to the room he shared with Ja'qui.

"Ooh, I heard you smashed youngin's head in," he said, laughing. "You goin' get it!"

"For real, Jayson? What he goin' do?"

"Probably give you a whipping, punish you for like two months, no dessert and no TV. You'll see."

"Dag," I mumbled, leaning back in the chair and crossing my arms over my chest.

"Nah, don't worry, shawty. He don't get down like that. He'll probably just make you read a couple lines outta the Bible or make you say you're sorry in front of everybody at church Sunday."

My eyes popped wide open. "What? I'm not talking in front of everybody."

"You're getting off easy," he said, smiling.

I guessed Jayson was right. I breathed a deep breath and rubbed my forehead.

"I'll catch you later."

The hours seemed to crawl by before I heard Mr. Big finally come home. Everyone was called to dinner, and I made my way out of the room and down the stairs. I can hear Mr. Big's voice before I reached the dining room, deep and loud like our preacher's. My stomach flipped over a few times. I can't tell if he knew what happened or not. I slid into an empty seat and fixed my plate. Jamal and Ja'qui had already started telling him about the seventy-six-yard catch that Ja'qui caught during football practice. Mr. Big was all smiles as he listened to the details. I sat pushing the peas around to the edge of my plate, then Jayson kicked me under the table. I looked up and wondered why he was smiling so hard. But then he made a fist and mouthed the words "Go, champ." I rolled my eyes and looked back at my plate.

"What's that, Jayson?" Mr. Big asked.

"Oh nothing, sir."

Danica shot me a look from across the table, and then I looked down.

"No. I know exactly what you're talking about, but I want Camille to tell me. What happened today at school, young lady?"

I took a deep breath and said, "I got into a fight. With a girl who been picking on me since my first day."

"A fight? Is that ladylike, for a young girl to be fighting like she ain't got no sense or no home training?"

"No, sir."

"So, why didn't you just walk away? Or why didn't you go tell a teacher if there was a problem?"

I shrugged my shoulders and played with the macaroni and cheese on my plate. Mrs. Brinkley got up from the table and went to the kitchen with the empty bowl of peas.

"I can't hear you!"

"I don't know, sir."

"Well, since you don't know, go to your room and take some time to think about it. Now!"

I got up and backed away from the table. I went upstairs and climbed up on my bed and lied down. It wasn't long before I fell asleep. A couple of hours had passed and the room had become dark with night. I could hear the laughter from everyone downstairs watching TV together. They sounded like a big happy family and I wanted to be down there, too. I rolled over and looked up at the ceiling.

Suddenly, my bedroom door opened, and even though it was dark, I knew it was Mr. Big holding a bag. I sat up. My heart was beating so hard, I thought he could hear it.

"I got you a present, Camille," he said before sitting the bag on the desk and closing the door shut with his other hand. The lock clicked and my heart jumped in my throat. It thumped harder and louder.

"This gift is just for you. I bought it on the way home after I found out what happened in school today. Now, I know you don't have much, but little by little you'll start getting some nice things that'll make you feel better, and maybe you'll start feeling more like a part of this family."

Mr. Big took a step closer, and then he put his huge hand on my knee. "Now, the Lord says in the Bible, you must honor thy mother and thy father, don't it?"

I shivered. All of a sudden I felt real cold and wanted to pull the blanket up over my whole body.

"Come here," he said, turning my body toward him. My legs dangled off the bunk bed and he took his rough hands and started rubbing them up and down the curve of my legs. "You are so pretty. Anybody ever tell you that?"

My mouth felt like it had cotton in it, and I couldn't say anything. I shook my head.

"You want to know what gift I bought you?" He went back over to the desk and took out two pair of jeans and three shirts. I couldn't see them in the dark, but I could smell the new fabric scent in the air. I ain't have new clothes since last Christmas, when Nana bought me a sweat suit and some underclothes. I put one of the shirts up to my nose and breathed in the smell. The stiff fabric felt nice in my hands. No one had ever worn this before. It wasn't hand-me-downs or from the thrift store like all the other stuff I had.

"You like it?" Mr. Big asked. "I can get you nice stuff all the time. Just like I do with Danica. All you have to do is be a good girl and real quiet."

I was scared as I listened to him, but I didn't want to let go of the clothes.

"Now, what I do for you got to be secret. You understand? No one can know, or I'll have to stop buying you nice things. You hear?"

I held on to the new shirt as Mr. Big pulled my body to the edge of the bed. I almost fainted when he pulled my sweatpants and my panties down and threw them on the floor behind him. I let him push me back on the bed and then I closed my eyes real tight as his cool lips touched my private part. He put my legs up on his shoulders and licked me. It felt like he was trying to kiss me down there, his tongue was doing weird things. I cried silent tears as he moaned. Just when I thought he was done, he put one of his fingers in me, sending a sharp pain down there. He pushed it in and out like a Q-tip. I cried aloud, and then I heard him unzip his pants. I ain't know what to do, but I knew Danica ain't cry when she was with him, so I wiped my face and waited for whatever was going to happen next. But nothing happened. I could hear his watch shaking against his wrist real fast. He moaned loud twice and then I could hear him zip his pants up.

"Sweet," he said. "Like fruit." And then he wiped his mouth, put his finger to his lips reminding me to be quiet, and then he unlocked the door.

I lied in the bed crying, before I finally wiped my face with one of my new shirts.

3

FEBRUARY 2002

We was piled up in Mr. Big's 1996 Nissan Quest headed down I-95 South to Richmond, Virginia. There was a big function with our sister church that Mrs. Brinkley couldn't stop talking about for weeks. She made sure everybody had on brand-new clothes and all the boys had fresh haircuts. Me and Danica was even sent to a hair shop on North Capitol Street, where I was finally allowed to get my first perm.

When the car slowed down out the blue, Mr. Big yelled out with an attitude, "Jesus H. Christ! We ran out of gas! The light must be broken."

He stopped the car on the side of the highway. The sign in front of us had the words CAROLINE COUNTY on it. I had never been this far away from D.C. before, and it felt real strange. Like I couldn't breathe or something. Mrs. Brinkley moved around in her seat, looking like she wanted to say something, but she held her tongue as usual.

"Jamal and Jayson, we're gonna have to take a walk," Mr. Big said.

"Why Ja'qui not going?" Jamal asked, sounding heated.

"Boy, just because you almost out of school don't make you grown! Who you think you are, asking me questions? Now get out the car!" Mr. Big shouted. "Rochelle, Ja'qui gonna stay here with y'all while we go find a gas station. One can't be far, since I haven't seen one for miles. We'll be right back."

"Ja'qui always has been your favorite," Jamal grumbled, shoving the side door open.

My eyebrows shot up, and I pinched Danica. Nobody ever talked back to Mr. Big before. Jamal was sure gonna get it. He stuffed his hands in his coat pockets and waited for Jayson to get out the car, too. But Mr. Big ain't do nothing but give him the eye. I couldn't believe it.

Danica shook her head and said, "Wow."

As soon as they left and started walking up the highway, Mrs. Brinkley turned the talk radio station to a gospel station.

"I bet we'll be here all day," she said, irritated. "I cannot believe that man didn't make sure we had enough gas before we got all the way out here."

Danica made a face at me, and I shrugged. Ja'qui laughed and rubbed the back of his head. We was surprised she was complaining about Mr. Big. She never, ever said anything. Sometimes, I seen her roll her eyes when he wasn't looking, or leave the table or the living room after he said something she ain't like. But she never, ever complained in front of us. She never even raised her voice in front of us.

Only one other time did I hear her get mad. Her and Mr. Big was in their bedroom arguing about a *policy* or something he wanted her to do. All I kept hearing her say, real clear, was "No, Frank! I'm not going to do it!" I ain't never know what they was talking about, but she was pissed for days.

"Mama, are we gonna get something to eat before we get to this thing?" Ja'qui asked. He was sitting right behind her.

"Who knows?" she said, twisting her necklace with her long fingers. "Your father's so stubborn. I'm sure he's going to keep going without stopping when they get back. Like it's our fault he ran out of gas and now we're running late. They were supposed to have a dinner at the church. That man . . ."

Ja'qui sucked his teeth, and Danica patted his knee.

"If any of you got to use the bathroom, I suggest you do it now," Mrs. Brinkley said.

"Man, it's too dag'on cold out there for all that," Ja'qui said. "I'll wait till we get to the church."

"Boy, you better watch your tone," she said, turning around looking at him. "Besides, your brothers are walking God knows how many miles in that cold weather."

"But, Mama, I—"

"*But, Mama* nothing! Stop sounding like a brat," she said, glaring at him. I pinched Danica again, and this time she pinched me back. I couldn't believe it. Mrs. Brinkley was finally pissed off for a change. *You go, Mrs. Brinkley.* I guess having to sit on the side of the road in the freezing cold did it.

"Maybe Jamal's right. Maybe we have spoiled you rotten," she said angrily. "Mr. Big-Time Football Star. I pray Jesus keeps you on the straight and narrow. I really do. You and your father."

Ja'qui sucked his teeth and looked out the window at passing cars. Danica shook her head and then lied it back on the headrest. I closed my eyes and finished taking the nap I had started before the little incident interrupted me.

Almost two whole hours had passed by the time we seen Mr. Big walking back with a big red container in his hand. Jayson was with him, but there was no sign of Jamal.

"Where's my child?!" Mrs. Brinkley yelled, jumping out of the car. "Frank, where's my son?!"

Mr. Big ain't say nothing. He just walked to the gas tank. Jayson climbed in the backseat and closed the door behind him, shaking his head at the same time.

"What happened, Jay?" Ja'qui asked right away.

"Man, it was crazy," he said, shaking his head and rubbing his palms together for heat.

We could hear Mrs. Brinkley's muffled voice rising up and down as she pulled on Mr. Big's arm. He pushed her away from him, but she was still asking where Jamal was, her voice was starting to strain out like she was crying dry tears or something.

"What happened, Jayson? Tell us!" Danica begged. We was all holding our breath, waiting.

"Jamal just went off on Daddy. Started talking 'bout he can't wait to move out and he ain't tryna be all the way out here for no church anyway. He said, ain't nobody ask him if he wanted to come. Daddy kind of like just turned into Incredible Hulk and tried to grab him up."

"You lyin'," Ja'qui interrupted. He looked out the window at Mr. Big trying to calm his mother down.

"Yeah, then Jamal was backing away from Daddy, right? Like back toward the woods, but Daddy caught him and went ballistic. I was scared as shit."

"Wait. What?" Danica asked, shaking her head, confused. "He hit him?"

Jayson nodded. "And then Daddy told Jamal to walk his ass back home."

I got real scared and stayed quiet. Mr. Big was a different man around the boys than he was with me and Danica. They usually got away with stuff that me and her could never get away with. At first I thought it was cuz we was foster kids, and they was his real kids, but it ain't have nothing to do with that. He treated them like that just cuz they was boys. Jamal was the oldest and he was the same height as Mr. Big. Not as wide but definitely more muscles. He was a senior wide receiver at McKinley Tech.

"Damn. Where he at, son?" Ja'qui asked, opening the door. I could tell he was getting angry.

"Man, I don't even know, but he can't be too far. Wasn't nothing out there but a gas station and a Subway joint," Jayson said.

Before Ja'qui got out the car good, Mrs. Brinkley climbed back in the front seat. She wiped tears from her cheeks and said, "Get back in the car. We're going to get your brother."

It was a quiet ride up to the gas station. We waited for thirty minutes to see if Jamal would show up before Ja'qui begged Mr. Big to let us get something to eat from Subway. Jamal showed up a whole hour later, shivering and looking pissed off. Mrs. Brinkley jumped out the car and hugged him. He hugged her back, even though it looked like it hurt him to do it. She said something to him, and Jamal nodded, and then she walked him back to the car with her arm wrapped around his waist.

"You not getting back in this car until you apologize. I don't care what your Mama said!" Mr. Big said.

Jamal sighed and said he was sorry.

"I'm the king of this nation, you hear me? What I say goes. Period. You understand me?"

"Yes, sir," Jamal said.

"Good," Mr. Big said and turned back to look out the front window.

Jamal climbed in the back of the van and tried to warm up.

Mrs. Brinkley was so upset about all the chaos that she told Frank to just go back home. Mr. Big opened his mouth to say something, but then he just shook his head and headed for the exit that said 95 North to Washington, D.C. It was a long hour and twenty minutes back to Rhode Island Avenue.

Later that night when Mr. Big came in our room, he took a long while deciding which one of us he wanted. I closed my eyes and prayed that it wasn't my turn, but when he told Danica to switch beds with me, I knew God was ignoring my prayers. It felt like Mr. Big was taking his frustrations out on me. He squirmed around in circles on top, pushing my legs open wider. As he grunted and moaned, I wondered if Danica did what I did whenever he was down here with her. I always prayed that he would hurry up and get out or that Mrs. Brinkley would walk in and catch him. Even though it never worked for me, I closed my eyes again and gave God another chance to save me.

4

MAY 2004

Danica had a little boy who looked exactly like Mr. Big, though she named him Ja'qui, Jr. That's when Mrs. Brinkley threw her clothes out on the street and made a phone call to Social Services with some lie that Danica had been stealing money from her. My caseworker, Ms. Lewis, came to the house to check on me a little after that, but there was nothing to tell her, except my best friend had been put out for no reason. All she had to say was, "Well, just make sure you don't be stealing from the Brinkleys, before they put you out, too." I hated her after that.

I cried for a few days after Danica left. She was the only real person who I trusted. We never, ever talked about what Mr. Big was doing to us. If anything, the secret we kept made us closer. She always covered for me whenever I forgot to do a chore, or I would come up with a quick excuse whenever Danica came home late from school, even though her and Ja'qui was out spending time together cuz Ja'qui had skipped football practice.

I knew that with her being gone now, Mrs. Brinkley would want me gone soon, too. I think the only reason Danica was really gone was because Mr. Big ain't want her there no more. He was done with her. I heard him call her "ruined" a few times when he was in the room.

Lately, I had been thinking about running away—before I got ruined, too. I just ain't know where to go. I mean, Mr. Big would be all over me now. Only Jayson still lived at home, since Ja'qui and Jamal was in college out of town. Mrs. Brinkley was still on a quiet rampage, looking at me from the corners of her eyes every other minute.

Jayson and I had gotten real, real close, especially after he told me he really hated playing football even though he was good at it. He hung out in my room just about every chance he got, going through fashion websites and music magazines. In the mornings before school, he even helped me pick out what hot outfit I should wear and I helped him, too. Jayson even walked with me to school in the morning since it was on the way to his school.

Ever since I joined the Ebony Fire dance troupe, I always had practice after school, so I got home late. Mr. Big said as long as my grades stayed good I could do any extracurricular activity I wanted. I did okay in school. I mean, I wasn't on the honor roll or anything, but I wasn't failing, either. I wanted to join Ebony Fire as soon as I seen the girls dancing during a neighborhood rec football game. They was the same girls who was popular. Everybody wanted to be them, and not the corny cheerleaders from school. I was popular already, just from that one fight I had with Nissa back in elementary. I came real close to fighting twice after that, but mostly my rep had everybody scared of me. Nobody never really tried me.

The only reason I ain't try out for Ebony Fire at first was cuz Nissa was the captain. She had been the captain for two straight years. But Danica knew how bad I wanted to be on the troupe, and one day after school she made me go over to their practice. At first Nissa wasn't trying to hear nothing about me joining up, but when I showed her how good I was at doing a split, she said, "Okay," even though she wore a stank attitude for days. We unofficially squashed our beef for the time being.

I was leaving practice with my girlfriend Shakira when this boy with this throwback Washington Bullets jersey said, "Hey, shawty. The brown-skin one with those sexy-ass legs! Let me holla at you real quick."

I blushed when I turned around and saw how fine that boy was, and he even called my legs sexy! Me? I could tell he was older than me, at least sixteen, but he looked good. Real good. He had on some fresh white Air Force Ones with the blue check, and he had long cornrows done up like Carmello Anthony. A caramel cutie, for sure. I was nervous, but then I thought, *What would Danica do?* No boy had ever tried to talk to me before.

"Girl, he's cute as a mug," Shakira said, giggling. "Ain't that Chu from Montana Avenue?"

Shakira was the kind of girl who always knew every-body and everything. She swore she looked like the singer Ashanti, and she did a little bit, but with big ole hazel grem-lin eyes. Nah, for real, she was cute.

I slowed down so him and his friend could catch up with us. "I don't know no Chu. Who is that?"

"You 'bout to find out," Shakira said, smiling and shifting her bag with her practice clothes in it.

"Hey, what's up?" he said before he lit a cigarette. "What's your name?"

Shoot. *What would Danica do?* It ain't like I could give him my phone number. Mr. Big would flip out if a boy ever called the house asking for me.

I smiled at him and said, "Camille. What's your name?"

"Chu. You gotta boyfriend?"

I shook my head.

"You want one?" he asked.

I blushed.

"Um, excuse me," Shakira interrupted, "I *am* standing right here. Damn."

"Oh, my bad. This my boy, Rob."

Rob nodded his head and took the cigarette from Chu. He was brown-skin, medium-sized, and had a little height to him, like he was over six feet tall.

"This is . . . ," I said, before looking at Shakira to see if she wanted me to give her real name.

"KiKi," she said, smiling at Rob.

"Y'all lying. That ain't your name," Chu said. "What's up with that?"

"Naw, my real name is Shakira, but that's my nickname."

"Oh, okay," Chu said. "How old are you, Camille?"

"I'ma be fifteen next month," I lied. My birthday wasn't until January, not June. "What about you?"

"Oh, you a young buck," he said.

"Don't sleep." I heard the words I thought Danica

would've said coming out of my mouth. I turned to walk away. "Come on, KiKi."

"Wait up, sweetheart," Chu said, grabbing my hand and pulling me back to him. "Let me get your number or something. You too sexy for me to let you get away that easy."

"Give me your number? I'll call you when I can," I said, holding his hand.

Rob laughed. "Man, these girls too damn young. I bet you she can't even get no phone calls."

Shakira pulled Rob's arm, and they walked near the corner store while Chu gave me his number. I wrote it on the inside of my D.C. government book.

"You goin' call me, shawty?"

I nodded.

"All right. I'ma be waiting," he said, walking over to Rob.

Shakira walked toward me, grinning from ear to ear, and then we hurried up across the street.

"Girl. Rob play basketball for Tech. His arm all muscular and shit. He's a lil' cutie!"

"He is, he is . . . but you gotta tell me about Chu," I squealed.

"I don't know much. Just that his brother Tep used to sell out Trinidad. You know, near Hechinger Mall? But his spot got raided and him and like six dudes got locked up last year. But you know them niggas still got paper, and that Haitian dude, Smurf, be still hooking Chu up with money and gear every now and then," Shakira said. "Shoot, I'd hit. That boy fine, too."

I looked at her and smiled, but she better not even think about it.

The next day Jayson sat in my room teasing me about the new hairstyle I was rocking. He said I looked like a brown Raggedy Ann baby doll with my new micro-mini braids. I had a few blond streaks in the front, like all the girls in high school had it, too. I blinked my fake lashes that made me look even more like Bambi. Hell, I knew I looked hot. Shoot, I'd even be jealous of me, if I wasn't me. I couldn't wait until Chu saw it.

"Mama said it looks too grown, but whatever—I love it!" I said, looking in the mirror.

"Yeah, it looks all right. It accentuates your high cheek-bones, your spindle neck, and your ethereal beauty," Jayson said in his fake British accent, trying to be funny. "I can't believe Daddy ain't say nothing about it yet."

"He ain't gonna care. Trust."

"Let me grease your parts," Jayson said. He picked up a few of my braids and pulled them away from my face real gentle-like, cuz he knew they was still tight at the roots. "Hand me the Kemi Oil."

I grabbed the oil off the dresser, but before I could give it to him, Mr. Big walked past the door and started going ballistic.

"I always knew you were a fuckin' faggot!" he yelled, grabbing Jayson by the neck and pressing him up against my bedroom wall. I never heard Mr. Big cuss before, and even as mad as he got, I never seen him that mad.

Tears was falling from Jayson's eyes while he did his best to push Mr. Big off of him. But even though Jayson was just as big as his father, he still was no competition. Mrs. Brinkley came running upstairs like the house was on fire, but she ain't do a thing to stop Mr. Big. She just stood in the doorway, rubbing the back of her neck and saying "Sweet Jesus" over and over again.

"Daddy!" I begged. "Please stop!"

Jayson was gasping for air. He had quit fighting Mr. Big off, and his feet wasn't touching the floor anymore.

"You're killing him, Daddy! Mama, please!" I screamed. "Do something!"

I turned to Mrs. Brinkley, who looked like an animal caught in a trap. But she was shaking and squeezing her cross necklace.

"Please, Mama, you can't let Daddy do this to him!" I yelled.

She paced the room, as if she ain't know what to do. But me, my arms was in the air, then by my side, and then out in front of me, reaching for Mr. Big. "I'ma go call the police if you don't get off of him!" I yelled, pushing Mr. Big as hard as I could.

Foam had started falling from the crack of Jayson's mouth and I got real scared. "Get off of him!" I yelled, pushing Mr. Big again. He ain't even blink, so I jumped on his back and wrapped my arms around his neck.

"Frraank, Frank. Let my son go!" Mrs. Brinkley yelled, like she just snapped out of it. "Let him go, Fraank!"

"Daddy, please!" I screamed. "He wasn't doing nothing wrong."

"Goddamn faggot!" he said before letting Jayson loose. Jayson gagged a few times, trying his best to catch his breath, and then he hollered real loud before kicking the wall three times. He ran down the stairs and out the front door without looking back. I ran behind him, and I ain't care what trouble I might get in for leaving the house without permission. I just wanted to check on my brother.

When I finally found Jayson down the street standing in front of the corner store, I ain't know what to say. I ain't know if he was gay. I never asked him. Hell, I ain't really care. I guess with Danica gone, I just felt like Jayson was taking her place. All the questions I used to ask her, I just started asking him. He *got* me just like Danica did, and he was comfortable around me like I was around him. That's all that I cared about.

Jayson was splitting a cigar open with his fingernails. I watched him let the middle stuff fall to the ground and then I followed him as he walked away. We walked together without saying nothing to each other for a long time. We stopped in the big park at the bottom of the hill. Right underneath a big tree, there was a broken-down bench with a piece of wood on the back part missing. Jayson sat on top of it, with his feet on the seat, and I leaned against the tree. I ain't notice until now that his eyes was bloodshot. I shook my head, knowing Mr. Big made that happen to him.

Jayson took out a tiny plastic bag filled with light green grass and carefully evened it out on the cigar skin.

"What you about to do?" I finally asked.

"Roll up."

"That's weed?"

"Yep. We gonna get high, high, high, high," he sang before licking and twisting the cigar. "You actin' like you ain't
never heard of weed before."

I had heard of it like in rap songs and stuff, but I ain't
never seen it in real life. I mean, I saw the big leafy thing
on people's T-shirts and on necklace charms and tattoos,
but I ain't never seen it look like that. It really did look like
weeds. Green ones. Except they was chopped up and stuck
together with seeds in it.

"You wanna smoke some?"

"Am I gonna go crazy or anything like that?"

Jayson laughed and then he took a lighter and ran the
flame along the sides of the cigar before lighting the tip and
then inhaling it deep until a big curl of smoke blew from his
lips. The smell was different than anything I ever smelled
before. Not that it was a bad smell, it just ain't smell like cigarettes or cigars. The scent was strong and thick. It seemed
like it was all over the park, in the trees, in the grass, and in
the sky. After he pulled on it two more times, he passed it
over without even looking at me. I put the cigar up to my
lips and tried to do like I saw him do, but I couldn't make
a long curl of smoke like he did. My nostrils was burning
something terrible, too.

Jayson said, "You gotta pull on it till you feel a funny feeling, and then you hold it in your chest for like two seconds.
Then blow it out. Easy peasy."

I tried again. This time when I did it, my face got numb
and I felt like my toes was twinkling like stars. I laughed and
then pulled on it again, this time longer. The light from the
tip lit up bright orange and then I started choking.

"Camille, put your arms up over your head!" Jayson said, laughing. I laughed and coughed until tears ran down my face, and then I raised my arms up, letting air fill my lungs again.

We smoked the whole cigar, which he called a blunt, until it was smaller than my fingernails. Well, Jayson smoked it when it got to that size. It was too tiny for me. I thought I was gonna burn my lips.

"Remember that day when I caught Ja'qui and Danica doing it in the laundry room?" Jayson asked, laughing.

I laughed because Danica told me Jayson had changed his voice like he was Mr. Big, and Ja'qui damn near passed out after he bumped his head running into the wall, he was so busy rushing to put his clothes back on.

"No, you should've seen how he tried to fit her big ass in that little-ass space beside the washing machine. He had her looking like a New York pretzel," Jayson said.

"I miss that girl so much."

"Me, too."

"She used to hook me up. Made sure I ain't leave out the house looking like a bama," I said, laughing.

"Well, hate to say it, but . . . sometimes, you still did," he said, joning on me.

"Boy, whatever," I said, shoving his thigh.

We sat quiet for a while. I knew what he was thinking about, but I wasn't going to bring it up.

"That man just tried to kill me," he said, shaking his head. "Can you believe it?"

"Nah," I said, putting my head in my hands as I leaned on my knees. But I *could* believe it. He did things to me at least once a week that I never thought was supposed to happen to a girl who tried her best to be good. If Mr. Big thought his own flesh and blood—his baby boy—was a faggie, then he was probably gonna do a whole lot worse if he knew for sure that he was.

"I'm not gay, Camille," Jayson said, like he knew I was thinking it.

"Okay. I believe you. But . . . I don't care if you is."

"Just because I like some of the stuff I do, don't make me gay."

"Jayson, I said I believe you. Dag."

He looked at his watch and then said, "We should start heading back before they change the locks."

I laughed and then gave him my hand so I could pull him off the bench.

"Let's take a long walk around the park after dark." Jayson sang a line from one of Jill Scott's songs, and I smiled. We were both high, high, high.

"Find a spot for us to spark . . ." I added another line.

"Oh, *now* you know about that?" Jayson said, surprised. "Better not tell nobody but God."

I giggled and held his hand as we walked back up the long hill. I ain't care if he was gay or not, I was just glad he was my friend even though I still hadn't told him my secret. Maybe that day would come.

5

A COUPLE DAYS LATER

Chu told me to meet him at the Rhode Island Avenue train station at nine o'clock. There was a breakfast spot he wanted to take me to in Adams Morgan, and he said he wanted to take me shopping downtown. Of course, I had to hook school to make this date, but it was worth it. I had only talked to Chu three times on the phone and met him once again after Ebony Fire practice, and he wanted to take me shopping already? Bet. I still can't believe it. But I wasn't gonna give him a reason to change his mind. When he showed up outside the train station riding in the passenger seat of a black truck Rob was driving, my knees locked up cuz I was nervous all of a sudden.

"Hey, Camille, what's up?" he said when I walked up to the truck. "Get in, sexy."

I smiled and climbed in the backseat. "Hey, Rob," I shouted over the loud music. He nodded at me and busted a U-turn. I ain't never been to a Go Go before, but my brothers always played Go Go music around the house, so I knew who some of the different bands was and that it was TCB coming from the speakers.

"He goin' drop us off after he make a run real quick," Chu said, turning back.

"Okay," I said, leaning back in the seat and checking my fingernails. Even though they were short, I had painted them dark purple. I dug in my purse and popped a stick of gum in my mouth, and then I looked out the window. I was jamming to the rollaton drums when I noticed we was going out Maryland somewhere. I ain't ask no questions, since I knew that was gonna seem corny. I just stared out the window.

When we pulled up in the gravel driveway at a big brick house surrounded by trees, I thought I was gonna stay in the truck while Rob did whatever he had to do, but Chu told me to get out and come with him in the house. It wasn't until that moment did I think maybe I should've asked Shakira to come with me. I climbed out with my book bag and my purse and followed both of them in the house. Inside, an old Jagged Edge song was blasting from somewhere, and a real, real dark-skin man in his thirties came out from the back with a green gym bag.

"What's up, Joe?" he said with an accent before handing the bag to Rob.

"Ain't shit," he said, taking the bag and giving him dap.

"Y'all wanna hit a Bob before you bounce?" the guy asked us.

"That's what's up," Rob said.

We all sat in the living room smoking and listening to music. I was glad Jayson had taught me how to smoke, cuz I would've looked real stupid in front of everybody, and that would've been real embarrassing.

"This shit is crucial," Rob said, coughing up smoke. He passed it to Chu, who puffed with ease before he passed it over to me.

As I inhaled, I thought about how crazy it would've been if something bad had happened while I was all the way out in Bum Fuck, Maryland, with people I barely knew. No one would ever know what happened to me. I passed the blunt to Chu and watched him smoke, then I thought about if anyone was even gonna care if I turned up missing. Who was gonna miss me? Maybe Jayson or Shakira. Maybe Danica, but I hadn't talked to her since she got put out, so she ain't count. Ja'qui told me that she moved out Virginia with her real family, so he never got to see her that much, especially since he was playing football at West Virginia University. Yeah, they would miss me, but only for a little while. A year or two, and then they'd forget all about me.

Chu and I was nuzzled together on a love seat with way too many throw pillows on it. He leaned over and slipped his tongue in my mouth and then I sucked it and kissed his lips. My head was clouded with weed and my skin was real warm.

"I feel like I know you, young."

"Huh?" I asked shook. *How did he know me?*

"Relax, not like that . . . ," he said, kissing me. "I can't explain it, I just feel . . . feel like we met before, or like I just know you already."

I raised my eyebrows, confused. "Why you say that?"

"It's hard to explain. I just do," he said, kissing my nose. "Something 'bout you."

"Hmmm . . . ," I said. "I'm special, huh?"

"You know it."

"Right?" I said, twisting my lips to the side. "Stop sycin' it up."

"What? I'm serious."

I smiled and kissed him on his nose.

"You wanna go to the basement?" he asked before dipping his tongue in my mouth and all the way down my throat.

I tried to keep up with him, but I needed to catch my breath, so I said, "What's in the basement?"

Chu laughed. "It's goin' be me and you in a minute."

I smiled and nodded, then he grabbed my hand and took me downstairs.

The basement was really plushed out like a mini-version of *MTV Cribs*. I mean, it was real nice. There was a big movie screen with a projector in one section, and a framed blue and red flag with a palm tree on a white square in the middle hung on the wall by the bar and pool table. I saw a room with high-tech gym stuff and a room that led to a Jacuzzi and steam room. One wall was all glass, from floor to ceiling, and I could see a big swimming pool and barbeque pit in the backyard.

"What's that guy's name?" I asked as Chu took me to a room with a bed. "Where he get all this nice stuff from?"

"If I tell you, I might have to kill you," he said, laughing.

I rolled my eyes. "Okay, be like that," I said, pushing him away.

"Nah, his name is Smurf."

"Why they call him that?"

"Cuz that nigga blue-black, that's why," he said, smiling.

I shook my head at the silliness.

"You havin' a good time?" he asked as he kissed me on my neck. Before I could answer, he started feeling me up and taking my shirt off. It was feeling too good to stop him. He was touching me real soft-like, and being real careful. He rubbed his hands over my body, massaging and squeezing, kissing and sucking.

"You a virgin, ain't you?" he whispered.

"Uh-huh," I lied.

"See, I'ma make you wifey, before anybody else start thinking about snatching you up."

"You are?" I asked, kissing him on his neck and running my fingers over his cornrows.

"Yeah, I see how them niggas be watching your sexy ass while you be out there dancing and shit."

I giggled. "You be watching me?"

"Always. Even when you don't know I be watching you."

"For real?"

"Mm-hmm," he mumbled, while pulling my jeans down. "You goin' let me taste you?"

"Okay, but I'm scared."

"Scared? It's not gonna hurt. You gonna love it. Watch," he said, licking my legs.

I lied back on the bed and looked up at the ceiling. I let him do the same thing Mr. Big do with his mouth. It even felt the same weird way. I kept still the whole time, since I ain't like this part at all. I wanted him to hurry up, but I ain't wanna seem like a little girl by telling him I ain't like it.

"What's wrong?" Chu asked, looking up.

"Nothing."

"You sure? You still scared?"

"Mm-hmm."

"Come here," he said, sitting up and pulling me to him. "Man, one day you gonna love it. We ain't gotta do nothing else."

I put my head on his chest and closed my eyes.

"Hey, I forgot. I got something for you."

I looked up and watched him dig in his pockets. "You do?"

"Yeah. Here." He fingered a gold necklace with the letters *C-H-U* spelled out in cursive.

"This for me?" I asked, surprised. "Oh, my God. When did you get it?"

"Don't worry 'bout all that," he said, grinning. "You like it?"

"I love it. Help me put it on." I'd have to hide it from Mr. Big, since he'd go crazy if he knew I was talking to a boy, especially one who was giving me gifts.

Chu crawled behind me and put the chain around my neck.

"I never knew that's how you spelled your name. I thought it was *Chew,* with a *W.* I thought it was a nickname for a silly thing you must've did when you was young."

He laughed. "Nah, it's Chu. Short for Chukwuemeka."

"Chu what?"

He laughed again and pulled me in his arms. Then he repeated it. "Chu-kwu-e-me-ka. It means 'God has done something great.'"

"Chu-kwu-e-me-ka," I repeated, letting all the vowels fall out my mouth. "Your family from Africa?"

"Yeah, my father is Nigerian."

"Oh . . . I like it."

"I like *Camille*, too."

I blushed and fingered my necklace. Rob yelled from the stairwell, telling us he was ready to go. Chu helped me put my clothes back on, and then we met Rob upstairs.

In the car, Chu asked me if I was hungry and if I still wanted to get breakfast. I nodded, but instead of going to Adams Morgan, Rob pulled up into McDonald's. After we got our food, he dropped us off at P. G. Plaza, cuz Chu still wanted to get me a couple of tops. I certainly wasn't going to complain about that. While we was out, he got me a pre-paid cell phone, so I could call him whenever I wanted and without my foster parents knowing my business. I couldn't wait to tell Shakira about my wonderful day.

Over the next few weeks, Chu and I started hanging real tough. I went over his crib after school just about every other day cuz I skipped dance practice. He would order Chinese food from the carryout around the corner. Chicken with garlic sauce or beef and broccoli and a fruit punch for me, and he always got wings and mambo sauce or a steak and cheese with fries and provolone cheese melted on top. He lived with Rob and Rob's older cousin Nut, who I never really saw much. He was in his twenties and was always in and out, usually with a different girl. They all looked skanky, too. He was a strange but cute-looking dude. Light-brown skin with a beard and mustache that he kept trimmed up. And he stayed fresh since he shopped at Up Against The Wall a lot.

I saw him staring at me a few times. I ignored him even though he never really said anything. One day, out the blue, he had the numbers 666 cut in the back of his head. I asked Chu about it, but all he said was that "nigga crazy, that's all." When I heard Nut blasting the same Three 6 Mafia song over and over again like he was going into a trance, I figured that nigga was more than just crazy. That shit always made me dizzy with the same beat and chants that repeated over and over. Nut walked around chanting, too. I decided to keep my distance since he seemed like he belonged in St. Elizabeth's Hospital with the other nuts.

Their place was in a rundown apartment building on Montana Avenue. It kind of reminded me of my old neighborhood in Wellington Park. It seemed like there was always a lot of people out and about. Dudes smoking on the corner or fixing cars in the parking lot with their radios turned up real loud. Women sat on the steps out front, gossiping and watching their children play or braiding hair. I got tired of hearing ice cream trucks come around every two hours waiting for greedy children to spend their parents' last dime on junk food. But that was their neighborhood.

It was nothing like where I lived now. My street had a lot of traffic going up and down it—Rhode Island Avenue was always busy, but no one really hung outside on their porches. Neighbors did yard work and that's about it. They came home from work and went in the house.

I liked it around Chu's way. People spoke to each other,

asked about one another's children and other family. Sometimes fights sprung up, but everybody knew everybody, so a lot of time the cops ain't even get involved unless it was a shooting. A few times fights came from inside the apartments and ended up all the way in the street—usually it was a chick angry at her man over another chick, or sometimes it was the other way around. Maybe a parent got into it with another parent cuz their child had started a fight with the other parent's child. Once, a girl got smashed in the head with a hammer by her baby father. It was even on Channel 4 News. I couldn't believe she survived.

In Chu's neighborhood, people seemed to look out for each other. Every time somebody new came on the block, it was like everybody noticed. I felt safe around his way for some reason, even though the girls stayed in our business.

Inside their apartment wasn't nothing much to talk about. They had a couch and a love seat with a plasma TV, where they played *Madden* or *NBA Live* all day. I spent most of the time there smoking with Chu and Rob until it was time for me to go back home.

Chu was really growing on me. We smoked weed and talked a lot about how the Brinkleys wasn't my real parents and about my Nana dying. I ain't tell him about Mama. That would hurt too much. He told me stuff, too. About his brother, Tep, being locked up for three years and how he wasn't talking to his mother since she kicked him out when he was fifteen. Chu said his father moved back to Nigeria when he was seven and he and his brother ain't seen or heard from him since. We kind of bonded when I told him I never even knew my real father. When he asked me about my mother, I just told him she was too sick to take care of me. I was relieved that he let it go at that. I could tell he knew I ain't really want to talk about it.

When I finally let him put the head all the way in, he took a few strokes but stopped cuz he thought he was hurting me when I started crying. But I wasn't crying cuz of that. I was crying cuz I was thinking about Mr. Big the whole time Chu was on top of me.

When I saw how Chu was looking at me, I almost wanted to tell him why I was crying. But he ain't say nothing, he just lit a blunt and started smoking it.

"Man, you gonna have to get over whatever it is you scared of . . . or I'ma have to . . ."

"You gonna do what?" I asked, pissed off.

"Man . . . shit," he mumbled and shook his head. He took another puff and then completed his sentence. "I'ma have to do something. Shit, Camille, you gotta suck me or something. I gotta get this nut out."

I rolled my eyes. I was mad at Chu, but at the same time I ain't want him thinking about being with nobody else. He was good to me. I crawled over to him and picked up his man. It looked totally different than Mr. Big's. Chu's was thick and long with smooth veins that ran around the sides. The top looked like a mushroom. Mr. Big's reminded me of a thumb, except the top looked wrinkled and like an elephant's nose. Sometimes I even had to pick lint off before I put it in my mouth. Chu's dick was three times the size of Mr. Big's and it hurt when he put it in me earlier. But Mr. Big's went in with ease, like I was putting on a tampon or something.

I held Chu's man in my hand and then put it in my mouth. He smiled and leaned back, before locking his hand on top of my head. I knew he was gonna like it.

"Damn, girl," he moaned as I sucked. "Fuuccck."

I smiled. I never got scared when I did this part. It was the only time I felt like Mr. Big was weak. As big as he was, he always acted different whenever I did that to him, like he just couldn't help himself. I always felt like what me and Mr. Big did wasn't right, but I ain't know how to stop, or if I stopped what would happen to me. Danica was God knows where, for real. I still ain't caught up with Mama. She wasn't out there looking for me, and I wasn't really looking for her, either. The Brinkleys made sure I had food and a bed to sleep in, but now that Chu was buying me my clothes and keeping money in my pocket, I ain't really need Mr. Big sneaking it to me no more.

That night when I got home, he came in my room like he always did, long after Mrs. Brinkley was in a deep sleep. When he climbed on top of me, I laid still as usual, listening to him grunt as he stuck his dick in and out a few times. He moaned real loud and let the sticky stuff get on my stomach.

"Hurry up and wipe that off, Nectar," he said, handing me a roll of toilet paper. "I don't want your Mama asking me about the sheets again."

I rolled my eyes and wiped myself off. Now I knew for sure that bitch knew what the fuck he had been doing to me. Mr. Big put his night pants back on and left something on my desk before he left.

The next morning, when I got up I looked at the wad of

bills. I sucked my teeth, counted the money, and stuffed the crinkled dollars in my purse. It was enough to get the cute pair of True Religions I wanted. I sent Shakira a text to see if she wanted to skip school and head up Georgetown. She hit me back: *DWN4 ?EVA*. School was almost over for the summer, so we was skipping like every other day anyway. As soon as I got out the house, I called her. We planned to meet at the bus stop on Rhode Island Avenue.

Her and Rob ain't become a couple like me and Chu. All Shakira ever wanted to do was talk about how Rob had fucked her and never called her back. I mean, I felt bad for her, but not really. She was a cute girl and could dress, so she could pull another dude easy. I wished she would stop acting like he was the only guy she could get.

We looked around for a while, and then after I bought my jeans and she bought a cute red pair of stiletto sandals, we went to get something to eat. After that we decided to go to the movies, just to pass time.

Around three o'clock, we went up to the rec center to see who was out there. We saw Nissa and Lauren and waved, even though we only spoke just cuz she was in charge of Ebony Fire.

"That bitch is so fake," I mumbled.

"Damn, like that? You still don't like Nissa?"

"Nope."

"Why not?"

"I don't know. I guess cuz I can tell she still be hating on me."

"You think?"

"Yeah. I be seeing her staring at me in practice. She don't think I see her, but I do."

"Hmmm," Shakira said. "I think she still scared of you."

"Maybe. Anyway, let's go. Ain't nobody up here."

Shakira followed me out of the building and we walked down the street, still carrying our shopping bags and book bags. Her cell phone rang and she started chatting away. I pulled my phone out, realizing Chu hadn't called me all day. I dialed him up and listened as his phone went straight to voicemail. That was strange.

"Hey, babe, it's me. Haven't heard from you all day. I'm about to go in the house like in twenty minutes, so you know it's gonna be hard to talk to you. Call me back."

Shakira and I kept walking till we got to her corner and then we separated. I stopped at the corner store to buy a fruit punch and some Doritos, hoping to give Chu more time. After a while, when he didn't call, I went in the house.

Mrs. Brinkley was sitting in the living room watching *Oprah* when I walked in the door.

"Hi, Mama," I said before going to the kitchen.

"You went shopping again?"

"Um, yes, ma'am," I said, opening the refrigerator out of habit, since it wasn't like I was hungry. "You seen Jayson?"

"No. He isn't home yet. Don't eat anything that'll ruin your appetite. I have a casserole in the oven."

"Okay."

"Come here. Let me see what you bought."

I was shocked, since she never seemed to care about what I bought. I walked in the living room, pulled the jeans out the bag, and handed them to her.

"One hundred fifty-eight dollars?" she asked. "Your father giving you that much money?"

I shrugged my shoulders.

"And you're spending it on jeans?" she asked.

Did she really want an answer from me?

"That's unimaginable," she said, shaking her head. She got up and went to the kitchen and checked on her food.

"Am I excused?" I asked, since Mrs. Brinkley looked liked she wanted to say something else to me.

"No. You're not excused. Take a seat here in the kitchen."

I rolled my eyes, got up, and walked over to the tiny table in the kitchen.

"So . . . tell me," she started. "What are you going to do with yourself?"

I was confused, and my face must've showed it.

"I've been watching you. Prancing around here in your high heels, and your tight clothes, all made up like some kind of common . . . What are you going to do with yourself? Or do you want to just keep doing what you been doing?"

"What's that?"

"Hmmm," she mumbled and slammed the oven door shut. "You must think I'm an idiot."

"Huh?" I said.

"You think I don't know what's been going on in my own house!" she yelled.

"Mama, I don't know what you talking about!" I shouted.

"Don't call me that!" she said, pacing the kitchen. "I don't want to hear it!"

"Mama . . . I . . ."

"I want you to start praying right now. Get up!" Mrs.
Brinkley yelled. "Kneel on the floor. Right now!"

I felt my eyes tearing up. She wanted to put all the blame
on me for what had been happening. Was she gonna put me
out like Danica? Where would I go?

"Hurry up! Jesus needs to forgive you," she said in a voice
I never heard from her.

I hopped out of my chair and crawled down on my knees.
I put my elbows in the chair I had been sitting in and closed
my eyes, too scared to even think about praying. I cracked
my eyes open to see what Mrs. Brinkley was doing. She
took a bottle of olive oil from the cabinet and came back
to where I was kneeling. I closed my eyes again, feeling her
make a cross on my forehead. She stood over top of me with
her hand on top of my head. "Father, Lord Jesus, we need
You today. We need Your forgiveness, Lord. We need Your
glory and Your mercy, Lord. There's evil all around us, and
we need You, Lord. Wash away her sins, Heavenly Father,"
Mrs. Brinkley called out, at the top of her lungs. Her hand
rocked my head back and forth. Tears fell, but not cuz I was
the one sinning. Mrs. Brinkley kept on praying, and I wiped
tears running down my cheeks.

"Yes, Lord, redeem her! Fill her with the Holy Spirit. Hal-
lelujah! Show her Your love and Your power. Father Jesus,
show her Your mercy! Deliver her from evil," Mrs. Brinkley
shouted.

Suddenly, the front door opened and closed. I could tell
it was Mr. Big, and he stomped into the kitchen, asking,
"What in the world is going on here?"

Mrs. Brinkley touched her chest and walked over to the stove. I wiped my face and got up from the floor.

"Rochelle? What happened?"

She shook her head and pulled the casserole out of the oven. "Nothing, Frank. We just had a little girl talk," she said and then cleared her throat. "How was work? You're home rather early."

The next day Mrs. Brinkley took me to get that birth control shot, the one that stops people from getting their periods. She never said what she knew was happening under her roof, but I knew she was letting me know that she wasn't blind.

6

AUGUST 2004

Chu called me collect two days after Mrs. Brinkley spazzed out. He had got locked up and sent to juvie up Oak Hill for sixty days for possession charges. The police had found a gun and two bags of weed on him back in May when they had pressed him and Rob out on the block. Now he was on probation until he turned eighteen, especially cuz of the gun. They don't play when it come to that, even if it was unloaded. He almost got charged as an adult. And because of the weed, now he had to check in with his probation officer and take a urine test once a week. That's the part that really pissed him off, cuz he couldn't smoke weed with Rob and the rest of his friends no more. He always talked about how bipolar he was and how he couldn't live without it. I was just glad he was home now.

Shoot, a lot of people was checking for me while he was missing in action. I missed him like I don't know what while he was gone. I had to spend more time at home, dealing with the Brinkleys. My summer was miserable without him, but I wrote him a couple times. He couldn't write me back though, cuz I knew Mr. Big wasn't gonna have no jail mail coming to the house.

I'm not gonna lie, I had started to really miss the money Chu was giving me, especially since Mr. Big had stopped giving me as much as he used to. My gear was starting to slack just a little, up until Shakira put me on to boosting. She showed me how to steal expensive little stuff like silk scarves and high-priced costume jewelry from Nordstrom and Lord & Taylor, so we could bring it back for credit slips to buy what we really wanted from the junior's section. I had to keep being on point. After all, I was Chu's girl. But now that Chu was gonna be on his best behavior, I wasn't sure what I was gonna do. Probably keep doing what I was doing while he was away, using my five-finger discount.

Smurf was throwing a big crab feast at his house on the last day of the hottest month on record. Chu was really looking forward to it, since he had missed most of the summer being locked up. I brought Shakira with me to the crab feast, even though Rob looked mad as hell. He ain't say nothing to her the whole ride.

As soon as we pulled up to Smurf's crib all the way out Upper Marlboro, we could smell the steamed crabs.

"Mmmm," I said. "I can tell they cooked them in beer, too."

Chu put his arm around my shoulder and kissed me on my neck. "You know I only eat the legs, right?"

"That's it? Boy, you crazy. I eat the whole damn thing," Shakira said, sashaying her hips ahead of us. "The mustard, too."

"That shit ain't mustard, you stupid bitch," Rob said,

shaking his head. He followed her into the party but turned around and made a face at me. I laughed.

"You know why Rob never called your girl back, right?" Chu asked, smiling.

"No, why?" I asked, surprised he was gonna tell me the deal.

"All right, but you can't tell her, though."

"I won't."

"Your girl gave my man chlamydia."

I opened my mouth, shocked. "You lying."

He shook his head but kept smiling.

"Wow," I said, viewing Shakira in a whole new light. "That's nasty."

It was so humid that I thought about jumping in the swimming pool myself, but I was too classy for all that, plus I ain't want to get my hair all wet. But a lot of the *rollers* wasn't holding back. Some of them was stripping out of their clothes and grinding in their bikinis. Me and Shakira stayed classy and cute in our summer dresses. I had on a white one that wrapped around my neck. Shakira had on a red halter dress, showing her butterfly tattoo on her shoulder. She wore the red stilettos she bought up in Georgetown. All the dudes looked paid. Fresh to death with their graffiti-print tees, brand-name jean shorts, and right-out-the-box tennis shoes.

There was barbeque ribs and chicken, corn on the cob, and potato salad, and everything looked delicious. Smurf was really doing it big. He even had a DJ with gigantic outdoor speakers, and he was gonna set off some fireworks later. A group of people was playing spades and another group was playing poker. There was a bottle or a glass of something in just about everybody's hand. I sipped on a Corona with a lime wedge floating in it. The lush smell of weed was heavy in the air, and Chu started worrying that it might affect his next piss test.

"Camille, baby, let's go to the truck for a little while," he said, smiling.

"For privacy?" I asked, giggling.

"Mmm-hm," he said, leading me in front of him. "You look so damn sexy in that dress, girl."

It was the first time I had ever been on top, and I couldn't believe how good he was making me feel. Chu stared in my eyes the whole time. As I eased up and down, he kept asking me if I was okay. But I was more than okay. I felt like it mattered what I was doing this time, like whenever I sucked him off. It was nothing like what me and Mr. Big had ever did.

When it was over, Chu made sure not to get anything on my dress and he handed me some napkins. He seemed to like it just as much as me, cuz he kept kissing me. I wanted to be on top from now on, and for some reason I ain't think Chu was gonna mind.

I climbed out of the truck and went in the house to use the bathroom. On my way, I saw Shakira kissing Smurf in the den. I shook my head and kept going to the bathroom. That man was entirely too old for her. But who was I to tell her that?

*   *   *

After everyone was full and drunk, and the crowd started dwindling down, Rob was ready to go. He must've been mad he ain't pull none of the girls at the party or something. I went looking for Shakira but couldn't find her. I knew she had to be somewhere in the house with Smurf since I seen her with him earlier. I tried to calm Rob down until I found her, but he wasn't trying to hear it.

"You must be crazy if you think I'm waiting for that dirty-ass broad," Rob said, starting up his truck.

"Please, Rob? Don't leave yet. Give me two minutes, please?"

"Come on, Rob. Hold up," Chu said.

"All right, I'm just waiting for you, though, Camille."

I wasn't gonna leave Shakira all the way out in no Bum Fuck, Maryland, with some dude she hardly even knew. I ain't care if he was Rob and Chu's friend. I walked around the house and called her name, but besides a couple of people playing pool in the basement, I ain't see nobody. *Where could that girl be?* I started to go upstairs, but I ain't see none of the people from the party going in that part of the house since we got there. I hesitated but kept going. I swear I wasn't trying to leave her.

When I got to the top of the stairs, I saw a strange glowing light coming from a cracked door. I started to go back the other way, cuz whatever it was, was none of my business. I heard Rob blowing his loud-ass Ford horn, telling me my two minutes was up, so I turned back and kept going down the hall. The closer I got to the dark room with the strange glow, the louder the moans.

I rolled my eyes, cuz I just knew this hooker wasn't screwing this man already. I stood in the hallway trying to decide if I was going to yell her name and tell her we was leaving or if I was just going to go back downstairs. Rob blew his horn again, long and hard, so I decided to hurry up and just shout real loud that we was about to leave.

But I was dying to know what the weird glow was. I peeked behind the crack and almost fell into the room when I saw Smurf standing over Shakira beating his dick, while one of the girls I seen by the pool with long hair ate my friend out. The glow was coming from a funny-looking lightbulb that made some of the stuff in the room, like Shakira's eyes and teeth, light up. I shook my head and decided if she ain't have a ride home after all that she was doing back there, then too damn bad.

In the car, Chu asked me if I found "KiKi." I just shook my head.

He smiled and said, "I bet you did. You look like you seen a ghost or something. What shawty was doing?"

"That damn girl," I said, shaking my head.

"Oh, Camille, you ain't got to tell us nothing. We goin' find out all about it tomorrow," Rob said, laughing. "KiKi better hope he ain't in there videotaping her ho ass."

I shook my head, disgusted at her. Obviously, I ain't know Ms. KiKi like I thought I did.

Chu laughed and lit up a Black & Mild as we pulled onto Route 223.

7

NOVEMBER 2004

I was so over school, and not because it was my first year of high school at McKinley Tech. Since I had stopped hanging out with Ms. Thang, I was pretty much staying to myself. Ebony Fire was starting to get on my nerves cuz they wanted to have double practices on Saturdays. Shakira and me ain't speak since Smurf's party, and I still had my issues with Lauren and Nissa. Nissa wanted me to quit cuz I was only showing up at practice whenever I wanted to. But what can I say? Chu needed me.

I even stayed the night by his crib for a whole entire weekend once. The Brinkleys thought Ebony Fire was having an overnight retreat for all the dancers out in Front Royal, Virginia. They believed my little lie, too. They ain't even ask me for a permission slip or nothing. I had a fake one made up, just in case they did, though. I was surprised when Mr. Big gave me four hundred dollars for the trip. I ain't even have to do nothing extra for it, either.

When I found out one of Nut's girlfriends, Peaches, was a senior at Tech, we both started leaving school together at lunchtime and going back to the apartment. She wasn't as skanky as the other girls he brought by the crib, but she still had that look about her. The look that said she'd been through a lot of shit and dared a bitch to try to take her man. I knew after the first time I met her that the other girls was gonna disappear. Peaches was marking her spot, cooking big dinners like steak and mash potatoes one day and smoked turkey wings and candied yams the next. I was watching her. Chu even had the nerve to ask me why I never cooked. He must be crazy—that mess ain't for me.

I walked in the kitchen one day just when Nut was killing a mouse with his bare hands. I couldn't believe it. Blood was running down his arms and everything. I gasped and ran back out. Peaches was in the living room squirming around, but I had no idea it was because her man was acting like Zeus on the dipper.

Howard University's homecoming was the very next week, and me and Peaches had talked about sneaking into some parties with my brother Jayson. She got me a fake ID from her aunt who worked at the DMV, so I was straight. At least, I could get in some of the "eighteen and up" parties.

The night we was getting ready to go out, Nut kirked the hell out and told Peaches she wasn't "going no god-damn where." Peaches kept right on getting dressed. She looked cute in her short chocolate brown Anna Sui dress and her leopard peek-toe pumps. Chu walked up behind me and kissed me on my neck while I finished putting on my makeup.

"You sure you don't wanna go?" I asked.

"Nah, I got some shit I gotta do. Me and Rob probably ride through and do a little parking lot pimping later," he said, laughing.

I sucked my teeth. "Whatever, boy. You better not be trying to holla at nobody," I said playfully.

"You know I don't want nobody but you," he said and kissed my cheek. "Look at how gorgeous my baby is."

I smiled. I felt so lucky to be with him. He always said the right things whenever I needed to hear it. Every time my foster parents got on my nerves, and I wanted to vent, he'd just say, "Tell Daddy all about it," and wrap his arms around me. He made me never want to leave when I came over. Since he wasn't smoking weed anymore, I smoked with Peaches whenever Chu and Nut was out on the block. Sometimes I bought my own bag and smoked it by myself or I smoked with Jayson in our favorite park.

The phone rang, and Chu answered the collect call from his brother. Chu was still grinding it out even though he was on probation. His brother, Tep, used to be the main breadwinner between the two of them, but Chu was picking up the weight now. Tep called the crib a couple times when I was there. I listened to Chu talk in codes and then he said, "Yeah, she's standing right here. Camille, here. Tep gotta tell you something."

"Me?" I asked, surprised.

He nodded and handed me the phone.

"Hello?"

"So you Miss Wifey, huh? How you doing?"

"I'm okay," I said, blushing.

"My brother can't stop talking about you. I had to see if you was real, slim."

I giggled and turned toward Chu. "Yes, I'm real," I said, feeling extra special.

"Okay, okay. Well, make sure you take care of him. He's all I got out there."

"Of course, I will. That's my baby. He's all I got, too."

"All right, all right. I hear that . . . Let me holla back at my man," Tep said.

I passed the phone back to Chu and then kissed him on his cheek. While they finished talking, I dug in my overnight bag and grabbed my accessories. I looked at myself in the mirror and smiled. I did look gorgeous, like Chu said. The turquoise top was doing magic for my brown skin. I turned and looked at my butt to make sure my Citizens was doing what I paid them to do. Yeah, they was doing just right. Chu palmed my cheeks and massaged them while he talked on the phone. I could tell he wanted to hit it before I left, but I just did my makeup, and my eye shadow was perfect.

"Camille?" Peaches called out right on time. "Girl, you ready?"

"Yep," I said, grabbing my purse, stuffing it with the makeup I was gonna need for the night. "Is Jayson here yet?"

"No. You need to call him and see where he at."

I dialed Jayson up. "Boy, where are you?"

"I'm almost there. This damn train taking so long. Peaches driving, right?"

"Yeah."

"Why she can't just meet me at the station?"

"All right, all right. I'll tell her, so stay there when you get off."

This was going to be the first time I stayed the night out with no explanation whatsoever. I was willing to take my chances on this. H2O was going to be cranking, and I was ready for whatever. All week long, WKYS had been naming all the different celebrities who was supposed to come out, and I wasn't gonna miss Lil' Wayne for nothing in the world. I wasn't too worried, since the Brinkleys knew I was supposed to be out with Jayson somewhere.

The line in front of the club was already snaking down the street when we pulled up. Peaches decided to valet park, so we wouldn't have to spend all night looking for a spot. Top-of-the-line cars of just about every model paraded up and down the street, with music blasting and sparkling rims spinning. The music was pouring out the door and the loud bass vibrated the whole building. I passed the ID test with security without a problem. We watched a couple of girls who looked like hookers prance by, wearing long tracks with platinum blond streaks down their backs. The duo had on bright sequined bikini tops and shorts that looked like satin panties.

"Skanky bitches," Peaches mumbled.

"No class," I said, watching guys follow behind with drinks filled to the brim in their hands and their tongues hanging out their mouths as they looked the women over.

"Dayum, it's live as shit in here!" Jayson yelled over the noise of the crowd and the music.

I nodded and then we all headed upstairs. None of us was over twenty-one, so Jayson disappeared to find someone who could cop drinks for us.

"Shawty crunk on the floor, wide open," one of the Yin Yang Twins sang.

"Girl, this my song," Peaches said as she dragged me to the dance floor. "Shake it like a salt shaker!"

There was so many people on the floor, bodies rubbing, hands touching, hips popping in and out, booties twirking. By the time, the DJ had stopped playing "The Whisper Song," I was drenched with sweat.

"You look like you need this," Jayson said, handing both of us glasses of something fruity looking.

"Ooh, boy, what's this?" Peaches asked, excited.

"Fuzzy Navels," Jayson said, smiling.

"Where you get this from?" I asked.

"Don't worry about all that. Just enjoy it," he said, looking away, sipping on his drink.

"Well, excuse me," I said and took a long sip from my own drink.

"I'll be back," Jayson whispered in my ear.

"Where the hell you going?" I yelled over the loud music. Nelly's "Hot in Herre" had people bumping up into the both of us. We swayed with the crowd for a minute, but Jayson ain't answer me. He waved bye and disappeared into the crowd again.

"Where the hell he just go?" Peaches asked, leaning into me.

"I don't know, but he's being real sneaky," I said and turned to look for him.

"Well, whatever. Let's just have some fun," Peaches said while swerving her hips.

We danced for hours. A couple of guys had offered to buy both of us drinks, which we gladly accepted. Peaches rolled her eyes and told some crazy-looking dude to get off of her after he tried to grind on her butt.

"I can see if the nigga was at least halfway cute," Peaches said in my ear.

I laughed and then the DJ started playing Lil' Wayne's "Go DJ" and the crowd started going wild, pushing closer near the stage area. A few minutes later, Lil' Wayne and some of the Cash Money Millionaires came out on the stage and killed it.

I could not believe Jayson was nowhere to be found the whole time. After the DJ made a last call announcement for drinks, me and Peaches started looking for Jayson and heading toward the door at the same time. When we got outside, we waited for a while to see if he would come out, but he didn't. I called him on his cell phone, but there was no answer.

"What you think we should do?" I asked Peaches. "You think we should leave him?"

"Jayson grown. He probably getting his dick wet somewhere," she said, scanning the crowd.

I sighed and then dialed his number again.

"Hey, Peaches? You have fun?" a voice called from behind us.

We both turned around to see Nut leaning up against his Cadillac STS with his arm wrapped around one of the hooker-looking girls who was inside the club.

Peaches' face formed a scowl and then her fingers turned to claws as she pounced on the girl, who had no idea what was coming next. Peaches pulled and scratched, until the girl's bra-like shirt was pulled down around her waist like a belt, and a blond track had been snatched out from the root. I tried to break them up, but two seconds later I felt the hands of someone tugging at my clothes. When I turned around to see who it was, I felt fingernails scraping my face. I went crazy, throwing punches and swinging at the girl, who must've thought I was jumping into Peaches' fight. I could hear Nut laughing as the fight went on, and I could feel the big, strong hands of security guards tearing us apart.

"Hey! You gotta get the fuck off our premises with this shit!" the big security guard yelled. Another big guy with SE-CURITY on his shirt was standing with pepper spray aimed at us. They ain't have to tell me twice. Police sirens chirped to break up the crowd and then Nut said, "Okay, okay. That's enough. Y'all get the fuck in the car."

I wobbled on one of my heels and looked for Peaches. She was walking the other way.

"Peaches, what the fuck?! I said get the fuck in the car!" Nut yelled. I ran behind her and jumped in her car when she unlocked the door.

"Who the fuck that nigga think I am?!" she yelled, wiping her face off. "I don't have to deal with this shit!"

I tried to call Jayson one more time, but again no answer. I hoped he'd be all right since Peaches was pulling off like a bat out of hell. Her tires peeled out, and I closed my eyes and held on to the door. We both had calmed down a lot by the time we got to Rhode Island Avenue.

"You want me to take you home or back to Chu's?"

"Just take me home," I said, not sure what I was gonna tell the Brinkleys. I just knew I wasn't trying to hear her and Nut fighting all night. I called Chu and told him what happened. He begged me to come stay with him, but I told him I wanted to find out what happened to Jayson first and to make sure my parents wasn't gonna be pissed.

We rode in a silent car for a few minutes, before Peaches turned the radio on. I looked out the window, and then I got a text from Jayson. It read: *I'm bunned up. Call you in the A.M.*

"This boy," I said out loud.

"Jayson?"

"Yep. He's out being a ho somewhere."

"I told you so."

Knowing Jayson, he must've been with whoever bought us that first round of drinks.

"All right, girl," Peaches said, smiling as she pulled up in front of my house. "That was an interesting night. See you Monday?"

I laughed and said, "If not before then."

She shook her head and laughed, too. She knew and I knew she would be right back over Nut's in the morning, even though she had more than enough reasons to leave him alone. Nut had even tried his hand with me on the sly a few times, but I shut him down. I saw him staring at me when he thought no one else noticed, but I ain't call it flirting. Since he was only looking, I ain't think it was enough to tell Chu.

But one day, when Chu and Rob was out front, I came

out the bathroom the same time Nut was walking down the hallway. Instead of him moving out the way, he made sure to stand right in front of me. He was blocking my path with a smirk on his face, waiting for me to squeeze by. I rolled my eyes and said, "Excuse me" twice, but he ain't move one single inch. I tried my best not to touch him, though I was so close I could smell Hawaiian Punch on his breath. But we never touched as I squeezed by. Nut just laughed. I could hear his lips smacking together, like he had just blew a kiss behind my back.

That made me know why Peaches had trust issues with his crazy ass and why I knew never to be in his house again without Chu.

8

MARCH 2005

You not doing it right!" Nissa shouted, standing over me, her hands stretching my arms straight out.

"Look, fuck this shit!" I yelled, twisting away from her. She was plucking my nerves telling me I wasn't doing the routine right after I tried to do it three times just the way she showed me. "I quit this silly-ass group!"

"Fine, quit!" Nissa said, turning away. "You act like you don't want to be here anyway. Ain't nobody beggin' your ass to stay!"

"What?" I asked, putting my hand on my hip. A few of the girls rolled their eyes and looked away from me. Shakira made a face and laughed. "What the fuck ever! Fuck y'all!"

I grabbed my bag and walked to the bus stop. When I got to Chu's block, I walked over and leaned up against Rob's Ford Explorer with the two of them.

"Hey, baby, guess what?" Chu asked after blowing smoke from his Black & Mild. "This nigga got a full scholarship to play ball for North Carolina A&T!"

I smiled. "For real, Rob?"

He nodded and smiled.

"Congratulations," I said and gave him a light hug.

"All right, all right. Don't be all up on my girl, nigga," Chu said playfully.

"My bad, my bad," Rob said, grinning. "I'm about to catch up with my folks, though. I'll holla at y'all later."

We watched him back his truck out the spot, and then Chu asked if I wanted to go for a ride.

"In what?" I asked, surprised. He smiled and nodded at the navy blue Escalade sitting on big wet tires across the street.

"Baby, that's you?!" I asked excitedly, jumping up and down. Chu had been leaning on Rob to get around ever since we'd been together.

He smiled and held my hand as we crossed the street.

We was sitting pretty in his new whip, riding through the city, down U Street, up Adams Morgan, down Connecticut Avenue. We passed the Lincoln Memorial and the Potomac River, and then Chu took me to Georgetown for dinner at Sequoia. I felt a little out of place in my practice clothes, but whatever. I got the macadamia crusted chicken and Chu got the New York steak. Delicious.

After dinner, we went for a walk on the waterfront. Chu pulled me to him and said, "You know I love you, right?"

"Of course, I do. I love you, too," I said, kissing him.

He smiled. "I need you to hold something for me."

I raised my eyebrows, confused. "What?"

Chu took a deep breath and shook his head. "When we get back to the crib, I'ma give it to you. But you gotta promise me you won't look in the bag or nothing."

I leaned up against the railing that separated us from the

river. He was testing me. Chu knew I couldn't tell him no. "Okay," I mumbled.

"Everything's gonna be all right. I promise," he said, wrapping his arms around my waist. "Me and Rob gotta make this run down to Greensboro this weekend."

"How long you gonna be down there?" I asked.

"Just Saturday. We'll probably get back late, like after three. You'll probably be sleep."

I crossed my arms. He always did this to me. Just up and left, either with Rob or that crazy nigga Nut.

"Come here, girl," he said, kissing me. "Let's break in the seats in my new whip."

I smiled and kissed him back.

Saturday was going to be a long day without Chu around. As soon as he gave me the Gap bag and I got in my bedroom, I opened it. Inside was a black plastic bag with a square hard powder wrapped in clear plastic wrap. *Is it coke or heroin?* I had never seen it up close before, since Chu kept all that kind of stuff out of my sight. I counted fifty thousand dollars in the bag, too.

"Whoa," I mumbled. I closed the bag up and stuffed it in the back of my closet. I ain't know he was rolling like that. I thought he was just selling a little weed on the side.

For the rest of the day, I tried my best not to think about what was in my closet. When Peaches called me up and asked what I was doing since Nut was nowhere to be found and she was bored, I jumped at the chance to leave the house. Mrs. Brinkley had been hinting about me cleaning the refrigerator out, but I hated doing that. All that nastiness that was in the cracks underneath the vegetable tray at the bottom blew me.

"I'm coming to get you," Peaches said.

I threw on some cute clothes, since I knew Peaches was gonna look cute.

"Where we going?" I asked.

"I just wanna go by this spot I know Nut be at sometimes."

I rolled my eyes. Peaches was forever hounding that nigga. "Oh, all right. Where it's at?"

"Out Southeast, over there on Alabama Avenue."

"Oh, okay. After that can we ride out to Iverson Mall? I want to stop by this little boutique they got in there. Get me something new."

"All right," she said, turning up the volume on Mary J's latest. We both sang along as she drove down Suitland Parkway.

"Hey, can you make a left right here first? I wanna ride past my old neighborhood. You mind?" I asked.

"Nope, we can do that. I wanna give that nigga plenty of time to get into some trouble," she said, popping her gum.

When we drove down the dead-end street, I couldn't believe how much had changed since I been gone. The buildings looked smaller to me and dirtier. More garbage was on the ground, and some of the apartment windows and doors was boarded up. I felt sad as we drove down the street, and I looked at the new but old faces. Some I recognized, some I didn't. My heart ached as I looked up at Nana's old apartment and saw another little girl's face looking out the window.

"You can turn around now," I said. "Ain't nobody out here."

"You sure?"

"Yeah."

Peaches turned the car around and headed back up the street. I was hoping, for some strange reason, that I would see Mama doing her usual. Standing on the corner or sitting underneath the big tree where all the old cars used to be with all the other crackheads. But no one was there.

Peaches drove down Alabama Avenue and slowed the car down in front of a white brick apartment building.

"There go that nigga car right there!" she yelled. "Over this bitch's house again."

"What bitch? How you know it's a girl he fucking with?!"

Peaches rolled her eyes and said, "I know he fucking with her, cuz I followed his ass over here before. That nigga thinks I'm fucking stupid."

"You know which apartment he's in?" I asked, just as Peaches jumped out her car. I climbed out on my side and then watched as this crazy chick took out a box cutter. She walked over to Nut's Caddy and slashed all four of his tires. I covered my mouth as I watched Peaches pick up the piece of a broken cement block near the mailbox on the corner.

"Peaches, no! Girl, don't do that shit!" I shouted.

"Fuck this nigga! He got me fucked up. I'm not one of these little-ass girls he be fuckin' with!" She threw the rock through his front window, making the alarm sing through the night air.

"And I want that motherfucker to come out here and say something to me!" she screamed.

"Oh, my God, girl!" I said.

"Yeah, motherfucker. Bring your trifling ass out here!" Peaches yelled. "Bring that bitch you fucking out, too!"

I saw the blinds raise in a few of the apartments, but one on the second floor fell all the way from the window. I saw Nut staring at us, and he was pissed, too. He was so mad, I swear I could see flames glowing from his head.

"Yeah, nigga what?" Peaches yelled as Nut came running from out the front door of the building with no shirt on.

"Peaches, what the fuck you do to my car?" he yelled.

"Tell that bitch you fucking to come out here, so I can whip her ass!" Peaches shouted back.

"Look at this shit!" Nut yelled.

A cute brown-skin girl with a short, curly hairstyle stood at the top of the stairs with her arms crossed. She looked like she was mixed with something like Philippine or Indian.

"Oh, are you his other bitch?" Peaches yelled, running up the stairs. I watched as Nut ran up the stairs two at a time after her, and then he snatched Peaches and dragged her back down the stairs.

"You better get that crazy bitch 'fore I put one up in her silly ass!" the girl shouted, pointing a silver gun at her.

"Oh, my God," I mumbled as my body froze in place.

"No, Leta! Put that shit the fuck up!" Nut yelled as he tugged Peaches.

"Get the fuck off me, Nut!" Peaches shouted and tried to

twist out of Nut's grip like she ain't even see the girl's gun. "Fuck you, bitch!"

I shook my head, but words was stuck in my throat and my feet had gotten stuck on the ground somehow.

"You think I'm playin', bitch!" Leta said, aiming right at Peaches.

"Leta, what the fuck I say?" Nut hollered over his shoulder and then to Peaches he said, "Calm the fuck down, Peaches."

She opened her mouth to say something, but before she could, Nut smacked her so hard Peaches' whole body turned around.

"No, you didn't," Peaches said, holding her face. "You goin' smack me, and not that bitch?!" I could see the tears swelling in her eyes.

"I told your ass to calm down and go home!"

"Peaches, let's go home," I finally called out behind her. "Come on, girl."

"Yeah, drive her ass home, Camille!" Nut said, pulling Peaches back toward the car.

Drive? I ain't never drive before. I mean, I drove the bumper cars at Six Flags and at Kings Dominion a few times, but that was it. I walked around to the driver's side since it ain't look like I had a choice. Peaches was so mad when Nut put her in the passenger seat, she was crying and punching the dashboard at the same time. Leta was still standing in the building's doorway waving her gun from left to right.

"Yeah, bitch! I don't hear your ass talking shit now!" she yelled.

"Shut the fuck up, 'fore I come whip your ass!" Nut

shouted at Leta and then turned to Peaches. "Baby, it ain't what you think it is."

"What you mean it ain't what I think it is?! You fuckin' hit me!" Peaches said, wiping tears from her face. "And I caught your motherfuckin' ass with another ho! I'm through this time, Nut, for real."

"No, you not. And stop saying that shit."

Peaches sucked her teeth and shouted, "Let's go, Camille!"

I looked at the car and tried to put the gear in drive, the way I seen people do it. The gauge clicked in gear.

"Y'all get home safe," Nut said, backing away from the car. "I'll call you later, Peaches. Let me just finish what I'm taking care of."

"Nigga, fuck you!" Peaches yelled as tears streamed down her face. "Don't ever fucking call me again!"

I pressed the gas pedal, and the car lurched forward before I could pull away from the curb. The car jolted a couple times, and then it eased out before jerking again. I kept forgetting which pedal was the gas and which one was the brake.

"Fuck that nigga," Peaches cried.

I felt sorry for Peaches. Her whole world had been built up around Nut. We was practically roommates, cuz we spent so much time at their apartment, and I saw how much she couldn't get enough of him. Nut was totally different from Chu. One minute Nut was talking to Peaches any kind of way, calling her bitch and tramp, and the next minute he was calling her baby and honey and buying her expensive things and taking her to nice places. If I was confused, hell, I knew she was confused. But Peaches did the same things to him, so I guess it was like they needed to hear those things, both the good and the bad.

I only drove a few blocks before I pulled the car over. I was too scared to keep going. Every time a car pulled up next to me, it made me nervous and I felt myself drifting into their lane. I was relieved when Peaches said she could drive now, if I wanted.

"Thanks, Camille," Peaches said after switching seats with me. She rubbed her jaw as she made a left onto Good Hope Road.

"No problem," I whispered. What else could I say? That was some wild and crazy shit back there. It was the first time I had seen a gun in real life and the first time I felt like somebody might actually use it, too. Wait until I tell Chu about his boy. Something told me Peaches wasn't going to leave Nut alone, even after all that drama. That's just the kind of relationship they had.

9

A MONTH LATER

Chu told me to put on something "cute and innocent looking." I frowned, cuz he never asked me to wear something *innocent*. When I asked him why, he said it was a surprise. *I swear he better not be trying to take me to no church function.* I went to more than enough of those with the Brinkleys. Especially with Easter being around the corner, it seemed like they wanted to go every other day. I dug deep in my closet for a soft pink sleeveless cowl-neck sweater and a pair of my favorite Seven jeans. I put on my gray Jimmy Choo stiletto boots and some pink lip gloss. Pink was innocent, right?

When I walked around the corner to meet Chu in his truck, he said, "You ain't put on a dress?"

"A dress?" I asked, confused, "Chu where the heck are you taking me?"

He shook his head and smiled. "You should've put on a dress."

"You want me to go back in the house and change?"

"Nah, that's okay. Your peoples will be all up in your business making a big deal out of you changing your clothes. You know how they are?"

"Of course, I do," I said climbing in the truck. I frowned my face up again and leaned back in the seat. *Where is he taking me?* I watched as he made a left on South Dakota Avenue. We rode down Missouri Avenue and then we merged onto Military Highway. We was headed way uptown. *Who do he know around here?* Chu made a left on Nebraska Avenue and then parked the car in front of a real nice white house. I could see straight into the living room cuz the curtains was wide open. The black wood furniture looked like it was straight out of a magazine.

"Where are we, Chu?" I asked as we walked up the stairs.

"You'll see," he said, smiling and holding my hand.

He rang the doorbell and smiled when a plump woman with auburn dreadlocks opened the door.

"Hi, son," the woman said, beaming. "Are you going to give Mommy a hug?"

Mommy? I thought the two of them wasn't speaking since she put him out. But he wanted me to meet her, so I really felt special. Chu smiled and wrapped his mother up in a strong hug. I smiled at his tenderness.

"Ma, this is Camille. Camille, this is my mother, Bernetta Abani."

I reached out to shake his mother's hand. She said hello and told us to come inside. I was confused. When did the two of them start speaking again? I looked around the house, while his mother teased Chu about me. She had African-looking wood sculptures and big, bright paintings hanging from the walls. In some pictures on the bookcase, Chu was doing karate when he was a little kid. I smiled at his toothless grin in another picture. A boy who looked just like Chu, only a shade lighter, was in some of the other pictures. I picked up one picture that was on a shelf of the two of them together.

"That's my Imhotep back when he was a good little boy," Chu's mother said, standing behind me. She smelled like vanilla and cocoa butter mixed, the same way Mama used to smell. I smiled and inhaled the scent.

"Come on, let's take a seat," she said. "I fixed something I hope you're going to like, Miss Camille."

I walked over to the table where covered decorated glass dishes waited for us.

"I made some of your favorite dishes, Chukwuemeka. Jollof rice, goat, and iyan," she said, smiling and lifting the tops. "Camille, iyan is just mashed yams."

"Mmmm. Make sure you try it," Chu said, turning to me. "Yummy."

I smiled. It did smell good, and it looked like something Nana would make. But I ain't know about eating no goat.

"What about my soup?" he asked, like it was candy or something.

"Your father used to love my groundnut soup," Ms. Abani said, raising a wicked eyebrow. "And that's exactly why I don't make it anymore."

Chu laughed. I thought he said his mother was born in D.C. She seemed to know a lot about African things.

"Ms. Abani, how you know so much about Africa?" I asked as I made my plate.

"Oh, good question, sweetheart. I guess I first became interested in it when I was in college. That was a long, long time ago," she said, laughing. "I had a class where I studied African philosophy, and it just opened my mind to so many different beautiful things about that culture. I couldn't wait to visit Africa. I heard so much about the Tarzan and jungle stuff before I began studying them, so I was so surprised when I learned about how vast the land was, about the gigantic waterfalls and serene mountains. The many beautiful rivers and lush valleys. About all the original species, exotic plants, and animals. And oh . . . the people and the many different native tongues. The gold and diamond mines. I just knew I had to go see it for myself one day. When I was a senior, I took a study-abroad class in Lagos, Nigeria, and ended up staying for three years after that, teaching English through the Peace Corps."

"Oh," I said, amazed.

"And that's how she met my father," Chu said.

"Yes, Lord," she said before taking a bite from her plate. "But that's enough about memory lane. So, Miss Camille, what grade are you in at school?"

"Eleventh," I lied. I didn't want her to know I was so much younger than Chu, since he was eighteen, going on nineteen, and I was only fifteen.

"Oh, so one more year, huh? And you're going to study in college?"

I felt like I had to say something besides what I planned to say, which was I wasn't going to college but cosmetology school like Peaches had said she was gonna do. While

I thought about what I was going to say, Chu answered for me.

"Camille's been thinking about a lot of different things. Right, babe?"

"Yes. I ain't really thought about it all like that," I said.

"*Ain't?* You mean *haven't?*" Ms. Abani said, correcting me.

I looked down, embarrassed, and played with my food.

"Ma, please don't start," Chu said.

"Son, I can't help it. I teach English, for Christ's sake," she said and then turned to me. "Don't take it personally, sweetheart. I'm only trying to help."

I smiled with my lips closed and nodded. I went back to eating, since I didn't want to make the same mistake again.

"Well, you should definitely start thinking about your future. It will be here before you know it. You don't want to be like my son. A high school dropout! Now how does that make me look, Chukwuemeka? An English professor with two high school dropouts and a convict for children! Nonsense," she said, shaking her head.

Chu cleared his throat, wiped his mouth, and backed away from the table. "Come on, Camille," he said.

"Your father would be so proud of you both!" Ms. Abani said with an attitude. "I tried my best, Chukwuemeka. God knows I did."

"Ma, we ain't come over here for all this," he said, helping me from the table. I looked at the two of them go back and forth for a minute, and then I told Ms. Abani it was nice meeting her and thanks for dinner.

"Take care of my son," she said at the door.

"I'll talk to you later," Chu said, walking down the stairs.

"You know I love you, son," Ms. Abani said with a sincere tone.

"Ma, I love you, too," Chu said over his shoulder.

In the truck, Chu was quiet for a minute and then he started talking about how he had decided to get back in touch with his mother as soon as he came back from North Carolina with Rob.

"I felt a little jealous when we got to A&T," Chu said. "When Rob was talking to his coaches and looking around the school, all I kept thinking was, that could've been me."

I rubbed his thigh as we rode down the street. Chu kept talking about his mother and her always being disappointed and how she always blamed him and Tep for everything, especially after their father moved back to Nigeria to marry a woman his parents had chosen for him.

"He actually wanted Ma to say she would be his second wife."

"What?!" I asked, stunned. "Second wife? What kind of crap is that?"

"You know how they do over there? Husbands can take on as many wives as they can afford," Chu said, shaking his head.

Well, at least he seemed to have a problem with it, thank God. I couldn't imagine what sharing one man would be like, especially knowingly. I shook my head, cuz I ain't never heard of no crap like that.

"Even though we all use my father's last name, they never got married," Chu admitted. "My mother still wants my father, but he never even looked back after he left. I feel sorry for her sometimes, but she forgets that he left me and Tep, too."

"That's sad," was all I could say. I knew a similar kind of pain. "I understand how you feel, a little. My mother never looked back, either . . . after she chose drugs over me."

Chu looked at me and then squeezed my hand that was sitting in his lap. Without even saying anything, I knew we had just shared something special with each other.

A couple days later Chu told me him and Rob was heading back to North Carolina and that he wanted me to hold something else for him. I told him okay, since nothing had happened the last time. Chu had put the stuff in another shopping bag like he did the first time, so it wouldn't raise any eyebrows. As soon as I came in the house with the Macy's bag, Mr. and Mrs. Brinkley, who happened to both be sitting in the living room watching *Jeopardy!,* looked up at me. I took a deep breath, before I cut through the living room to the stairs.

"Jayson called looking for you," Mrs. Brinkley said, looking up from the scarf she was knitting.

I forgot I had turned my cell phone off when I went with Chu. Jayson had moved out at the beginning of the year, cuz he said he couldn't take them all in his business anymore. Mr. Big had given Jayson the blues about not going to college, and especially about not playing college football. He was working as a waiter at a five-star restaurant on Capitol Hill. I wasn't supposed to tell the Brinkleys where he was living at, either. There was something like a mini-war going on between the three of them, and I wanted to stay as far away from it as possible.

"You went shopping, yet again?" Mrs. Brinkley asked, just as I was about to put my foot on the first step.

"Um, yes, ma'am," I said, becoming nervous.

"What you get?" Mrs. Brinkley asked.

"Where she get the money is a better question," Mr. Big said, rising from his armchair.

He hadn't touched me since March, a long stretch for him. I was starting to hope he changed his mind about what he had been doing. I wasn't sure why, but I did notice that him and Mrs. Brinkley had started staying around each other a little longer than usual. Just like now. She was actually watching TV *with* him and not in the den reading her Bible like she used to do. I guess life was different now with all of their children out the house.

"Come here, Camille," Mr. Big called.

I turned around and walked back to the living room. *Be calm. Don't worry. Just be normal.*

"Let me see what kind of money you have to spend these days. What's in the bag?"

"Huh?"

"If you can *huh*, you can hear," Mrs. Brinkley said.

"It's nothing. Just some pajamas that was on sale. I saved my money up for this," I said.

"Let's see," Mr. Big said, reaching for the bag.

I snatched it back and said no.

Mr. Big's face frowned and he reached for it again. "I said, give me the bag!"

"No!" I screamed and backed away.

"Camille? What's your problem?" Mrs. Brinkley yelled and stood up. "Do what your father says!"

"He's not my damn father, and you're not my mother! So get off my back!" I shouted.

They both gasped. Mrs. Brinkley covered her heart with her hand, and Mr. Big took off his glasses.

"Little girl, you better watch who you're talking to and what filthy things come flying out of your mouth!" he yelled. "In my house, you honor and respect us! How dare you say I'm not your father and she's not your mother!? How dare you!?"

"Spare the rod, spoil the child, Frank," Mrs. Brinkley said, standing behind him. Mr. Big looked like she had just given him permission to do what he had been wanting to do for a long time. He began unbuckling his belt and snatched it from his pants loops like a whip. Fear crept over me.

Oh, hell no, he ain't. I ran through the living room and out the front door, as Mr. Big stood yelling from the porch for me to come back. But I ran all the way to Rhode Island Avenue.

Not on top of everything else he did to me. No, he wasn't going to start whipping me, too.

Once down the street, I called Chu, but his phone went straight to voicemail. I knew he was still in North Carolina, but I needed to talk. I sat under a bus stop shelter for a minute, clutching the Macy's bag and thinking about calling Peaches. She could let me stay with her and Nut at the apartment, but I wasn't really trying to be there without Chu or Rob. And something told me Chu ain't quite want to leave his stuff around Nut anyway, since every time he went out of town, he called me up to stash it.

"Oh, that's right," I said, remembering that Jayson had called. Maybe he was home. I dialed his cell.

"Where you been?" Jayson asked without even saying hello.

"You will not believe what just happened, Jayson!" I shouted, out of breath and holding back tears.

"Whoa, whoa. Calm down," he said. "Where are you?"

I inhaled and then let the tears fall. "Rhode Island Avenue. I just cussed them out and ran out the house."

"Whoa," he said again. "Meet me at Kerry's. I'm on my way back home."

"Okay," I said, wiping my face.

I hopped on the bus and caught the train to Minnesota Avenue. When I walked out the station, I crossed the street and headed to the Capitol Terrace Apartments. I had been there twice since Jayson moved. I knocked on the door to their second-floor apartment. Kerry opened the door.

"Hey, Camille. Come in. Jay's not here yet, but he told me you was on your way," he said.

"Hey, Kerry," I said, walking inside and sitting on the love seat.

"You want something to drink? We got some lemonade, some cherry Kool-Aid, some blue Gatorade. Shit, we got every kind of aid you need," he said, laughing.

"Kool-Aid is good," I said, flipping the TV channel from VH1 to BET.

I could tell they had added more decorations from IKEA and Pier One. It looked nice, with lots of shades of purple and gold. Kerry was in his early twenties and a dancer with the Washington Ballet. He taught children's dance classes at a school in Rockville. He was cute, with his goatee and short haircut. It was really Kerry's apartment, and Jayson was living with him in a one bedroom. Even though Jayson had never said the words, it ain't take a rocket scientist to see that they was lovers.

"Hey," Jayson said a few minutes later, with two Whole Foods grocery bags in his hand. "What the hell happened?"

"I can't go back," I said, shaking my head. "I'm not living there another day."

"Okay, okay! But tell me what happened, Camille!" Jayson said angrily. "What the hell happened at the house?"

"*Your* father called himself about to *whip* me with his belt, that's what the hell happened!" I said, crossing my arms.

"What?! Rewind, rewind," Jayson said, moving his hand from side to side.

"All because I said him and your mother wasn't my *real* parents!"

"But where did that come from? I know they can be . . . ridiculous, but . . ."

Kerry stood up. "I'm going to go in the bedroom and give you two some space."

We watched him walk across the room and then close the bedroom door.

"Listen, Camille, you know I got my issues with them, too, and I'd be the first to tell you they crazy. But I can't believe you'd even say that after all these years and all the stuff they did for you."

"Jayson, stop acting like your parents adopted me, or that they ain't kick Danica out just for being pregnant! Shoot, your father did a lot, all right. Don't even get me started," I said, rolling my eyes. As much as it hurt, I couldn't bring myself to tell Jayson just what those things was. Saying it out loud would make it true and real for me somehow, and I wasn't ready to admit that, either.

"Okay, okay. I get the point, Camille. I just wanna know what made you say enough was enough, that's all."

"I'm just tired of not having any privacy. Like you. I want to be done with it already. I brought a damn shopping bag in the house and they wanted to trip and make a big damn deal about it."

"Hmmm . . . they think you stealing again?" he asked.

"Probably," I said, thinking about that one time I got caught trying to pull another one of those tricks I learned from Shakira. The undercover cop took me to the back of the store to see the manager, and since I was so young, instead of calling the police, they made me call my parents. I called Mrs. Brinkley hoping she'd go easy on me. But of course, after she told Mr. Big, I got punished in other ways.

"You stealing again?" Jayson asked.

"Hell no! Chu takes care of me."

"Hmmm . . . so what you wanna do?" Jayson asked. "I mean, this place is too small for three of us, but I'm sure Kerry won't mind squeezing you in."

I shook my head. "No, I won't do that to you. I just need somewhere to sleep tonight. At least until I get in touch with Chu. He's out of town right now."

"When he coming back?"

"In the morning."

"Well, you know you're welcome to share the pullout with me," Jayson said, patting the couch.

Yeah, right. He ain't sleep on no damn couch. I smiled and said, "Thanks. And Jayson, thanks for talking to me, for real. You know you're like the only person I can trust, right?"

He nodded. "No problem, little sis. As long as you don't start hollering about I'm not your *real* brother and shit," he said, trying to tickle me.

"Stop it!" I laughed and kicked to get away from him. "Kerry, come get your boy! Please!"

10

MAY 2005

I ended up staying with Jayson two more nights, since Chu and Rob got caught up in some minor drama with some Greensboro dudes. Something about a fight and a car accident at a club. He wouldn't tell me details, but I knew he was still angry about whatever went down, and he said he probably wouldn't go back for a while. He was overjoyed that I was moving in with him, and he even told me to leave whatever I left at the Brinkleys, cuz he was buying me all new clothes. Now that made my day. But I wanted to get some pictures I left behind of me and Mama and Nana back when I lived around Wellington Park.

There was pictures of Danica, Jamal, Ja'qui, and Jayson, too. Pictures of me in Ebony Fire and old pictures from elementary school. I couldn't just leave it behind. The pictures reminded me of who I was in the world. Since Jayson wasn't talking to the Brinkleys much these days, the only way to get the pictures back would be facing them.

The day I decided to stop by happened to be a clear sunny day. Not one single cloud in the sky. Flowers had already started blooming in the front yard. Chu got out of his truck to come inside with me. I knew Mr. Big wasn't home from work, so it was the perfect time for Chu to show up. I tried my key, but it wasn't working.

"No they *ain't* change the locks already," I said, pissed and looking at Chu.

Mrs. Brinkley swung the door open. "Do you need something, young lady?" she asked with an attitude. She looked me up and down and then glared at Chu.

"I just want to get my stuff out of my room. That's all."

"We sent those things to Social Services weeks ago," she said, twisting her cross necklace. "Try calling your case worker."

Mrs. Brinkley was closing the door before I could even move my mouth. I put my foot in the door and said, "You did what?"

"Move your foot!" Mrs. Brinkley snapped.

"You crazy bitch!" I said, pushing the door, making Mrs. Brinkley jump back. "How could you throw my stuff out?!"

"Get out of my house, you skunt!" Mrs. Brinkley shouted.

Skunt? Chu tried to pull me out of the house, but I couldn't help what was about to happen. My hands was up over my head and then latching onto the neck of the woman who had ignored everything that went on in that house with me and Danica since Day One. "Fuckin' crazy bitch! Call on Jesus now!"

"Camille!" Chu yelled, ripping my hands up off of Mrs. Brinkley.

She rubbed her neck and tried to catch her breath, suck-

ing in air like she was a vacuum. "Get out, get out!" she
whispered, while pointing at the front door.

"You sat, and you watched what that nasty motherfucker
was doing to us. You think I ain't know, but I did. You knew
it the whole damn time. You was the one changing the dirty
sheets and washing my dirty panties. So I know you knew.
The money? You knew. Danica's baby was his, and you
knew that, too!" I yelled. Chu held my arm and pulled me
toward the door. "Fuck you and him. And you can tell that
nasty motherfucker I'll see his ass in hell."

I cried in the car like a baby curled up under Chu, wailing
loud and blowing my nose on his shirt. I cried for my secrets
and for Danica's. I cried for all of my pictures and for my
pain. Chu shushed me and kissed my forehead and wiped
my tears. He tried to make me feel better the best way he
could, but the hurt was so fresh. He didn't bother asking me
anything about what I had said on the Brinkleys' doorstep,
but he heard me. A part of me felt ashamed and another
part of me felt relieved that he finally knew what I had been
going through and bottling up inside all this time. I never
really thought about how my secrets would hurt him, too,
until now.

Back at his apartment, Chu lit incense and a special blunt
just for me. He left me in the room to smoke it by myself. I
fell asleep and woke up with him holding me so close, I felt
like I was going to suffocate.

*   *   *

That weekend, Chu took me to Hagerstown to pay his brother a visit. I had only gone once before, but this time we was going with his mother since it was Tep's twenty-third birthday. It was weird seeing the three of them try to act like everything was okay, just for the sake of getting through it. I knew Ms. Abani hated every single minute of being there. Her eyes looked like she was a blink away from losing it. I think I was a good distraction for what they was all feeling, cuz just about everything any one of them said revolved around me and Chu's relationship.

I hadn't been back to school since I moved in with Chu. The semester was almost over anyway and wasn't no way I could pay attention in class with everything that was going on. Jayson had been calling my cell phone nonstop for two straight days. Almost every hour on the hour. His voice messages was surreal: *"How the fuck you goin' put your hands on my mother, smut!"*, *"Wait till I find out where the fuck you stayin' at, cunt!"*, *"Bitch, you better watch your goddamn back!"*

The one person who I thought would still be in my corner had turned his back on me without even hearing my side of the story. Maybe Jayson wasn't supposed to ever know about the evil his parents did to me. I was sad every time I listened to my messages. A few days went by with no calls from Jayson. And then one day I got another message. This time, he was crying loud and breathing hard into the phone like he was drowning or something. *"Daddy dead . . . you gotta call me back, Camille. Daddy dead!"*

Dead? I stared at the phone for a long time wondering if it was a trick. If Mr. Big was dead, how? I lit a blunt and thought about the first time he touched me and how he used to call me Nectar whenever he was inside of me. I closed my eyes, thinking about his grimy hands touching my body and his rough lips kissing my skin. I felt my stomach knot up, and the feeling of throwing up made me run to the bathroom. I stayed in there for a long time but nothing ever came. I walked out to the living room and sat on the couch to stare at Jayson's missed call on my phone for a while. *Should I call him back?*

Peaches was in the kitchen washing dishes when she stopped and sat beside me on the couch.

"Hey, girl, what's wrong with you? You been staring at that damn phone forever."

I shook my head and frowned. "Nothing."

"Hmmm . . . Let me do your hair while you sitting here. I'm so bored I could scream. Nut supposed to be buying some crabs from the wharf, but he taking all day long. Can I do it? I need some more practice," she said, scratching her fingers in my hair. She had started going to hair school and was taking night classes to finish getting her high school diploma, unlike me. I was probably going to fail my last semester classes since I had missed so much school.

"I don't care. Do it if you want to."

"Yes!" she said, excited. "How you want it? I already got some human hair. You want it straight or curly?"

I shrugged my shoulders and played a game on my phone.

"Damn, Camille. Get yourself together. What's wrong

with you? Tell me something or I'ma call Chu up in here. Maybe he can come dick you down real quick," she said, laughing.

I smiled and tossed my phone on the couch. "Okay, give me something long and straight. Maybe like a bang. That would be cute, right?"

"Yeah, that sounds hot!" Peaches said. "I'll hook you up."

Hours later, Chu showed up with long-stem pink roses in his hand at the same time Nut showed up with the crabs.

"Aww, baby, you're so sweet," I said, kissing him and taking the flowers.

"I like your hair. Peaches did it?" he asked, touching the long strands.

I nodded.

"Damn, Nut. Where the hell my flowers at?" Peaches asked playfully.

"I got your flowers right here," he said holding his nuts. "Come and get 'em."

Peaches sucked her teeth, and Nut laughed before opening a beer he took out the refrigerator. He turned around and winked at me. I just knew she saw him, but I wasn't so sure.

"It's for our anniversary," Chu said, grabbing me and turning so my back was pressed against his chest in front of him.

I frowned. "Anniversary?"

"Yep. We met one year ago today."

I smiled and turned around. "You really remembered the day?"

He nodded but smiled. "Well, something like that. I just remember it was at the end of May."

"Aww . . . see, you messed it up," I said, teasing him. "Thanks anyway. They so pretty."

He laughed and turned around to get a beer, too.

Peaches was busy making her special crab dipping sauce, though it was nothing but mayonnaise, ketchup, Old Bay seasoning, hot sauce, a little bit of mustard, and a drop of vinegar. It was real special, all right——that's how just about everybody made it, minus or plus a couple things. But it didn't matter, since it was always good.

I spread out old newspaper on the dining room table and then opened all the windows that had screens on them. Nut turned the TV to ESPN, so we could watch an NBA playoff game while we ate. My cell rang twice, but my hands was too messy from cracking open shells, dipping crabmeat in sauce, and sucking it off my fingers to stop and answer it. Plus I was in a crab-eating mood, and everybody knows you don't just stop eating crabs to talk on no phone. I don't care who it is—you ate until the brown paper bag was empty.

After the crabs was all gone, I cleaned up and then I checked the new messages Jayson left on my phone.

"Camille, I really need to talk. We all at the house, Jamal and Ja'qui, too. Call me."

"Who was that?" Chu asked.

"Jayson."

"What he say this time?"

"He called earlier, before you came home. He said Mr. Brinkley dead."

Chu's jaw clenched. "You believe him?"

"I think he might be telling the truth, cuz he calmed down a lot from the other calls."

"You gonna call him back?"

"Should I?"

Chu paced the bedroom and then lit a Black & Mild. "I don't know. Why should you care that he's dead after what he did to you? I mean . . . however he died, he probably deserved it."

I bit my lip since I was thinking the same thing, but Jayson was my friend way before any of this craziness. Maybe if he just knew what really happened he wouldn't be so pissed. But then again, it *was* his father, just like it *was* his mama I attacked. He'd never believe me, and now that Mr. Big was dead, he couldn't defend himself.

"Let Jayson deal with that shit by hisself. If he was really your friend, a lot of stuff would be different. That lady wasn't the only one acting like she ain't see what was going on in that house!"

Chu was right. Jayson, Jamal, and Ja'qui had to sense something not being right sometimes.

"I'm changing your phone number today! So all that shit he doing can be squashed," Chu said angrily.

"Y'all niggas ate crabs without me," Rob said, standing in the doorway. "Damn. See how y'all do a nigga?"

I smiled and watched him give Chu a duffle bag.

"That's everything?" Chu asked.

"Yeah," he said. "Smurf said we should go down there the day after tomorrow."

"Oh, all right. That's what's up," Chu said, putting the bag in the closet.

I raised my eyebrows. I guess they was going back to Greensboro soon.

"Guess who the fuck I saw the other day, Camille."

"Who?" I asked.

"Your girl KiKi."

"For real?" I hadn't really had much to say to her since that incident at Smurf's cookout. I saw her around the way every now and then, but we ain't even speak to each other. "Where you see her at?"

"She was at the Tradewinds, when I went to see Back last Wednesday. And she looked like a straight-up hooker."

"Ugh, for real?" I asked. That hooker did love her some Go Gos, and Backyard was her favorite band.

"Yeah, and you know she was trying to holla at me again, right? But I wouldn't fuck that bitch with three condoms on, even if she douched with bleach."

Chu and I cracked up laughing.

"Hey, you gonna miss me when I go to college?"

"Nope," I said, smiling, but I would miss him. He was pretty funny and kept us rolling whenever he was around. I saw him play basketball once, and he wasn't too bad, either. He could dunk and everything.

The house phone rang and Peaches came in the room to pass it to Chu. "It's your brother."

"Oh, all right," he said.

Rob walked out the room behind Peaches, and I listened

to Chu talk in codes while I played with my new hairstyle in the mirror.

"Tell Tep, I said hi, baby."

Chu told him and then passed the message that Tep said hi to me. "He said he liked that picture I sent of us and that care package you helped me put together."

"Oh, for real? Good," I said.

Peaches knocked on the door. "Hey, Camille, you want to run to the mall with me real quick?"

"Hell yeah. Give me a second," I said, walking over to Chu. He reached in his pocket and passed me a wad of bills without even looking up or skipping a beat on the phone with Tep. I kissed him and put the money in my pocket.

"Thank you, baby."

Peaches drove to City Place in Silver Spring cuz her favorite nail salon was in there and she wanted to go to a couple of stores. I'd rather we went to Pentagon City instead, but I wasn't driving. We both got our nails done and then she saw something in the window at Rave she wanted to check out. I rolled my eyes. The stuff in that store was so not my taste, but whatever. I followed Peaches around the store, since I knew it wasn't nothing I was gonna want in there, but she was taking too long, so we went our separate ways.

"Hey, Camille," someone said. I turned around and was surprised when I saw Nissa.

"Hey, how you doing?" I asked, not really caring.

"I heard about what happened to your father. That's terrible. I hope they catch whoever did that shit to him."

I frowned and mumbled, "Thanks." I guess Jayson had been telling the truth. *What happened to him?* I ain't want her to know I ain't even know what was going on. That would look fucked up. I tried to change the subject. "So, how long you been working here?"

"Like since I was sixteen." I had forgot she was a couple years older than me.

"Oh, okay."

"You know I graduate this year, right?"

I was shocked. How could that be if we was both in the tenth grade? Well, I would be in the tenth if I was still going. "No, I ain't know that."

"Yeah, girl, I been busting my ass going to night school all year so I could catch up to graduate with my class. I gotta go to summer school, but after that I'm done. And then I'm going to FIT in New York."

Damn. I had no idea. "Oh, good for you."

"Well, let me get back to work. Oh, I forgot to tell you, I saw Danica like a month ago. Her son is so cute."

I lit up. "You did? Where?"

"I was out Potomac Mills with my mother."

"Oh, damn. I've been trying to catch up with that girl for a while."

"For real? You should try MySpace, see if she on it."

"I might," I said. Ain't nobody I know have no damn computer. "All right, well I guess I'll see you around. Take care."

Ms. Trinissa Drummond had it going on, I guess.

Peaches bought two wide belts, a sparkly gold tank top, and a pair of leggings. I wanted to call Jayson to see what happened, but I ain't want to do it while we was out shopping.

"You all right?" Peaches asked. "You been zoning out all day."

"Just a few things on my mind. Don't worry about it."

"All right, if you say so," she said. "Let me get a pretzel or a Cinnabon or something. Shit, I'm hungry."

When we got back to the house, Chu was standing outside in front of the building talking to Rob, Nut, and some other guys from the neighborhood.

"What you get me?" he asked, smiling.

"Um, well," I said, and I smiled, too. "I got you something, but you gotta come in the house to get it."

"For real?" Chu said. He plucked his Black to the ground and followed me in the house.

As soon as we got in the bedroom, I told him about what Nissa told me about Mr. Big.

"Damn. You goin' call Jayson to find out what happened?"

"You think I should?"

Chu sat on the bed and then said, "I guess."

"All right," I said, taking my phone from my purse. I sat on the bed beside Chu and dialed up Jayson.

"Camille? Somebody killed Daddy!" he said before I could even say hello.

"Huh?" I asked, confused.

"At a gas station in Capitol Heights. Somebody shot him right after he came out the store."

"Oh, my God. When this happen?"

"Last night, on his way home from work."

"Damn."

"You should come around here. Everybody's here."

I looked down. There was no way I was stepping foot back up in that house. "Jayson, I really don't think that's a good idea."

"Mama not gonna care right now. She's too . . . too depressed."

"Still . . . not after what happened. I can't come over there," I said and then sighed. "I'll have to catch you later. Maybe I'll come by your house tomorrow. Will you be there?"

"Yeah, for a minute. But I gotta help Mama plan the funeral and everything. A lot of family coming up from South Carolina. I can't believe you not gonna come," he said. I could hear the disappointment in his voice.

"We'll talk tomorrow. I promise."

Chu squeezed my thigh and rubbed my knee.

The next afternoon, Chu asked if I wanted him to go with me over Jayson's, but I told him no. I ain't think Jayson was gonna try to hurt me, not with his father dead and him grieving. Kicking my ass for trying to stomp the dog shit out of his mama was probably the last thing on his mind. I knew I'd be okay. Chu dropped me off and then gave me money to call a cab so I could get back home.

When Jayson opened the door, he looked like he had been crying for days.

"How you doing?" I asked.

"I feel like shit. Come in," he said, opening the door.

"So do they know anything about who did it?" I asked, sitting on the couch.

"No, the cameras was too fucked up. But they said it wasn't a robbery, cuz all his money was still on him."

"Damn." I shook my head, then I said, "How *she* doing?" not sure if he would be offended if I called her Mrs. Brinkley instead of Mama.

"She's been crying off and on, but she's okay. Her sister came up yesterday."

I had never met any of their other family the whole time I was there. One summer the Brinkleys sent the boys down South to spend the break with relatives in South Carolina. Danica and me was in the house together that whole summer. It was one of the best and worse times ever. It was the best cuz the boys wasn't around teasing us. We got spoiled with desserts "just because" and we went to Six Flags three times. But it was the worst, cuz Mr. Big had plenty of time to make his way on down to our room without the boys' usual distractions.

I sat with Jayson for a while, listening to him talk about memories he had of his father and why he hoped they caught the person that did it.

"People don't just get shot in the head by accident," Jayson said after he blew his nose.

"In the head? Jesus."

"Why would somebody just kill him like that?" Jayson asked before crying all over again.

But I had no answer for him. I listened to Jayson go on reminiscing about the good and the bad. He remembered how Mr. Big once tricked Jamal into letting Jayson beat him in a race down their street.

"Jamal was talking so much trash that Daddy told him to race me in his Timbs. Jamal was stupid enough to do it, too. All that mouth he had. Man, I smoked that boy something terrible!" Jayson smiled as he spoke. "It felt so good to finally beat him at something. You know, even though me and Daddy had our problems and our issues, I loved him. He ain't deserve that shit."

I rubbed his leg, not sure what to say since I definitely ain't have no love for him. I stayed with Jayson for a while longer and then I told him I had to go. He told me the funeral was gonna be in two days, at the same church we all used to go to every Sunday before Jayson moved and before I left. But I already knew I wasn't going, and I had already decided not to tell Jayson what Mr. Big did to me. Wasn't no use in me trying to change how he felt about his father. For now, the past was going to stay in the past. I couldn't change it anyway. When I left out the door, I knew me and Jayson would never be as close as we used to be, ever again.

EVEN THE SUN GOES DOWN . . .

11

AUGUST 2005

African accents bounced off the dingy walls of the hair-braiding shop at the corner of Eighth and H Streets. I was getting Senegalese twists, but I hated when they spoke that stuff couldn't nobody understand but them. I tried thinking about Chu's mother and what she said about Africans, but I just thought what they was doing was rude. I looked around at the five other girls leaning to the left and then the right, as the African ladies tugged and stitched fake hair extensions tightly on their heads. The braiders' dark, rough fingertips was cracked and peeling like they had been scrubbing floors with their bare hands.

Strands of hair floated through the air, landing on any and every thing. Hair was clogged in vents, wrapped around ankles, and even under my clothes. I knew some might be in my damn panties, too. Don't even ask me how it gets all the way down there.

I was lucky enough to get a chair at six in the morning since it took five hours to do the style I wanted and I only made my appointment the day before. Chu was out of town driving Rob down to Greensboro, since he had to move

into the athletic dorm at A&T a couple days earlier than
the other college kids. I was trying my best to stay out of
the house while he was gone. But it wasn't like I could've
went down North Carolina with them—Chu and Rob was
too busy building a little hustle down there with Smurf. Tep
was about to get out in a couple months, so a lot of stuff was
about to pop off for them.

Just as the lady doing my hair reached for another pinch
of the sandy brown synthetic weave I wanted added for
streaks, the front door swung open. In walks Shakira looking like a slut with some super-short booty shorts, a yellow
tank top with "Super Star" written in black glitter, and her
stiletto sandals. It was way too early for all that extra. I ain't
seen her in a minute, not since Ebony Fire, and she looked
real different, like she been there and back again. She had a
few scars on her face that ain't used to be there, and her lip
looked a little swollen. She was carrying a bag of blond hair
extensions that was oozing out of her plastic bag.

"Can I get some micro-minis?" she said to one of the
braiders sitting on a stool gossiping in the front of the store.

"How long you want?" the African lady asked.

"To here." Shakira pointed to the middle of her back.

"Two hundred and seventy-five dollars," the woman
said.

"Psst, you crazy," Shakira said and then turned to leave.
"*And* I brought my own hair. Nah. I'll just go to the African
Hair Gallery up in Silver Spring."

"Two fifty," the lady called to her back.

"Two twenty-five," Shakira said, stopping in her tracks
and turning around. "And I don't want two people doing

my hair at the same damn time, neither. That shit don't never look right."

The lady sucked her teeth and said something in her crazy-sounding language and then the other Africans laughed but kept their eyes locked on the scalps of their customers. Shakira put her hand on her hip and eyed the lady, who twisted her lips up and pointed to the empty chair next to me. As soon as Shakira recognized me, she rolled her eyes before dropping her body into the spinning chair. *No, that trick ain't just roll her eyes at me like I give a kitty that we still don't speak.*

I watched as some girls came in and out, making appointments and getting loose braids re-plaited back in. A couple mothers dropped by to feed their hungry children who had been sitting in the same seat for hours. Men walked through the door, too, boyfriends and husbands who needed to pay up for the hairstyles that cost anywhere from $150 to $500, depending on what the women got.

I was almost done, except for the ends. The lady still needed to burn them off to seal the tips. But just as she was running the sizzling flame over the synthetic hair, melting them down, the front door burst open with a loud thud, hitting the wall. A skinny man, wearing a black baseball cap and a blue bandana over his nose and mouth, tightened his grip on the black gun in his hand. Two ladies screamed out, making everybody look at the door.

"Y'all shut the fuck up and get on the floor!" the man yelled. He was shaking worse than some of us.

"Oh, my God!" Shakira hollered.

"Bitch, I said shut the fuck up! Now get your motherfuckin' ass on the floor. All of y'all!" he shouted, pointing the gun at her. I watched the man scan the room with his eyes as everybody jumped to the floor, and then he told one of the hair braiders who was sitting to get up.

"Get your ass over here, Nefertiti!" he yelled.

I laid my head on the dirty floor and waited for whatever was gonna happen next. Some of the women was crying and saying prayers. The slender lady wearing a turquoise head-wrap flinched as he pointed the gun in her direction.

"Get me all the money in this motherfucker! All the money!" he yelled at the top of his lungs. He was scratching and sweating. I was scared and wished Chu was here.

"Hurry the fuck up!" the man yelled.

I could hear the lady running around the shop and the sound of her flip-flops smacking the floor. I could tell the guy was high on some white, cuz he kept scratching his arms and was real hyped up. He was behind the lady every single step of the way.

"Yeah, yeah!" he yelled. "I knew y'all kept a lot of cash in this bitch!"

One of the women screamed something in African, and the man said, "Shut the fuck up! I want the money from all the American niggas in this bitch, too! Get it for me, Nefertiti!"

The woman was crying when she came to get the money I had.

"I'm scared," I heard Shakira mumble beside me.

"Me, too," I admitted.

"All right, now everybody take your bottoms off! I want

all bottoms. Pants, skirts, dresses if you in 'em, and I want big drawls and little drawls. I want them all!" the man yelled.

A few gasps went up in the air. One lady cried out like someone had just died, and then Skinny Man yelled, "Now! Take 'em off!" To make his point clear, he shot off a round in the ceiling.

Everybody started jumping around and snatching their clothes off. Some people cried aloud. I pulled down my jeans, and Shakira tore off her shorts.

"Hurry up! Nefertiti, give it here. Get all of 'em!" Skinny Man said as the African lady with the headwrap gathered everybody's stuff.

"Hurry up!" he yelled again.

We huddled up, hiding our private parts while Skinny Man backed out the door.

I watched the door for a few seconds before I realized that the man was really gone. Everybody ran around the store in circles. The Africans took their headwraps off and wrapped them around their waists. Everybody else looked for other things to use. Plastic bags with fake hair in it or hair magazines.

"Come on, Camille, let's get out of here!" Shakira shouted.

"Oh, my God. I can't believe this shit just happened!" I yelled, fumbling for my phone. The crackhead was so worried about taking our bottoms and the cash that he ain't even take our purses. I was gonna call Chu or Peaches— somebody.

"Let's go, Camille!"

"I can't go out there like this!"

"Hold on, hold on, hold on . . . I'ma call my cousin Marcha. She live right around the corner," Shakira said, digging her cell phone from her purse.

By the time Shakira's cousin finally came with shorts for both of us, someone had called the police and they was passing out yellow plastic blankets for everybody. We answered a few questions, gave a description of Skinny Man, and then we left the store.

"Girl . . . ," Shakira said, shaking her head. "I can't believe that mess."

"Me either," I said.

"That shit was wild. Come by my spot for a minute and get your nerves together," Marcha said. "I got some green at the crib."

"That sounds like a plan," Shakira said. "You coming, Camille?"

I nodded. What was I supposed to do? Even though Marcha looked a little suspect with her gold nose ring, her wet set hairstyle, and her spaghetti-strap green summer dress, when she knew her big ass needed, at the very least, a bra, I ain't feel like just going straight home. My nerves was still bad and I could still feel my hands shaking. Smoking weed was definitely a plan.

When we walked in Marcha's apartment, I was surprised. It looked halfway decent for it to be in the projects. As soon as we walked in the door, she turned on some old Rare Essence, and then she rolled a fat-ass J. After she took a few puffs, she passed it to Shakira, and then it came to me. I sunk deeper into the couch and closed my eyes.

"Y'all should've seen your faces when I got there," she

said, laughing. "Looking like somebody's newborn puppies, all scared of the world."

"Shit, your ass just don't know. That nigga was geeking like shit!" Shakira said. "I thought he was goin' shoot somebody on an accident."

I laughed cuz I was thinking that, too. "And if his ass scratched hisself one more damn time with that gun in his hand . . . he was gonna shoot his damn self!"

Shakira laughed and blew a smoke ring in the air.

"I thought that was it for us," I said, laughing again. "For real."

"Look at it this way," Marcha said. "At least your hair looks good."

"True," I said, smiling.

"And look at Shakira's fucked-up head," Marcha said, and she laughed. "Looking like a wet cat died up there. You sure that lil' nigga don't got rabies?"

I laughed and puffed on the blunt. Even Shakira had to laugh at that. "Leave me alone. I was trying to get the shit done. I know it look crazy."

"Well, you better hurry up and do something to it 'fore *you know who* get here."

"He coming here?" Shakira asked, looking obviously scared and running her fingers through her hair.

"Yeah, he said he was gonna be here around three, and it's what . . . ?" she said, looking up at the clock on the cable box. "Ten minutes to three now."

"Shit, let me get the fuck outta here. Come on, Camille!" Shakira jumped up and was at the door before I could even get off the couch. "Shit, shit, shit. I owe that nigga some money! Let me borrow one of your scarves."

Marcha tossed her an oily yellow head scarf and said, "You better hurry up and get out. And wash my damn shorts before you give 'em back. I don't know what your ass got!"

"Fuck you!" Shakira said as she closed the door.

"Who coming?" I asked as we walked down the street.

"Girl, this dude I do some work for."

"Work?"

"Yeah, you know. I gotta do some stuff every now and then to make ends meet. Ain't nothing."

I left it at that. Part of me ain't wanna know no more than that. The other part of me wanted to know all the damn details. But before I decided to ask any more questions, Shakira said, "So does this mean we're friends again?"

I tucked my lips into a straight line and then shrugged. "I guess."

"Why you stop talking to me in the first place?" she asked, stopping and turning to look me in the eye.

I took a deep breath. "I don't know. I just thought maybe we was growing apart." That wasn't quite a lie, but of course, it wasn't the whole truth.

"Oh . . . I guess we could've been. Ever since you got with Chu, you been different."

"What you mean by that?" I asked, feeling the heat rising up my neck.

"I don't know . . . I guess he just made you see things differently. I'm not saying it's a bad thing, just different."

"Hey, KiKi," someone called out of a passing car as we walked down H Street. Shakira waved and flashed a smile.

"You going back to school next week?" she asked.

"Naw," I said shaking my head. "You?"

"Girl, I ain't been to school all year."

I looked at her surprised. "Why not?"

"Girl, please. School ain't putting money in my pockets, and I gotta eat, so . . ."

And then I remembered that Shakira grew up in a house with all girls on Saratoga Avenue. Her oldest sister, Sadonna, was only twenty when their mother died. Instead of letting her three little sisters get shipped off to foster care like me, she was taking care of them herself.

"What you been doing for money?" I asked.

"Psst . . . any and every thing. You don't even want to know," she said, shaking her head. "But hell, it's money, so I don't give a fuck. What you been doing?"

I wasn't surprised to hear her say that, even though it seemed mighty suspect to me.

"Ay, KiKi, wassup?" a guy yelled from the passenger seat of a red Lexus that was crawling down the street.

She smiled and waved. "Hey, Boo! We goin' get up later."

"Yeah, all right," the guy said before the car pulled off.

"Nothing really," I said when she finally stopped cheesing. "I just been chilling."

"Chu must be taking care of you something good."

It was my turn to stop cheesing, cuz he was, but I ain't need her to know all that. "Something like that. I do all right. I still got family," I lied.

"And they know your ass ain't been going to school? I can't believe that."

I stayed silent.

"Well, I'm about to catch the bus, so let me give you my number, in case you want to hang out or something."

I listened to her give me the number, and I typed it in my phone even though I knew I wasn't gonna call her.

"What's yours?" Shakira asked.

I gave it to her, but I hoped she wasn't really planning to use it.

"All right, girl, I'll talk to you later." Shakira reached over and gave me a hug. "We was lucky as shit today, wasn't we?"

"Yeah, we was," I said, hugging her lightly.

"All right, girl."

I waved and kept walking, glad that I still had my Smart-Card so I could catch the bus home, too.

As soon as I unlocked the door, I knew I should've turned right back around since Peaches was crying on the floor in the living room with Nut standing over top of her smoking a cigarette, looking pissed off. I slipped my keys in my bag and said, "What's going on? Everything okay, Peaches?"

"That bitch always crying for some stupid shit," Nut said as he walked to the kitchen, putting his cigarette out in the ashtray.

"Don't call me no bitch, you lying muthafucka!" Peaches yelled.

"You better watch your damn mouth!" Nut shouted. "Or you can get the fuck out my crib!"

She gasped. "You goin' put me out? Even after I just told

you I'm pregnant?!" Peaches screamed, using the couch to balance her as she pushed herself up off the floor. "You fuckin' crazy muthafucka. You goin' put me and your child out?"

I looked between the two of them, shocked and waiting to hear what Nut would say or do. When he said, "How I know that's my baby?" I almost lost it just like Peaches did. She ran up on Nut and started swinging and scratching. Nut grabbed her shoulders and forced her to sit down on the couch.

"Wait, wait!" I yelled, trying to break them apart, but Nut was too strong for me. "Don't hurt her, Nut!"

Peaches clamped her teeth around Nut's wrist somehow, and then he hollered out in pain and just as quickly punched Peaches in her face.

"Oh, shit!" I cried, as I watched her slump to the floor, passing out.

"Fuckin' stupid bitch," Nut said as he rubbed his wrist and headed to the bathroom.

"Peaches? Get up, girl!" I yelled, shaking her. When she ain't move, I ran to the kitchen to get a cup of cold water and then I ran back to where she laid on the floor and dumped it all on her face. She coughed a couple times and twisted her head from side to side.

"You okay, girl?" I was bending over her, scared to death.

She coughed, nodded, and then started crying. I helped her sit up as I heard Nut leaving out the apartment. He ain't even look back to check on her. Bastard. I shook my head.

This had been a long day. First, robbed at gunpoint, now this.

"You gotta get away from that crazy nigga before he seriously hurt you!" I said. "And you pregnant?"

She wiped her face and nodded again. "But where the hell am I gonna go?"

I had no words for her. I barely had a place to stay. Chu was acting like he wanted to move to North Carolina these days, and Peaches was already living on her own since her stepfather had been trying to fuck her on and off for the past couple years. Nut was all she had.

"I don't know," I said. "I wish I did."

12

TWO DAYS LATER

When Chu came back in town, I told him all about my wild and crazy weekend. He seemed more quiet than usual and he ain't say much about anything I said. It wasn't like him.

"What's wrong with you?" I asked. "Why you so quiet?"

He shrugged and lit a blunt in the dark bedroom. "You want some?"

I shook my head.

"Come here," he said. "Put your head right here."

I crawled over and laid my head across his lean chest, just like he liked it. He held me close and rubbed my hair as he puffed on the Bob. "If anything ever happen to me, right, I want you to look for my brother, okay?"

I frowned. "What you talking about?"

He shook his head and said, "He'll know what to do. I just want to make sure you're all right."

"Baby, you scaring me," I said, sitting up and looking at him. "What you talking about?"

"I don't want to talk about it, Camille," he said before blowing out a long puff. "You trust me, right?"

"Of course."

"You love me, too, right?"

"Chu? Why you acting like this?" I asked, confused. I reached for his blunt and took a couple long puffs before giving it back to him. "You know I love you."

Chu stayed quiet for a long moment and I sat listening to his heart beating.

"Baby, you got me shook. You gonna tell me what's going on?"

"Nah, it ain't nothing to tell," he said, smashing the blunt out in the ashtray. He turned around and kissed me on my lips. "I just miss you, baby. You miss me?"

"Do you really have to ask that question?" I said, rolling him over on his back and sliding on top of him. "Of course, I miss you. You wanna see how much?"

Chu nodded and smiled.

Smurf really was a dark-skin dude. Nut called him "blur-ple" behind his back since that was black, blue, and purple mixed in his book. I was staring out the window at Smurf leaned up against his white E-Class Mercedes Benz, smiling and talking to Chu and Nut in the parking lot. I saw some of the neighborhood groupies trying to get Smurf's atten-tion, but he wasn't paying them no mind. They wasn't even in his league.

There was a lot of people outside since it was still warm. Children riding their bikes, a group of girls playing double

Dutch, some women sitting on the stoop gossiping. Two dudes riding a little tiny motorcycle, neither one of them with a helmet. The ice cream truck had just left, and I was mad because I wanted a Bomb Pop but was too lazy to go outside and get it. Chu was too busy to buy one for me.

"What you doing?" Peaches asked, leaning beside me, playing with my twists.

"Girl, just being nosey," I said. "So when was you gonna tell me you was pregnant, tramp?"

She smiled. "I just found out."

"Sure."

"For real."

"How far are you?" I asked, staring at her swollen jaw where Nut punched her a couple days ago. It was so dark brown it looked black.

"I don't know. Maybe about two months. I'm gonna go to the doctor on Tuesday."

"Wow. You keeping it?"

"Hell yeah! How you goin' ask me that?" she said, shoving me.

I smiled.

Pop! Pop! Pop!

Three loud gunshots rang out. I snatched Peaches to the ground and crawled away from the window.

Pop! Pop! Pop! Pop!

We crawled to the bathroom and shut the door.

Pop! Pop! Pop! Pop!

I dialed Chu's cell, but his phone just rang.

"Oh, my God," I mumbled. "Oh, my God . . . oh, my God."

"Let me see," Peaches said, reaching for my phone and dialing. "Nut, answer the phone! Answer the damn phone, baby!"

I shook my head from left to right and then cracked open the bathroom door. I listened to hear if they was still shooting, but it was quiet except for Peaches redialing Nut's number. I crawled out the bathroom and into the living room on my stomach. I could hear a woman crying so I rose up from the floor and peeked out the window.

As soon as I looked out the window, I blanked out until I heard my own voice screaming, "Aaaiiiii!"

I can't remember how I got downstairs, but somehow I did, and Chu's body was lying in my arms and my tears was mixing with his blood.

Police and ambulance sirens blared.

Peaches screamed at the top of her lungs beside me.

A woman across the parking lot clutched a little girl who was covered in blood, too.

I choked on tears and cried until I was hoarse and couldn't even whisper his name no more.

Strange hands yanked me away.

A deep voice shouted, "You got to let him go, miss."

My mind replayed all those times Chu made trips for Smurf, the packages I kept safe, the duffle bags Rob carried, the money, the coke, and everything else. I thought about how whenever Chu came back from being out of town, his mind always seemed like it was out of place.

"The doctors said he goin' be all right," Peaches said,

plopping in the chair next to me in the waiting room. "You can go home now if you want to. I know you're tired."

I shook my head and leaned forward, putting my elbows on my knees to hold my head up. "I won't be able to sleep," I said, wiping away a tear. We had already been here ten hours for surgery upon surgery.

Peaches rubbed my back, since now that Nut was going to be okay, she could breathe. But Chu was dead. Ms. Abani had to be drugged so she could finally stop crying. Smurf was in ICU holding on to his last breaths.

I stood up, and my legs felt numb, but I wiped my face and tried to walk.

"You goin' home?" Peaches asked. Her eyes cried for me, even though she wasn't shedding any tears.

I shrugged. "I just gotta get outta here."

"Call me, if you need me," she called to my back.

I ain't need her feeling sorry for me while she had her own pain to deal with. As I walked out of Providence Hospital, for the first time since the day I arrived at the Brinkleys' doorstep, I felt alone. Like no one loved me and like I had no plan. I wiped another tear from my face and started walking down Allison Street. I walked until the sun disappeared behind the houses. I thought about the first time Chu kissed me over Smurf's house and the little gray kitten he tried to sneak past Nut for me, not realizing Rob was allergic. We ended up getting rid of the poor thing anyway. I remembered the time me and Chu went to Unifest in Anacostia Park and he dared me to get my face painted like the kids. Of course, I won and he owed me a foot massage later. I thought about everything we did

together. The long walks, the long rides, the surprise dinners, and all the shopping. I thought about how he made
me feel special even when everything else in my world felt
wrong and unimportant.

I still couldn't believe he was dead. Just like that, he was
gone. And for what?

I walked to South Dakota Avenue and flagged down a
cab. I couldn't go back to the apartment. Not tonight. I ain't
wanna smell Chu's Bvlgari Aqua splashed on everything,
and I ain't ever wanna sleep in his bed again without him.

"Where do you want me to take you?" the cab driver
asked.

I looked at my cell and then out the window. I ain't know
who to call. Rob's phone kept going straight to voicemail.
I was trying to tell him what happened, even though he
couldn't get here right away since he was at school. I ain't
know how else he'd find out about it.

"Just drive," I said, drained.

"You sure you got some money on you?" he said with an
attitude.

I rolled my eyes and gave him twenty dollars.

Jayson popped in my head. I ain't talk to him for months.
A surprise visit wasn't cool, especially since I ain't show up
to his father's funeral. I knew if I asked, he'd let me stay
there cuz as mad as he was with me, he still cared about me.
But I felt so guilty about not being there for him when he
most needed it that I couldn't just call him now. How was
my loss more important than his?

I scrolled through my phone. *Shakira.* Yes, yes. She won't
be asking no whole lot of questions. Thank God I still had

her number. When I asked her if she was busy, she said no and gave me the address to the apartment she lived in on Nineteenth Street. I told the cab driver and leaned back in the seat.

Imagine this. Me going to Shakira Scott's spot. She ain't even sound surprised to hear from me.

When the cab pulled up in front of her two-story apartment building, she was sitting on the stoop with two other girls. They all looked like hoes.

"Hey, Camille!" Shakira said, giving me a hug like we was best friends. She was dressed as wild as usual. She had on some black spandex booty shorts with two big gold buttons and a gold halter top that tied up behind her neck. Her stiletto cheetah sandals was wrapped up her legs.

"Hey, girl," I said, hugging her back.

"This is Trina Boo and Wynika," she said. The two girls looked just as freaky—long stringy tracks down their backs and tiny, fitted bright-colored summer dresses. One looked like she was pregnant, though. "Camille been my girl since what? Elementary?"

I nodded. "Something like that."

The two girls smiled.

"You all right, Camille?" Shakira asked, taking a step back and staring me up and down. "Come on, let's go inside. You look like you need to talk."

I nodded again, near tears.

I walked up the one flight in the building that had four apartment units. Shakira had a small, near-empty one-bedroom apartment. There was an old raggedy couch in the living room with a small crochet blanket on top, and I'm sure it was covering holes or stains. I could smell burnt chicken grease with a hint of Ajax coming from the bathroom.

"Make yourself at home, Camille," she said, clicking on the fan that stood in the middle of the floor. She took her sandals off and said, "You want something to drink?"

I walked over to the couch and sat down. "Some water?"

"All I got is tap, unless you want one of these wine coolers? I got kiwi-strawberry and grape."

"Okay, either one," I said, knocking a roach off my pants leg. I tried to do it on the sly, but she saw me.

"Girl, I can't help it. Wynika trifling ass and them dirty-ass kids downstairs," she said, smiling as she went to the refrigerator.

I smiled, a bit embarrassed for her.

"I used to bomb the apartment like once a week until I decided to stop fighting them muthafuckas. You see that white shit all along the walls? That's boric acid. They say that shit's supposed to work, but what the fuck you see crawling everywhere?"

"You live here by yourself?"

"Yeah, something like that."

"What you mean?"

She gave me a bottle and she opened one for herself and then she sat on a big purple beanbag that was in the corner. Shakira crossed her legs Indian style and then swung her golden blond extensions over her shoulder.

"It hot in here to you?" she asked, fanning herself with her hand, her bangles click-clacking against each other.

Hot wasn't the word. It felt like Egypt in this bitch. It was stuffy, and I could feel sweat beads popping up on my nose. I pressed the cold bottle to the side of my face and nodded.

"Yeah, I know. An AC is next."

"How long you been living here?"

"Since the beginning of the summer."

"For real? You doing it then."

She looked sad, but I had my own problems. "Girl, please. This dude is paying my rent."

"Oh, yeah?"

"I mean, I work, but he got me covered for most of it," she said, taking a sip from her bottle. "So what's up with you?"

I took a deep breath and blew it out. "Chu got killed today."

"Stop fucking playing with me!!" Shakira said, jumping up and running over to sit beside me. She put her hand on my knee. "Girl—oh, my God! Are you okay? What happened? I am so sorry, Camille!"

The tears started back up and I let them fall as I sipped my cooler.

"Girl, you don't have to say nothing. Nothing at all. Just let it out the best way you feel like doing it."

She got up and lit incense and then I watched her roll a J through tears. I sipped on the cooler until the bottle was empty.

"Can I have another one?"

"Sure, girl. Just grab it from the fridge."

I walked over and grabbed one and then listened to the noise coming up from the street. Children was still running up the block as dark as it was outside. Some was setting off firecrackers even though the Fourth of July had come and gone over a month ago. Cars drove down the street with music blasting from the speakers. A man kept coughing like his lungs was about to collapse. Trina Boo and Wynika's laughter carried upstairs through all the open windows.

"Here, girl, smoke this shit," Shakira said.

I walked over and took the tightly wrapped cigar from her hand. I took a long pull before falling back onto the couch. Shakira was only sixteen and she was living in an apartment by herself. I couldn't understand it, but my mind was too full with other stuff to even worry about it.

"And ain't your father just got killed, too?" she asked, shaking her head.

"That muthafucka wasn't my father," I said, crossing my arms.

"I mean your foster father? I saw it on the news back when it happened. Did they ever find out who did it?"

I kept my mouth closed and waited for her to pass the blunt back to me. It was all too much. I ain't wanna think about Mr. Big. Not right now. As soon as the blunt ran out, Shakira rolled another one and we smoked until I was so tired I passed out.

13

THE DAY AFTER
THE WORST NIGHT EVER

Knock! Knock! Knock!

"KiKi?!" a girl's voice yelled from the other side of the door. I wiped the sleep from my eyes and sat up from the couch. I almost forgot where I was, but I saw the purple beanbag on the floor and remembered that I was over Shakira's apartment. I watched a roach crawling on the ceiling, hoping he wasn't headed my way. Another roach was scaling the wall and headed behind the big picture of the African woman with the basket on her head.

Knock! Knock! Knock!

"Girl, wake up! You got some eggs in there?" the girl called from the other side of the door.

Shakira came from her room wearing a pink satin robe. "I know this bitch done lost her muthafuckin' mind. What, Wynika?" she asked, snatching the door open.

"Tell me you got some eggs I can borrow?"

"Do I look like Safeway, bitch?"

"Look, do you or don't you?" Wynika said, rolling her

eyes and planting her hand on her hip. "Why you always gotta be so nasty?"

"No, I don't. Now, why you always begging, bitch?"

"Shut up . . . I ain't goin' be too many more of your bitches. Hey, girl," she said waving at me.

I waved back. They must go through this every day, cuz I just knew a fight was about to take place, but nothing jumped off.

When she left out, Shakira gave me a hand towel that was almost to shreds and a washcloth. "Sorry, girl, this all I got that's clean. You can borrow some of my clothes, if you want."

I said thanks, but I really ain't wanna wear nothing of hers even though I knew she was really trying hard to be nice. I guess she never really was a bad person. I just chose not to be friends with her no more.

After I got out the shower, some eggs mysteriously showed up. She also had toast and bacon on a plate for me. I was shocked.

"You know, you can stay here as long as you want. You goin' through so much right now. I wouldn't wish that shit on nobody," she said, shaking her head. "I'll even help you get your stuff later, if you want."

I nodded. I couldn't even think about what was going to happen the next hour, let alone the next day or two.

For the next week, I slept on Shakira's couch. Well, I spent most of the time tossing and turning. She was gone most of the time, mostly at nighttime. A few nights she brought back company, but they went straight to her bedroom. I was half sleep, but I could hear them laughing and the headboard banging up against the wall.

One night I woke up drenching in a cold sweat from a nightmare. Chu was running and I was chasing behind him, but I could never catch up. When I woke up, I thought I felt somebody standing over me, but when I strained to see in the dark living room, wasn't nobody there.

I had lost my appetite, so Shakira's empty fridge wasn't a problem. I never went to get any of my things from Nut's apartment. I just couldn't do it. Peaches called me a couple of times, but I kept the conversation real short. A part of me was jealous that Nut and Smurf both survived. It hurt to hear her talk, even though she was saying nice stuff. I just ain't wanna hear it.

The day of Chu's funeral, Shakira had to talk me into going. I ain't wanna remember my baby like that, but she made me realize that it wasn't about me. It was about his family and honoring his memory, so I put on a decent dress from her closet and caught a cab to the funeral home by myself, even though she offered to go with me. Nut was in a wheelchair and he had his arm wrapped up. For whatever reason, the 666 number was cut in the back of his head again. I shook my head when I saw it. I just thought it wasn't appropriate. Not today.

Before the service started, Peaches told me Smurf was still in intensive care at the hospital, but the doctors said they was about to upgrade his condition at the rate he was going.

I heard a loud shout in the front of the church from a

woman. Just when I looked up to see who it was, she shouted, "Chukwuemeka! My son! Oh, my son!"

Chu's mother was all to pieces as she stood in front of the casket crying. Two women with big black hats tried to hold on to Ms. Abani as she slumped to the floor. My stomach knotted up and tears slid down my face watching her. I hadn't seen her since the night he died, when she rushed up to the hospital, all hysterical and angry.

Out the blue, Ms. Abani threw her hands up in the air like she was waiting for something to happen, but she was quiet for a minute and everybody watched her. She called Chu's name again and then she said it again.

"Oh, Chukwuemeka! My son, why?" she cried until her voice cracked. Other people around me cried aloud, too. An old lady started singing a song to no music. She was off-key and her voice was cracking, but it only made me cry more.

After the women took Ms. Abani to her seat, Chu's brother, dressed in orange and shackled around his ankles and wrists, shuffled up to the casket. There was two guards on both sides of him. He was so close to being released, and he had been doing so good, that his parole officer must've agreed to let him come say his good-byes. Tep stood silent for a long moment. Ms. Abani cried out loud again and raised her arms in the air. After a few minutes, the guards escorted him back out the door. He couldn't even say anything to his mother. It was so sad.

I thought about what Chu said about getting in touch with Tep if something ever happened to him. It was too ironic. Chu had to know something was about to happen, and I knew it had to do with whatever the hell he had been doing in North Carolina. When Rob walked by Chu's casket, he cried just as loud as Ms. Abani was. I wanted to hug him and tell him it was going to be all right, but I really wasn't so sure. They had been friends for a long time. Chu had told me how they first started being friends cuz him and Rob kept getting sent to detention for being late to school every day. Soon, Chu asked him if he wanted to spark after they got out, and that was how they first started being tight.

I still ain't wanna see Chu looking like that. It just ain't feel right. So I stayed in my seat when it was my row's turn to view his body. When a man with an all-white embroidered two-piece African outfit, who was sitting in the row in front of me, came back from viewing the body, my heart jumped. It was Chu, only a lot older. That had to be his father. All the way here from Africa.

I played with the CHU necklace around my neck and closed my eyes as a soloist sang "Amazing Grace." The tears kept slipping from my eyes. All I could think about was the last time we kissed and the last time he held me. No one else knew just how hard it was to be so close to someone and to have them snatched away just like that. I knew how Chu tasted. I knew how his body would flinch if I touched him softly in just the right spots. I knew how he was when no one else was looking. He ain't have to play a role around me, like he was hard or like he was never scared. He was just him. And now he was gone.

After the service, I walked over to Ms. Abani and gave her a long, tight hug. She wrapped me up with her big arms and squeezed me. "I know you loved my son," she whispered. "He loved you, too."

"He loved you, too, ma'am," I said as tears streamed down my cheeks. She couldn't possibly know just how much I was gonna miss her son. He knew all of my secrets and he still loved me.

"Be strong," she said before turning to greet other people.

I wiped away tears and put the program in my purse. I was just his girlfriend, and my name wasn't even in it. But I knew I meant a lot to him. Hearing her say that meant the world.

I tried to catch up with Rob, but I couldn't find him any-where. I waited for a while to see if he was in the bathroom, or if I would see him smoking outside with the other peo-ple huddled around the outdoor ashtray, but he was gone. Peaches caught me on my way out the door.

"How you doing, girl?"

I shook my head.

"I know. I know. You gotta come by the house soon. Okay?"

I nodded.

"All right, shawty," Nut said as Peaches rolled him away.

I felt a pinch in my heart watching them together.

I slept for two straight days after they buried Chu. Sha-kira ain't bother me, either. I woke up smacking my face cuz I thought I felt something crawling across it. I sat up and realized that it was only sweat running down my forehead. I exhaled, relieved. My T-shirt was so sweaty it was stuck on my body.

Shakira was in the bathroom humming a song with the door wide open. I stretched and walked over to see where she was about to go.

"Hey, you finally up, huh? You hungry?"

"Nah, not really," I said, yawning. She was styling her hair. "Where you about to go?"

"Girl, I gotta go to work."

"Work?" I asked, confused. "Where's that?"

Shakira sucked her teeth and said, "Trust me. You don't wanna know. Shit, I been working just about every day since you been here."

I frowned, cuz I ain't never seen her in no uniform. "No, tell me. Where you work at?"

"Nah, not yet," Shakira said, dabbing lip gloss on top of her already pink lips. "What time is it?"

I looked at the time on the microwave in the kitchen. "It's ten o'clock."

"Shit, my ride is probably here," she said, rubbing glitter lotion on her arms and neck real fast.

"You a stripper or something?" I asked.

"I wish . . . too young for that," she said, stepping away from the mirror, looking at herself. "All right, girlie, I gotta go. You gonna be all right?"

I nodded, but I still was confused.

"Okay. Oh, yeah. I got that new Tyler Perry movie on DVD. You should watch it."

I stared at her slipping into her clear stilettos, before she grabbed her purse and walked out the door. I went to the window and watched her, Trina Boo, and Wynika climb into a silver Excursion.

I lit a cigarette from a pack that Shakira had on the kitchen table. I never really smoked cigarettes until lately. Shakira always had them around, more than the weed, so I helped myself to one here or there. I stayed in her room, smoking and drinking wine coolers as I watched DVDs. I fell asleep in her bed and woke up when Shakira came home. I looked at the digital clock by her bed: 6:15. I listened to her jump in the shower and then she came back out twenty minutes later and climbed in bed.

"I am so tired," she said as she pulled the sheet on top of her. "See you in the morning."

But I laid there thinking that it *was* morning.

14

SEPTEMBER 2005

Shakira looked nervous. I saw her chain-smoking cigarettes at the kitchen table and fidgeting with her hair. I noticed when she came in the house her left jaw looked like it was swollen or like she was sucking on a jaw-breaker or something. I knew it wasn't food because she was smoking back-to-back cigarettes. Maybe she had a tooth-ache. She started tapping the table with the lighter over and over again, and it was annoying me.

"Shakira?!" I shouted from the living room.

"Huh?"

"What the heck's wrong with you?" I asked.

She pulled on the cigarette and blew out a cloud of smoke, then flicked some of the ashes in the tray.

"What's going on?" I asked, walking over to the table. I pulled out the chair across from her and sat down. "Why you acting like this?"

She shook her head and said nothing.

"Your jaw swollen?" I asked, looking closely.

She looked away. "Lucifer said he's coming over here to see you today," she said. "He wanna talk to you."

"Who?" I asked, jerking my neck back.

"That's what I call him," she said, blowing a puff of smoke across the table.

"What the hell he wanna talk to me about?"

"He seen you a few times, sleeping on the couch," she said, flicking more ashes in the tray. "He just wanna talk to you."

I rolled my eyes.

"Just listen, okay? It's time you find out some things, and he's on his way, so—"

"So what?"

"Just listen to him," she said, tapping the table with the lighter again.

I frowned, cuz I was too confused. *Lucifer?* I touched her hand to make her stop tapping the lighter. When she stopped, I went to the kitchen to make me a sandwich. I kept thinking about the dude's twisted name and shook my head. After I got the ham and cheese out the fridge, I sat across from her and waited for the nigga with the scary name to show up.

A couple hours later, I heard someone struggling up the stairs and then a few taps on the door.

"Open the door, bitch. I know you hear me coming!" I heard a familiar voice yelling. But say it ain't so.

Shakira opened the door and said, "Hey, baby. What's up?" before she kissed Nut on his lips.

Baby? I shook my head and leaned back on the couch as he hobbled in the apartment on his cane.

"Camille, Camille, Camille. How you doing, shawty?" he said, limping over to the couch. He plopped down into the seat beside me. "So I see you like it over here, huh? KiKi hooking you up?"

I was too stunned to talk.

"Oh, you don't have to say nothing. I already know you like it over here."

I crossed my arms over my chest.

"You ain't have to pay for no food, no weed, no cigarettes, no nothing," he said, counting on his fingers. I turned to face him, surprised he knew all my business. "KiKi treating you real good, ain't she?"

He smiled and then ran his tongue across his lips. I rolled my eyes and turned my head. Shakira passed me a cigarette right on time, cuz I saw I was gonna need it talking to this jerk. Nut offered to light it. I leaned down for the flame, even though I ain't wanna be so close to him. When I came back up, I blew smoke in his face. What the hell was he doing over here with Shakira?

Nut bit his bottom lip. He was trying to hold his tongue, cuz I guess he ain't like what I just did. But he just laughed.

"You can always come home. Ain't nobody say you can't. It's just me and Peaches now. But she miss you."

I shook my head. The nerve of this dude.

"I miss you," he said, grinning. He put his hand on my knee and squeezed.

I knocked it off and rolled my eyes again.

"But . . . I know you still don't feel right about that, and I can't say I blame you. Chu was my man, one hundred fifty grand."

I cocked my head sideways, listening to the bullshit coming from his mouth.

"Me and Chu been tight since when? Like he was thirteen or something. Him and Rob running the streets and shit, playing football in the parking lot. Shit, I used to teach that little nigga how to play. I was like his coach," he said, laughing. "Yeah, I'ma miss that dude."

I couldn't stop shaking my head. I hated hearing him talk about Chu, knowing he was still trying to see if he could fuck me.

"But shit," Nut said taking a deep breath, "I almost died that day, too, remember? I'm trying to live my life something big now, you feel me?"

I took a long pull from the cigarette and then stood up to walk across the room. I walked from one side of the living room to the other.

"Who did it?" I asked, feeling a tear ready to fall. "Who was shooting at y'all?"

Nut shook his head. "Man, who knows. Everybody wants Smurf's spot. All that gwop that nigga got? Shit, niggas stay plotting on his ass."

I rubbed the back of my neck and walked to the other side of the room. Shakira sat at the kitchen table watching us. She was still chain-smoking, too. I stood in front of the window and looked outside. The same silver Excursion I saw Shakira jump into that night was parked right in front of the building. Wynika was leaned up against it, talking to Trina Boo. They was laughing about something.

And that's when everything hit me. "Is that your truck, Nut?" I asked, shocked.

He laughed and I turned back to look out the window.

"That's my work truck," he said, like something was funny.

"Your what?" I asked, since I never seen him in it when I lived over on Montana Avenue. I always seen him driving the light blue Caddy.

"I gotta little hobby and shit. Nothing big. Just a little something something."

"Huh?"

Shakira walked across the room and gave me another cigarette.

"You looking real good, Camille. Did I tell you that yet?"

I jerked my head back. This nigga was really trying his hand today. "What you want me to do, Nut? Fuck you?"

He smiled and licked his lips again. "In due time, Ms. Lady, in due time. Especially if you want a place to stay."

I sucked my teeth and shook my head at Shakira and then I looked Nut up and down. "You sick muthafucka! How can you keep doing this to Peaches?"

"Youngin, how you think me and Peaches met? She my bottom bitch now."

My eyes almost popped out of my head. *Bottom bitch?* But then I started thinking about all the women Peaches was chasing off and how they kept coming back. I thought about the girls we fought at H20 last year at Howard's homecoming, and then the girl who pulled the gun out on Peaches in Southeast, with no fear in her eyes.

"She likes to forget every now and then, that I'm about my business, but that bitch gonna catch on real soon." He pulled a set of keys out of his pocket and held it in his hand. "You want these? They for the apartment across the hall . . ."

I sucked my teeth and crossed my arms. I knew Nut ain't really hustle, not like Chu and Rob did. I never really thought about where he was getting his money from. He was always in and out. I thought he was too busy chasing pussy to be doing anything else.

"If you can keep a secret."

I rolled my eyes and walked to the other side of the room. "You can just get that shit the fuck outta my face." *Who the fuck he think I am?*

"Listen, bitch," he said, standing up and walking toward me with his cane. "Who the fuck you think killed that nasty muthafucka over there on Rhode Island Avenue? Your fairy godmother?"

His words jumped over me like a thunderstorm.

"Yeah, I know what that nigga was doing to you. Shit, Chu shot him, but I'm the one who made sure that bitch-ass nigga was dead. I shot him in his muthafuckin' head," he whispered in my ear. "You gotta love a nigga for doing some shit like that."

He smiled and stared me up and down.

All of it was news to me and too much to handle. I took a few steps back and finished the cigarette before dropping it in a half-empty soda bottle.

"I ain't telling you to do nothing you ain't never did before anyway. Chu was my man, and God rest his soul. I felt his pain about that shit. He was real fucked up behind that sick dude."

I started shaking, and then I rubbed my forehead. Everything was just too much.

"Shit, I feel yours now," Nut said. "I know you hurting and shit. Chu gone. That nigga ain't coming back, either. Who else you got? What you goin' do without him?"

I rubbed my arms and walked around the living room. I stopped in front of the picture of the African lady with the basket on her head. *What the fuck?*

"You gotta take care of *you* now," Nut said, standing behind me.

"Here," Shakira said, passing me a wine cooler. I took a long-ass sip, and then my face felt numb for some reason, but I couldn't shake it. I walked around the room. My neck started feeling warm and my head was spinning. It was just too much. "So you knew all this, the whole time, Shakira, that I lived with Nut? You knew he got shot with Chu and everything? All this time?"

She nodded and I started shaking. I looked at Nut, who was grinning. "E pills, sweetheart."

I frowned and looked at the wine cooler. I scratched my face and my neck cuz it wouldn't stop itching. The room was so hot and humid, hotter than usual, and the sweat was making me itch more. The room started whirling around and around, so I fell to my knees to get my balance. I was too dizzy.

"Yeah, go head, KiKi, take her clothes off," I heard Nut say and then the sound of his pants unzipping.

Shakira stood up and started peeling my T-shirt off. I wanted to stop her, but my mouth felt stuck. I reached up and touched my lips to check that they was still there. Of course, they was, but no words came out. My arms felt like wet noodles. I ain't have no control of them whatsoever. I couldn't even feel them. My heart was too busy racing. I could feel her tugging on my shorts, but I couldn't do nothing to stop her. My whole body was dead. I felt like I was watching everything happen to me, looking down from the ceiling. It was like slow motion.

"Our secret, right, Camille?" Nut said, taking his shirt off.

Our secret. Just like Mr. Big.

The last thing I remembered was Nut's big, thick dick in my face.

When I woke up, I was naked on the floor. My panties was by my head beside a wad of bills. My neck ached like I pulled a muscle, and my thighs felt sticky, like glue. My head thumped by the temples, making me feel woozy.

Shakira was wearing her pink satin robe when she walked from the kitchen with a glass in one hand and a cigarette in the other.

"You all right?" she asked.

I opened my mouth, set to curse her ass out, but a sharp pain went through my head. I laid back down and waited for the pain to disappear. I couldn't remember nothing.

"Here, drink this and take these."

I tried to sit up on one arm to say, "fuck you," but no words came out.

"I know and I'm sorry. But . . . ," she started.

"But what?" I finally whispered. My head was pounding so hard it hurt to open my eyes. I rubbed my forehead again.

"Take these. It's painkillers. Eight hundred milligrams each. You'll feel better. I promise."

I snatched the pills and tried to read them, but it was too blurry. I faked like I knew what it meant and threw the pills in my mouth before I drank the juice. I closed my eyes. I ain't wanna take nothing from her skanky ass, not after they had just tricked me, but the pain was so intense. I hurt all over.

I could hear her shuffling around the apartment in her bedroom slippers. When she came back, she had a long T-shirt with her.

"Here, put this on."

"Oh, now you want me to put my clothes on? How could you trick—I mean . . . why?" I asked. I felt so defeated, tears wasn't even coming even though I wanted to cry so bad. My life had changed so much. So fast. Why was it happening to me?

"Listen, Camille. I ain't have no choice."

"You could've warned me. You could've told me something!" I tried to yell, putting the shirt on. I shook my head.

She lit a cigarette and sat on the couch. "Me and you . . . we different . . . but not that different," she said, crossing her legs. "Don't act like you ain't know what I was doing all this time. I know you saw me in Smurf's room at his cookout last summer. He told me he saw you."

She pulled a long drag from her cigarette. "I been doing

this shit since I was twelve. It's not so bad. At first it is, but it gets better."

I rolled my eyes and pulled my knees up to my chest. I wrapped my arms around my legs.

"Camille, sometimes you just do what you gotta do. What you wanna do, get back in the system? Get another foster family? Or what, live in the streets, go from one shelter to the other? A group home?"

I shook my head.

"I thought about doing that shit first, too. It ain't worth it, believe me," she said, looking at her nails. "I don't think you really got a choice, if you ask me."

"I ain't asking you," I said angrily. I was pissed off. I knew Nut raped me, but did Shakira touch me, too?

She rolled her eyes. "Well, at least here you'll have your own apartment. All you have to do is give Nut a cut. He'll pay all the bills and he'll make sure nobody fucks with you. What else can you ask for?"

I looked away from her and back at my knees. Chu would never believe this was happening to me. "Did he do that to your jaw?"

She rolled her eyes again and sucked her teeth.

"He fuck you when he want to, too. Don't he?"

"Look, I ain't making you do nothing you don't wanna do!" she yelled and got up. She walked toward her room, but then she turned around all of a sudden. "All I'm saying is, it's easy, Camille."

I felt a tear running down my cheek. I reached up to wipe it away.

"But . . . it is your choice. You can make a lot of money,

girl. And I know you used to having nice things. You ready to give all that up?"

"He tell you to say that, too?"

She stormed in her room and slammed the door.

Maybe this was the plan God had for my life. All this stuff—Mama disappearing, Nana dying on me, Mr. Big doing whatever the hell he wanted, Mrs. Brinkley acting like it was my fault. And now Chu. Dead. After loving me so much.

I shuddered and then another tear slid down my face.

An hour later, Shakira came back out the room. I was still lying on the floor crying. The tears wouldn't stop, no matter how hard I tried.

"It's not that bad, girl. We got each other," Shakira said, handing me a tissue. She reminded me of Danica when she said that. For a split second, I couldn't help but wonder if maybe it wouldn't be that bad.

15

A FEW DAYS LATER

Trina Boo had a little piece of car. It wasn't nothing much, just an old 1994 Honda Accord, but it ran good enough to take us around the corner to Safeway. Wynika brought her two badass four- and five-year-old sons with us, Ra-Ra and Meko. They terrorized Safeway the whole time we was in there, screaming and hollering, yanking food off the shelves and throwing it on the floor, trying to fight other people's children. And Wynika was acting just like she ain't give a damn. I couldn't wait to get the heck out of there and away from them.

When I came back from the grocery store, I couldn't believe who was sitting on the couch. Peaches. She looked like she had been crying, but I wasn't gonna ask her what was wrong. I ain't know what to expect out of her mouth. Was she sad cuz she knew the whole damn time what her man was into, or was she getting herself together so she could try to whip my ass? But then I thought about it: Peaches was in Shakira's apartment cuz she already knew what was up. How else she get in?

"Hey," she said as I walked to the kitchen. "I brought all

your stuff over. Shakira told me to put it in the hall closet. Hope you don't mind. Something told me you wasn't coming back to get it. I can't say I blame you."

I pressed my lips together and started unpacking my grocery bags.

"Camille, I know you mad at me."

She damn right. I rolled my eyes at her stupid-ass comment and put a bottle of spaghetti sauce, some cans of tuna, and some packs of Oodles of Noodles in the cabinet. I tried my best to ignore her.

"Camille, don't be mad at me. You don't understand."

"How many fights did I jump in for you, cuz of some silly-ass broad?" I snapped.

"What was I supposed to say, Camille? 'My man is trying to be a pimp, just bear with me for a moment while I beat this bitch back'?"

I shook my head and put some Hawaiian Punch in the fridge.

"Come on, Camille. You my girl. Don't be mad at me."

"Do you know Nut drugged me up and then raped me, right there on the floor where you standing at?! Did you already know that shit was gonna happen?!" I shouted, crossing my arms.

Peaches looked like every ounce of her soul was drying up. I saw her shudder and then clench and unclench her fists.

"What? You wanna whip my ass now, Peaches?" I asked, rolling my neck. I took a stance, ready for anything. She would be one stupid bitch if she thought she was gonna win. I knew where all the knives was at in that kitchen. I was ready to kill a bitch dead.

She stared at the floor for a long time, and then she looked up. "Camille, I'm here to convince you to stay and work for Nut."

"What?" I asked. "What you mean, you here to *convince* me?"

Peaches shook her head.

"What kind of chick are you? I swear I thought more of you than that . . . all this time, I had no idea." Here I was thinking she was in night school and in hair school, and really and truly, she out tricking. I never really paid that much attention to her comings and goings, cuz I used to be with Chu. Maybe she had been changing her clothes over here, with Shakira and the other two girls all this time.

"You think you better than me, Camille? You used up. Just like me," she yelled. "Bitch, you *been* fucking for money. Don't get it twisted!"

I took a step back.

"Yeah, you was fucking Chu for money. Fucking him for clothes, fucking him for nice dinners, fucking him for jewelry and for whatever else he was doing for you! So what's the big fucking difference? You need to wake up, sweetie!"

I shook my head and pulled a wine cooler out the Safeway bag and opened it. I sat down at the kitchen table. Peaches sat down across from me and opened a wine cooler, too. I lit a cigarette and passed her one. We sat for a long time, not saying nothing.

"When I first met you, Camille, I ain't know all this was gonna happen. You had Chu. I thought I was gonna talk Nut out of doing this shit. I was scrounging for money, when me and him met. Nut took me off the street and told me I deserved more. I did. Now, I got a place to stay and he give me just about anything I want. I knew he slept with women—hell, he was paying to sleep with me at first," she said, sipping the bottle and flicking an ash. "But, girl, I thought he was goin' change. That it was just goin' be me and him now."

"Hmmm." I sighed. That was a day I ain't seen yet.

"I thought he loved me and that he would change if I showed him I could be everything he ever needed. But then he started telling me about his plans for us. At first, I tried to talk him outta doing this shit for a long time, but Nut ain't no drug dealer. That nigga a hustler."

I twisted my lips, cuz I wasn't sure what the difference was really.

"He about making money, a lot of it, without taking no whole lot of risks," she said before taking another sip. "I thought I wasn't gonna have to sleep with dudes for money no more, but—"

"Nut let you fuck other dudes?"

"I ain't proud of it. Just some regulars I had before I hooked up with him. These old white men that work on Capitol Hill. Their little dicks don't count," Peaches said, laughing. "They pay me a whole lot of money. All I gotta do most of the time is just suck their dick. That shit ain't nothing."

Nut was a sick dude. I shook my head. No wonder Shakira called him Lucifer behind his back. "And you okay with doing all that?"

"Whatever gonna make him happy, shit, I'm gonna do it. Nut got a lot plans for me and him. He wants to start doing real estate, right? He gonna buy us a house first. Then he gonna start buying other houses and fixing 'em up to sell

them for twice the money he paid for 'em," she said. "He say
he even wants to make sure all his girls got houses, too."

I guess that wasn't a bad idea. Nut had something like a
plan. "But what about your hair school?" I asked.

"Girl, I already know how to do hair. You know this. Fuck
hair school. What the hell they goin' teach me I don't already
know by now? I don't need no license to tell me what I can do.
I was tired of paying for those classes anyway."

She had a point.

"See, Camille, the way Nut see it, you gotta look at it like
we a family. He like that kinda stuff. You know he used to
hate being by hisself when he was young."

Peaches lit another cigarette and inhaled.

"Every chance he get to be around a lot of people, he always ready for that. That's how he felt about Rob and Chu
living with him. They was his family."

I had thought about that. If Nut was doing all this and that,
why had he been sharing an apartment with Rob and Chu?
Clearly, it wasn't about the money. Rob and Chu was starting
to make some real cake, and Nut ain't seem like he was hard
up, either.

"But now Rob away at school and Chu . . . well, it's just
me and him now at the house. He keep talking about how he
want to buy this little shitty-ass building so he can rent out all
four of these apartments."

"Oh, for real?"

"Yeah, it's a part of his plan. It's gonna be his first rental
property."

"Wow." I couldn't even fake. I was stunned.

"And then he gonna try to get everybody who work for

him their own house eventually. But we all gotta work together first. Everybody gotta do their part and put money in
the pot."

My own house? I never thought I'd have my own apartment,
let alone my own house. But even Shakira had one. I was
really starting to think about it. How different could it be
from what I was doing with Mr. Big?

"If that's what he gonna do, then . . . I guess it's not that
bad."

Peaches smiled. "I ain't want you to be on the streets by
yourself, girl. Struggling. I know you ain't got nobody. Shit,
you know I been there. My mother's husband, man, don't
even get me started," she said, shaking her head and blowing
a puff of smoke in the air. I knew she was thinking about her
pedophile stepfather. "We're a family now. Me, you, Nut, and
the other girls. Okay?"

I smoked my own cigarette, until it was a nub. I dug in the
glass dish in the center of the table and got out the keys to the
empty apartment across the hall. Hell, I could do this. Easy
peasy.

Nut gave me six hundred dollars to get a bed and some other
furniture from the thrift store on South Dakota Avenue. Shakira rode with Trina Boo, and I rode with Peaches to pick it
up. Everything was so broke down—a missing knob here or
there, a cracked shelf, or a splintered door—but the dresser
and the chair for the living room was all mine, and the beat-up
mattress would just have to do.

Trina Boo's voice sounded so high pitched, like Dino from

The Flintstones. She was getting on my nerves. Every time she opened her mouth, she sounded like she was saying, "Rile! Rile! Rile!" I just wanted her to shut up.

"You should get this nightstand and maybe this little thingamajig," she said holding up a crazy-looking mirror decoration.

"Ah, no, thank you," I said. "Just the basics."

"Go to National Wholesale Liquidators for your sheets, towels, and stuff like that. They real cheap," Peaches said.

It felt strange to be out with all three of them. Shakira and Trina Boo looked like they just came back from a club, in their loud outfits. With their long hair extensions and accessories, no one would ever believe they was helping me move into my apartment. Peaches wasn't too far behind in her fitted slim-leg jeans and baby T. Why did she have to wear stilettos just to go shopping for furniture? I shook my head, cuz I could feel the eyes on us as soon as we walked into the store.

We bought as much as we could with the six hundred dollars and headed back home. The rest of the stuff I'd need I'd have to buy later after I made some money for Nut.

We was cleaning the apartment when Wynika came across the hall with Ra-Ra and Meko.

"Stop running, you two! I swear to God, I'm gonna whip your little asses," Wynika yelled as her kids ran back to the bedroom where Peaches and Trina Boo was cleaning up. They ran to the bathroom and then back out the front door to their apartment. "Them little badass kids get on my fucking nerves!"

I shook my head and went back to wiping the windows off. Shakira was sweeping the living room. I still couldn't believe wasn't nobody in here older than nineteen and they all had their own place. Now I had mine, too.

"Girl, you better set some bombs off before you get all comfortable. Them goddamn roaches ain't nothing to play with, and they ain't doing nothing but just hiding in the cut," Wynika said, laughing.

"Yeah, we bought some. But I think we should *all* do it at the same time," I said, spraying more Windex. "So, I got some for you, too."

"Bitch, what you tryna say?" Wynika said. I could tell she was just kidding, so I ain't look back at her. "Whatever. Anyway, Miss Thing. What name you goin' go by?"

"What you talking about?" I asked, turning around.

"What name you goin' use? Cuz *Camille* ain't goin' cut it," Wynika said, laughing. "Bitch, you ain't all innocent."

Shakira laughed. "Like my name KiKi on the streets. Peaches, well, she Peaches, and Trina Boo, that's enough already."

"Yeah, and I'm Patience," Wynika said in her sexy voice.

I cracked up laughing. "Patience?"

"What's so damn funny?" Wynika asked, as if she ain't get the joke.

I just shook my head—if she ain't know by now, then she'd never know. Shakira was giggling, too.

"What y'all laughing at?" Trina Boo asked in her squeaky voice, coming in the living room. She was so skinny, like those models where you could see their spines and ribs. But she had a big butt that ain't even seem like it was supposed to be there. She had a big chest, too, but her butt made a lot of dudes stop every time we was out.

"Wynika's street name," Shakira said, taking off her yellow plastic gloves and leaning against the kitchen counter.

"Oh, I know. That shit is funny as hell," Trina Boo said.

"Bitch, you know you ain't got no damn patience," Peaches chimed in. "Them kids running all through this building like they at a zoo."

"Do you see me busting a sweat about it?" Wynika asked. "See, patient. Just like a virgin."

We burst out laughing.

"Bitch, you wish," Trina Boo said.

"Anyway," Wynika cut in. "Like I was saying, Camille, what name you goin' use?"

I thought about it, cuz she was right. *Camille* just wasn't gonna cut it. Plus, I ain't want people knowing my real name. I can be somebody I'm not with a different name. Like I'm acting. That's what I was gonna be doing anyway. I did it before.

"Nectar," I said.

"Damn, bitch," Wynika said. "That shit is hot!"

"Okay," Peaches said, nodding. "You can definitely pay the bills with that name."

I smiled.

"Nectar?" Shakira asked, confused. "I don't get it."

"You don't know what *nectar* mean? You stupid," Wynika said.

"Fuck you!" Shakira shouted. "No, I don't know what the shit mean."

"It's like fruit juice, or something like that," Peaches said.

"Why not just say Juicy then?" Trina Boo asked, smiling like she had invented the word.

"Everybody use that name. Think out the box, ladies, damn," Wynika said, rolling her eyes.

"She's right. Nectar *is* sexy!" Peaches said.

"Where you get that shit from?" Shakira asked.

"It just came to me," I said, and then I turned back to wipe the windows.

"Well, Nectar it is," Shakira said.

But as I stared out the window at the cars speeding up the one-way street, I knew it couldn't be that simple.

Later that night, Nut came by to see the apartment. He was using his cane, but I ain't think he still needed it, cuz he wasn't limping that much. He looked around and ain't say nothing but, "All you really needed was a bed."

I rolled my eyes and leaned up against the counter in the kitchen. He smirked and then walked over to stand in front of me. I could feel his breath on my face. Nut stared straight into my eyes, like he was waiting for me to look away, but I ain't do it. I wanted him to see Chu in me.

He laughed and then palmed my butt with his free hand. I twisted away from him a bit. He grinned and then pulled me closer to him. "Friday payday. I want you to go out with the girls. Peaches will show you what's up," he said just as he leaned in to kiss me. "Nectar, right? That's what we calling you now, right?"

It took everything in me not to wipe my mouth off with the back of my hand. I rolled my eyes and looked past him.

"You mean to tell me you still got a little attitude? After all I just did for you? Come on now, Camille," he said, leaning against the refrigerator. He held my chin with his finger and thumb and turned it toward him. "What a nigga gotta do? I'm trying to do you a favor. You do wanna do this, right?"

How could I say no when my only other choice was really no choice at all?

I crossed my arms over my chest and nodded.

"I said I'm goin' get you a house. Probably by next summer. Then you ain't gonna have to do it no more. This shit we doing, shit, we can make a lot of money. Before you know it, you'll be straight. Feel me?"

I bit my lip as I listened. My arms still tight across my body.

"I'm setting up savings accounts for all of y'all and I'm goin' pay all your bills. Rent, electric, gas, water. I bet you don't even know how to write a check or how to get a money order yet, do you?"

I shook my head. That wasn't something I ever had to worry about before. I couldn't tell you the first thing about a bank account, either. I was scared to even think about asking somebody how to do anything official. They was probably gonna look at me like I was stupid or wonder why I was asking.

"See," Nut said, rubbing my cheek with his hand. "You need me, shawty."

I nodded. Nut was right.

16

FRIDAY

Shakira's closet was filled with all kinds of hooker gear. Coochie-cutter spandex shorts, backless mini-dresses, and bra shirts. I let her pick me out a white, skin-tight dress with sparkling glitter that came just below my panty line.

"That shit looks hot!" she squealed after I finished squeezing the spandex tube over my butt.

"Wait, put this on, too," she said, reaching for a wide black belt. TCB was blasting from the radio as Shakira jiggled her hips in the mirror behind me to the pounding congo beat. "You goin' make that money tonight, girl!"

I looked myself over, more nervous than impressed, and then slipped into Shakira's clear stilettos. She had on a black and red halter dress with black strappy sandals. Peaches ran her comb through my hair—a long, brown lace-front wig she made for me, gold highlights and all.

"I hope you ain't got no panties on. You ain't gonna need them. Here," Peaches said, reaching into her bag to give me a small pack of baby wipes. "This is what you're gonna need. Put this in your bag."

"She ain't lying," Shakira said, stuffing her own bag with a pack.

"And here are some condoms," Peaches said.

I ain't never use one before, but I remembered my sex-ed teacher rolled one over a banana, and Nissa had asked if it was true that you could still get pregnant with a condom. When the teacher said it was rare, but possible, I knew it wasn't gonna matter one way or the other if I told Chu to use one, since Mrs. Brinkley had me on the shot. So we never did.

Peaches had on a gold one-piece catsuit I had never seen her wear. Even though she shopped at Rave, this ain't look like something she would ever buy. But then again, I ain't know Peaches like I thought I did.

"You nervous?" Trina Boo asked, walking into the apartment, standing beside me in the full-length mirror. She looked innocent in her green-and-white striped halter dress, like she was going to a club or to a concert in the park. I gave her a closed-mouth smile and raised my eyebrows. Of course I was nervous.

"She look good, don't she?" Peaches asked, fingering my hair.

"She sure do."

"All right, y'all, let's go. Nut told us to be ready at eleven, and I ain't trying to hear his shit," Peaches said. "Trina Boo, go tell Wynika to hurry up and meet us in the truck."

"Okay," she said, disappearing down the steps.

"I hope Andre can watch them boys tonight. His mother likes to trip every now and then," Peaches said on her way to the door.

"Who is Andre?" I asked, filing behind Peaches and Shakira.

"Wynika's nephew. Her sister live right across the street in that apartment building," Peaches said, pointing.

I could hear Wynika telling Ra-Ra and Meko goodnight as she walked to her front door. I walked out to the truck, where Nut was waiting in the driver's seat. I could feel eyes on my back, probably from some of the dudes in the neighborhood I had been ignoring every time they tried to holla at me whenever I stepped one foot out the building.

"She refuse to watch Wynika's kids for her," Peaches mumbled as we climbed in the truck. She got in the front passenger seat. I sat all the way in the back row. Shakira sat beside me and Trina Boo, and Wynika sat in the next row.

"We gotta stop to get Marcha," Shakira whispered in my ear.

I nodded, remembering her cousin, who had saved us from walking home half naked from that hair-braiding shop the day we got robbed. I guess she was working for Nut, too. We all waited for him to pull off. He hadn't said nothing to any of us since we got in the car. After a second, he pulled off and headed toward H Street, then turned down Sixth Street, and pulled in front of Marcha, who was standing in front of her building at the corner. She was a little chunky, not as chunky as Wynika, but she looked sloppy in her red-cropped leggings and her bright orange tank top. Her nose ring was still killing me.

"Hey, y'all," she said, climbing in the back row to sit beside Shakira.

"Hey," some of us said. Nut still ain't say nothing. I looked at him and saw that he was staring at me in the rearview mirror. I looked away for a second. He smiled and looked at Peaches, who had turned around to see what he was smiling at. I looked out the window and watched as Nut made a left onto Florida Avenue heading toward Northwest. He jumped on New York Avenue and drove pass the Convention Center. Nut pulled up on Fourteenth Street, near Logan Circle, and double-parked his truck beside a hotel.

"All right, bitches, make that ass clap and clear your throats," Nut said, looking in his rearview mirror. "Get the fuck out and make that money."

Everybody climbed out and fixed their clothes in the middle of the street. There was steady traffic, and a few other women was already out, walking up and down in similar outfits.

"Peaches, take care of Nectar," Nut said, leaning out the window. "She the pick of the litter. And now she your responsibility. Ya hear me?"

I saw her roll her eyes before she said, "Okay, baby."

Shakira handed me a tiny bottle of Grey Goose from her bag. "Drink that shit ASAP. Trust me when I say you goin' need it out here."

I twisted the cap and swallowed the hot liquid in one take.

Shakira giggled. "Here. Put this one in your bag for later. You nervous, ain't you?"

"She should be," Wynika said, stepping into the street. "Ain't nothing out here but monsters."

I felt chills going up my back as I watched her cross the street. Her wide hips stretched the seams of her hot pink dress. Marcha and Trina Boo walked on opposite sides of the street, their hips switching hard.

Nut bust a U-turn and drove back down the way we came from.

"Where he going?" I asked, watching his backlights fade until he was totally out of sight. "He gonna come back and get us later?"

"He might. It depends," Shakira said.

"On how much money you make tonight," Peaches said, combing her fingers through her hair. "Come on."

I bit my lip and walked between the two of them.

"Oh, don't worry. He's around here watching," Shakira whispered. "He like Santa Claus. That nigga knows when you've been sleeping."

A white Sentra crept up beside Shakira and stopped a few feet ahead of her. She waltzed over to the car and giggled a few times before climbing in the passenger side.

"She going make him take her around the corner, in the alley on L Street," Peaches said. "Make sure you always make them niggas use condoms, girl. Even if you giving head. 'Half and half' is a little head and a little sex. Charge no less than eighty for that. If a nigga just wants sex, charge fifty. Make him come as fast as you can. Don't prolong that shit. If he wants head, charge forty. If you wanna do anal, that's up to you. But I don't do that shit. Fuck no. I gotta save something special for Nut. Make a nigga pay a hundred for that shit, for real."

I couldn't believe I was hearing her.

"Make sure you always ask that nigga two questions. Is

you a cop or is you a pimp?" she said. "You need to stay the fuck away from both of 'em."

Peaches seemed like she changed to me. Ever since I found out she had been selling her body long before she met Nut, it was like she stopped acting like she was somebody she wasn't. She was still nice to me, but something about her seemed different. Maybe she just seemed more hardcore to me.

"You goin' keep the baby?" I asked her.

She cocked her head and said, "I told you yeah already. Why you keep asking me that?"

I shook my head and looked away. We walked to the end of the corner without saying another word.

"Wait. There go one of my regulars," Peaches said, waving at an Italian-looking guy in a gray BMW. "I'll be back in like twenty minutes. Time is money," she said, scooting toward the car. Her heels *clack, clack, clacked* on the smooth pavement.

"Hey, you. How you been?" I could hear her say before she hopped in the car.

Now I was all alone, standing under the lamppost, watching cars crawl down the street like a club was just letting out. There was all kinds of cars—old ones, new ones. Clean ones, dirty ones. A few had made a couple rounds, I guess to see which one of us they wanted. I rubbed the backs of my arms as I walked back up the street, listening to the *clack, clack, clack* sound of my own heels and trying to remember everything Peaches just told me. I was scared and nervous. How was I supposed to remember all of that, and what if somebody tried to hurt me? Rob me? Kill me?

I lit a cigarette and watched Marcha and Trina Boo walking on the other side, taking turns walking out in the street, doing tricks with their butt to get cars to stop. Trina Boo turned around with her back toward a stopped Impala, and then she bent down to touch her ankles. Her innocent-looking green-and-white striped dress flew up above her waist. That bitch ain't have no panties on. I shook my head. Wynika was nowhere to be found, so she must've disappeared with somebody. I watched other girls I ain't know walk all the way up the street. A blue Civic inched up beside me, but I kept walking. I ain't wanna do this shit.

"What's wrong, sweetheart?" the guy asked. He looked to be in his thirties with his thin beard and mustache. "You want to talk about it?"

I took a deep breath and planted my feet. I thought about Nut lurking behind a tree, watching me, and wondered if he would try to hit me or something if I ain't make some of the money back he already gave me. I seen him beat Peaches and I know he was the reason Shakira's jaw was swollen that day.

"Hi," I said.

"Come here, baby girl."

I strolled, reluctantly, and stood in front of the passenger side.

"What's your name?"

I cleared my throat and said, "Nectar."

"Nectar." He sang it like the name had just quenched his thirst. "Nectar, can I get a little t.o.p.?"

"You a cop?" I remembered to ask.

"Naw, baby girl. I ain't no cop."

"You a pimp?"

He laughed and squeezed the top of his steering wheel with both hands. I could tell he was just as nervous as I was, so I took a deep breath and put my hand on my hip.

"What's your name?" I asked.

"Kevin."

"Hey, Kevin," I said opening up his car door. "What you want?"

"You," he said.

His car smelled like he sprayed that new car scent that comes in a bottle, cuz his car definitely wasn't new. There was plastic CD cases on the floor under the dashboard. A McDonald's cup was in the cup holder and some papers was hanging from the visor.

"It's gonna be a hundred," I said, hoping he would change his mind.

"A hundred? That's a lot."

I stared at him for a second and then squeezed the latch on the car door to get back out. I ain't wanna do this shit.

"Nectar? Where you going?"

"You goin' pay up?"

He sighed and then dug in his pocket to get his wallet. I watched him count his money. "All I got is eighty?"

"I guess I'll suck you for that much," I said. I knew it was double what Peaches told me to charge, so maybe Kevin would just say forget it, since it was too high.

He looked at me like I was crazy, but then he said, "Fuck, okay, baby girl. Let me just run to the ATM real quick."

The ATM?

Nah, he was kidding. He was leaving for real. He just

changed his mind. Good. I nodded and reached for the latch again. "See you when you get back," I said.

"No, ride with me," he said, pulling off from the curb. "It's just going to take one second. A Wachovia is right down the street."

I took a deep breath and sunk down in the seat. I looked in the side mirror at the place we was leaving. I could see Marcha's orange tank top and red leggings getting smaller. I hoped God wasn't going to let nothing happen to me.

A minute later, I watched as Kevin put in his pass code and waited for the money to spit out the machine. I opened the other tiny bottle Shakira gave me and swallowed the Goose. When he got back in the car, he asked me where I wanted to go. I told him on L Street. I took another deep breath and waited as he parked behind a car.

"Can I kiss you?" he asked.

I shook my head.

"Well, can I touch you at all?"

"Give me the money," I said. He gave me five twenty-dollar bills and I put them in my bra.

"You all right?" he asked.

I took a condom from my bag and gave it to him.

"I need to touch you or something so I can get him hard," Kevin whined.

I nodded and let him squeeze my breasts and then rub my thighs. He was just as rough as Mr. Big used to be with me, not gentle like Chu was. Kevin moaned as he put the condom on with his other hand.

"All right, baby girl. Come to Papa," he said. "He hard as a rock for you."

I crossed my chest with one hand, saying a quick prayer, and then climbed over to Kevin's side of the car. I slowly positioned myself on top of him and closed my eyes so I ain't have to look at his face. He smelled like the cologne they sold at CVS, where the whole aisle smelled the same. Kevin had an average-size dick. He moaned a couple times as I slid up and down and then he started to shake. The whole thing took no more than four minutes.

"Damn, Nectar. That shit was good," he said.

I rolled my eyes. Was I supposed to thank him? I wiped myself off with one of the baby wipes and pulled my dress back down. "Take me back around the corner please."

"No problem," he said before knotting the condom and throwing it out the window. "You goin' be here tomorrow?" he asked after he pulled up to the spot where he found me.

I nodded, but all I could think about was how easy it was making that money. I climbed out of Kevin's car as he said, "See you tomorrow."

I smiled and turned to walk down the street. I caught up with Shakira and Marcha. Wynika was sitting under a bus shelter across the street rubbing her feet. I knew those stilettos was killing her, cuz mine was killing me and her hefty butt was three times my size.

"How it go, girl?" Shakira asked.

I smiled.

"That shit was easy," I confessed. I decided not to tell no-body I charged double, cuz I was gonna keep my own savings, just in case this shit with Nut ain't work out. I figured if any of my customers had a problem with my prices then they could go pick somebody else. Nut was probably gonna give me a break for a little while since I was new, if I ain't make him a lot of money.

"Told you," she said, lighting a cigarette. "It gets easier."

I bit my lip and thought about her words. Somehow I ain't quite believe her.

A couple weeks later, Nut called a Sunday afternoon meeting. Peaches cooked a big dinner in Trina Boo's apartment. Fried fish, collard greens, wild rice, and buttermilk biscuits. We ate over Trina Boo's, since Wynika brought her table across the hall so we could all eat together. Ra-Ra and Meko ate on the floor, where Wynika had laid out newspapers. Her nephew Andre stopped by to get a plate, before going back across the street. He looked like he was a little older than me, but I wondered if he was a special-ed case or something, cuz he ain't seem to have it all together. I saw him playing outside, like he was nine or ten with the other kids in the neighborhood. Shakira's cousin Marcha was there, too. She had caught a cab over from Sixth Street. I was wondering why Ra-Ra and Meko was in the same room where Nut was about to make his announcements, when Nut stood up.

"Business doing real good," he said, leaning against his cane, looking down at all of us seated around the table. "Y'all doing real good. Keep it up. I just want y'all to know that I got some badass youngins working with me. And cuz of that, I got a surprise for you."

A surprise? I looked at Shakira and then Peaches. They both shrugged their shoulders. Nut pulled out his Blackberry and sent a text, and then he said, "Anybody know why those big-ass companies like Coke and McDonald's do so good?"

We all looked at each other. I looked across the table at Wynika, who was buttering her biscuit. No one knew where Nut was going, and ain't nobody offer him an answer.

"They brand theyselves with logos and shit. A nigga in China know what Coke is, just like a nigga in Germany or India do," he said, laughing.

Somebody knocked on the door and everyone looked in the direction of the sound.

"Get that, Trina Boo," Nut said.

She got up and walked over to the door.

"Nut here?" the person asked.

When she stepped back, a short white guy with crazy tattoos etched up one of his arms and a big black earring that made his earlobe droop walked in with a black case.

"Brands, ladies," Nut said proudly. "That's what makes *small* businesses *big* businesses."

"Hello, girls," the guy said.

"This is my man Dave. A hot tattoo artist who just moved here from New York. So who's first?"

Trina Boo sucked her teeth and walked to the bathroom.

"That nigga crazy. I ain't getting no fucking tattoo for his ass," Shakira whispered.

"What, bitch?!" Nut said, pointing his cane at her. The end of the stick was a few inches from her mouth. "I hear your ass talking slick out your mouth. Don't make me knock your muthafuckin' teeth out!"

"Whoa, whoa . . . let me show you what I designed first. I bet you are going to love it," Dave said, opening up his bag and pulling out a pad.

Shakira leaned back in her seat.

"Hey, Meko, take your brother back in the room and watch TV," Wynika said. He sucked his teeth and grabbed Ra-Ra's hand before dragging him down the hall.

Dave walked over and put the pad on the table. I leaned forward to see what it was. A butterfly.

"But I already got one," Shakira said, frowning.

"But not like mine, and it ain't where I want it," Nut said, pissed off. "And I'm getting sick of your muthafuckin' mouth!"

The butterfly was cute, but there was three tiny sixes on one wing.

"Dave gonna put it right here on your back," he said, pointing to the center of his waistline. "That shit is so sexy, and your ass ain't got a choice."

I frowned and leaned back in my chair. I ain't want no damn tramp stamp.

"Everybody gonna know y'all work for me. High-class, top-of-the-line young dimes," Nut said, boasting.

Marcha stood up and pulled her chair to the center of the living room. She raised her shirt up and pulled her sweatpants down a little bit. "I'm ready, baby," she said, bending over the back of the chair, shaking her butt.

Wynika laughed and said, "Well, fuck it. I'm next."

So I guess I had to be after her, or else.

17

OCTOBER 2005

I was standing on the block smoking a cigarette in my usual spot on Fourteenth Street when a brand-new 2006 black Denali with dark tinted windows pulled up beside me. The rims was spinning like crazy and I could hear congas pounding from the speakers. When I got to the truck, the dark-skin guy with a low-cut fade was wearing a navy blue suit with an orange tie.

"You Nectar, right?" asked the dude. He was kind of cute with his big white smile.

"Hey, cutie," I said, leaning in the window. He was puffing a J and had his whole car smelling good. "Yep, I'm Nectar. What's up with you?"

"Ain't nothing. How much for you to stay the night with me at the Renaissance?"

"You ain't a cop, are you?" I asked coyly.

"I'm sitting here smoking a blunt, and you asking me if I'm a cop. Come on now, sexy."

"Can I hit that?" I asked.

"If I can hit that," he said, smiling.

I licked my lips and smiled back. Then I fluttered my fake

eyelashes Peaches insisted I wear to help me look older and said, "What's your name?"

"Joe."

"Well, Joe, you can hit this shit all night long for a G."

"A G? Shit, I got that," he said, digging in his pocket. "I'll give you half now."

I said a G only cuz nobody never asked to spend the whole night, and I thought he was gonna say it was too high, but he just handed me the cash. I tried not to look too shocked. "Okay, well let me just text my man. He gonna follow us around the corner, okay?"

Joe nodded as I sent the text to Nut and then climbed in his truck. He sent a text back to make sure I sent him the room number when I got inside. He wrote that he was gonna come up and get half the money. But I ain't tell him I was charging the dude a whole G.

As Joe drove down K Street, I puffed on his blunt and let that good old Backyard Band take my mind away. I double-checked to see if Nut was behind us in the side mirror. I could see his silver Excursion trailing behind us.

When Joe turned down Ninth Street, he said, "So how long you been out here, sexy?"

"Not long. Why?" I asked, blowing smoke in the air.

"Just asking."

"Why you *just* asking?"

"You look young, that's all."

"But you like me young, right?" I asked, smiling.

He smiled and reached for the blunt. Joe looked like he was around twenty-five. I wondered what he did, cuz he certainly ain't look like a hustler, and he was young and clean.

But I knew it wasn't my place to ask how he made his money, and it really wasn't any of my business as long as he paid me.

Once inside the hotel lobby, I waited as Joe checked us into a room. It was a nice hotel, and nothing like the cheap, dirty-ass motel on New York Avenue where niggas always tried to take me. Wynika called it the "No Tell Motel," cuz shit was always happening there, and whenever the cops came around asking questions, nobody knew nothing.

On the elevator, I let Joe palm my butt, even though he ain't give me all my money yet. He was so damn sexy, I wanted to fuck his ass for free. He kept licking his lips, like he knew he was gonna fuck the shit out of me. I smiled.

As soon as we got to the room, I sent Nut a text and told him the room number. He was there in no time, tapping on the door. I gave him $250, and before I could close the door behind me, he put his foot in the doorway.

"Don't fuck him like you fuck me. You hear me?" Nut said.

I rolled my eyes and nodded.

"I ain't playing with your ass, Nectar," he whispered.

"Okay, okay," I said.

"I'ma pick you up around seven, too. So don't let that nigga think he treating you to breakfast. It ain't even going down like that. No, sir."

I nodded as Nut stepped away and then I closed the door, pressing my forehead against it. I was actually a little nervous since I ain't never been with nobody who wanted to pay so much to be with me. What was this dude really into? When I turned around I thought I was going to see him pissing in a cup or lining up knives to cut him with or some other wild, crazy shit like Peaches told me those old white men on Capitol Hill liked to do with her. But Joe was just sitting on the edge of the bed, still with his suit and tie on.

"So what's up?" I asked, sauntering over to him.

"You," he said, licking his lips.

I took off my cream Baby Phat jacket and sat it on the chair across from the bed. Then I turned around and peeled off my purple sleeveless dress.

"Can you keep your boots on?" Joe asked.

"Mmm-hmmm," I said, rubbing my legs.

"I just want to eat your pussy."

I smiled and lied on the bed, but he motioned for me to sit on the love seat across from the bed. Joe dropped to his knees and threw his tie across his shoulder, before spreading my legs apart. He pressed his mouth against me, sucking, kissing, and licking with his fat tongue for what felt like an hour. When he was done, he made me take a shower with him, but all he did was rub my body down with soap. It felt so good.

He ordered vanilla ice cream and chocolate cake dessert from room service cuz I said I had the munchies. We sat up watching Jimmy Kimmel and then a rerun of *The Wire* until we fell asleep in the king-size bed.

I woke up when I heard someone knocking on the door. I looked around the room and saw the sun shining behind the curtains. *Shit. Nut.* I jumped up from under Joe's arm and ran to look out the peephole. *Peaches?*

I cracked opened the door. "Hey," I whispered, confused.

"Girl, Nut outside waiting for you. He been blowing your phone up for damn near an hour. What the fuck you doing in there?" she said.

"Shit. Okay, okay," I whispered. "Let me just put my clothes on and get the rest of the money."

"Hurry up, 'fore he want to come up here and yank your little ass out of that room!" she said in a low voice. "And you was supposed to get all the money before you fucked him! The fuck is wrong with you?"

Damn, did I just fuck up and tell on myself? I nodded and tried to play dumb, and then I closed the door. I tried to remember if I told Nut that Joe was only paying half up front and half after, but I couldn't remember. After I hurried up and put my clothes on, I squeezed Joe's shoulder.

He woke up and smiled when he saw me.

"Hey . . . I gotta go," I said.

"Already?" he asked. "I wanted to spend the rest of the day with you."

I bit my lip and said, "Maybe next time. But ummm . . . I'm gonna need the other half before I go."

"Oh, all right," he said, sighing. "Let me get that."

I waited as he dug in his wallet and handed me five crisp one hundred-dollar bills. That's when I remembered that Nut knew the deal.

"Do you have two fifties?" I asked. I ain't want to give Nut no more than what he was expecting.

Joe smiled. "No, why?"

I frowned. "Never mind."

"So, can I get your number?"

"My number?" I asked, biting my lip. He was sexy and

he had money, but I couldn't chance it. Nut would find out, somehow.

"Yeah, so I can call you and see you whenever I want to see you."

"But you know where I'll be," I said, walking to the door. Nut wouldn't like that shit at all. He ain't want nobody calling us like we was in relationships. I could hear his voice in my head now: *No free pussy.* So I said, "Just come see me around Fourteenth Street."

I opened the door and walked out before he could say anything else.

"Damn, girl. He gonna be pissed the fuck off. I can hear his ass now," Peaches said, grabbing my arm.

We hurried downstairs and outside. Nut was pushing his Caddy today and I could hear Three 6 Mafia chanting before we even reached the car. *"Just kill yourself / Go 'head and kill yourself."*

I had never been inside of the Caddy. As soon as I climbed into the backseat, I noticed a weird-looking hairy thing about the size of an apple dangling from the rearview mirror. It was twisting left and right but never all the way around.

"You must've had a good-ass time, wasting my muthafuckin' time!" Nut shouted as soon as I got settled. "Where the fuck my money at?"

I rolled my eyes and handed him three one hundred-dollar bills.

"Oh, that corporate nigga gave you a tip, huh? You prime shit, then, huh?" he said, smiling. "But that don't change a goddamn thing. When I tell your ho ass to be ready at seven, that's what the fuck I mean."

He pulled away from the curb and made a right at the light. "I'll fix your ass when we get back to the crib," he said.

Peaches smiled. I could see her cheeks rising all the way from the backseat. What the fuck was she so happy about? I crossed my arms and waited for whatever was next. He dropped her off at the apartment on Montana Avenue, though it was clear she had a problem with it. But she knew better than to say nothing, and she just marched up the crumbling stairs that led inside the beat-up building.

"Get in the front," Nut said.

I opened the back door and went to the front seat. He drove down the street and made a left. I stared at the hairy thing twisting back and forth and then I leaned in to look closer.

"Didn't I tell your little ass I don't fuckin' play that shit?" he said, just as his fist flew toward me, crushing my face against the window. The car was still moving, but he hit me again. "I'm not that bitch-ass nigga Chu. I don't give a fuck about you!"

I grabbed my jaw, stunned that he actually hit me the way I had seen him hit Peaches. I could feel the pain growing and then throbbing as a tear fell down. I wiped it away and then looked out the window.

"Don't make me have to smash your ass again. It ain't good for business," he said, turning down Rhode Island Avenue.

When he made a left on the same street the Brinkleys

lived on, my breath got caught in my throat. Nut parked the car in front of the house. But how did he know? The light blue house sat looking cold and empty. All the leaves had fallen from the tree in the front yard, and the cobblestones that lined Mrs. Brinkley's plants was all out of place and scattered around the yard. The soil looked like a dog or a raccoon had been digging in it.

"We followed his ass for a couple days to see where he worked at," Nut said. I could hear him lighting a blunt. He inhaled it and blew the smoke out. "His ass was big as shit and greedy, too. We watched him stop at Dunkin' Donuts after work every day. His fat ass had a cup of coffee and three jelly donuts every single day we followed him."

I could hear him inhaling another whiff before blowing it out. The car got real smoky, so I cracked the window to let some air out and massaged my stinging jaw with my other hand.

"Rob was the one who said we should beat his ass, but nah," he said, laughing, "Chu wanted that nigga dead, for real. But . . . he ain't have the heart to kill him, though."

I looked at Nut and noticed that the hairy thing that kept swinging back and forth was now facing me. It was a dried-up, tiny animal head. I covered my mouth to keep from screaming out loud.

"Oh, that shit dead already. A spider monkey. You ever watch National Geographic?" he said, plucking the dangling head. I watched it swing back and forth and then spin back around to face the front window. "You ain't gotta worry about this."

This nigga was crazy. Where in the hell did he find that

shit? My hand was still covering my mouth, horrified, staring at the lifeless thing spinning.

"Only thing you gotta worry about," he said blowing out another puff of smoke, "is fucking up my money. You feel me?"

I nodded and wiped the tears that began flooding my face no matter how hard I tried to stop them.

A couple days later, me and Shakira was laying in Trina Boo's bed watching videos when Trina Boo plopped down beside me. Sometimes, I couldn't understand her. Trina Boo was eighteen, a year older than Peaches, but she was a little ditzy. She mentioned stripping, cuz she said she could make more money, especially since she was still gonna work on the side. But she wanted that house like Nut promised us.

"That's my shit," Trina Boo said, jumping up and dancing to the remix of Snoop's "Drop It like It's Hot." "I'm telling y'all I'm going to New York. I'ma be in one of these videos."

"Nut will fuck you up," Shakira said, smiling.

Trina Boo sucked her teeth. "Fuck him. Look at this ass! Them rappers are gonna love this shit," she said, wiggling and popping.

I raised my eyes, since even I had to admit Trina Boo had a big old booty that looked like she bought it. She was cute, like a dark-skin baby doll. Nut treated her like she was an Anna Nicole Smith or something, like he ain't expect her to know anything. She was clueless sometimes.

"You should try it, though," I said. "I'm not gonna hate

on you, girl." Maybe that was the best chance she had to get the hell away from Nut. Sometimes I wished I had another plan. Hair school went out the window a long time ago. When Peaches stopped going, I lost interest.

"Thank you, Camille. At least you got faith in my skills," she said, smiling and wiggling her butt cheeks again. "See, all I ever asked for was some support from you hoes."

Shakira stuck her tongue out and walked over to grab a bottle of nail polish off of Trina Boo's dresser. "Hey, did y'all hear Nut told Peaches to get an abortion?"

"No, sir?" Trina Boo said, sitting down.

"For real?" I asked and sat up.

Shakira nodded and then twisted the cap off.

"Why?" I asked.

"Why you think? He don't know if it's his!"

"Damn," Trina Boo said, shaking her head. "But I can't blame him."

"She said she never use condoms with him, but she do with her tricks," Shakira said.

"Who told you?" I asked.

"Wynika told Marcha the other day."

"But ain't she too far along?" I asked.

Shakira rose her eyebrows and kept on polishing her fingernails. "I remember one time, this girl got pregnant by her pimp and he made her get an abortion that late and her ass ain't never make it out of surgery."

"She died?" I asked.

"Mm-hmm," Shakira said.

"Yeah, well, I wouldn't want to have his goddamn baby

anyway. His crazy ass walking around with the Mark of the Beast," Trina Boo said.

"Bitch, you are, too, now," Shakira said, tapping her tattoo.

Trina Boo rolled her eyes. "Well, I'm getting that shit removed as soon as I get my big-ass modeling contract. Tyra Mail!"

"Girl, you silly," Shakira said, laughing.

"I feel sorry for Peaches, y'all," I said.

"I don't know why. She think you wanna take her crazy-ass man," Shakira said.

"What?" I asked, stunned. "Please!"

"Don't act like we ain't hear him call you the pick of the litter, bitch."

"Please, that don't mean nothing. He pick whoever he want up in here, whenever he want. Plus, we all fuckin' for dollars. What real man gonna let his girl do this shit?" I asked. "I ain't thinking about him."

"True," Trina Boo said.

"So what you saying about Peaches?" Shakira said.

"What? You asking trick questions?" I asked.

"Hmmm," Shakira said, before blowing her wet nails.

"What? I'm lost," Trina Boo said.

"Like always," Shakira said.

"What?" Trina Boo asked again, confused, but then she was distracted by another BET video. This time Lil Jon and the East Side Boyz. "Aw shit, this my other shit. Turn it up, Shakira!"

I laid back on the bed and thought about how messed up Peaches must've been to have tried to be in a relationship with Nut in the first place, even after she met him as a trick. On top of that, why would she want to have his child? But then I thought about all the girls who worked for Nut and how we all needed something from him and how we found strength from each other, despite the madness. It was weird, but we really was a family. Just a messed-up, crazy one.

18

NOVEMBER 2005

Loud screaming and thunderous pounding on the door woke me up out of a deep sleep. I jumped up and grabbed my robe and then ran to see what was going on. I saw flashing police lights on my living room wall.

"Shakira, what's wrong?" I asked, pulling the door open and tying my robe at the same time. My body was still so tired, but I knew it was some kind of real emergency.

"Girl, they just locked Wynika up and took her kids!"

"Huh?" I asked, wiping sleep from my eyes.

"Come on! Trina Boo about to take us up Fifth District to see what the fuck is going on!"

I ain't even try to ask questions. I threw on a pair of jeans, a hoodie, and some tennis shoes.

"We goin' be in the car!" Shakira yelled from the hall stairs.

"Did y'all call Nut and Peaches?" I said, putting on my jacket and grabbing my keys.

"Yeah, but ain't nobody answering the phone!"

As soon as I got in the hall, I saw the blue and red lights flashing in front of the building. Wynika was in the backseat

of one of the police cars. Shakira and Trina Boo was waiting in front of the building, and Trina Boo was on her cell
phone.

"Them niggas ain't trying to tell me shit!" Shakira said.
"I don't know what the fuck's going on!"

"Nut said he was going to meet us at the station," Trina
Boo said.

I looked back and forth between the two of them. I was
anxious, but I ain't know what to do. I could see Wynika
leaning her forehead on the back of the seat in front of her.
I knew she was crying.

"I'm so pissed off! They act like they can't tell us shit!"
Shakira shouted. "How the hell they goin' just barge up in
here and take her kids like that!"

She seemed like she wanted the Feds to hear her. "You try
to call her sister?" I asked. "Maybe she know something."

"Nataki ain't goin' know shit!" Shakira said. "That bitch
act like she better than us, like she ain't got her own fuckin'
issues!"

The police car Wynika was in drove off. Two other of-
ficers paraded back and forth, taking notes. We jumped in
Trina Boo's Civic and headed in the direction of the police
car.

A few hours later, after Wynika had been processed, we
found out more than I think anybody wanted to know. She
was being charged with child neglect. Ra-Ra and Meko had
a doctor's appointment earlier that morning, cuz they had
been crying about having sore throats for days. When the
test came back later that afternoon, Child Protective Ser-

vices was called in to discuss the results since both kids had tested positive for gonorrhea.

Couldn't be nobody but Andre's trifling ass. Nut shook his head and walked straight out the door after Wynika's lawyer told us the news.

"Money fuckin' lost," Nut mumbled.

It was a long, quiet ride back to Nineteenth Street. With all the drama, Nut said we ain't have to go out tonight. Wasn't nobody in no mood to work no way. I ended up falling asleep in Trina Boo's apartment, cuz we stayed up all night talking about everything—if any of us had ever seen any signs from Andre, if any of us thought Wynika was being blind the whole time, and what we thought was going to happen to the kids. We even talked about who Nut might get to take Wynika's place. All that talking made us sleepy.

The next morning, around eleven o'clock, the three of us jumped in Trina Boo's car and headed to the Denny's on Benning Road and East Capitol Street to grab breakfast. I hated going there, cuz it always seemed to be crowded no matter what time of the day or week. But my vote for The Diner in Adams Morgan was cast out.

"We all look like shit," Trina Boo said, scooping eggs into her mouth. She was the only person I ever knew who ate sunny-side-up eggs, and that shit in the middle looked disgusting.

"No, bitch, *you* look like shit," Shakira teased.

"Y'all think they goin' let her go, or what?" I asked, cutting my waffle and taking a bite.

"Hey, KiKi," a guy said, sitting down at the table across from us.

"Hey, how you doing?" she said, smiling.

"Ain't nothing. We need to get up again, one of these days," the guy said.

Shakira smiled and nodded, but she turned back to us. "His dick is about the size of this sausage," she said, sticking her fork in the link and raising it up. The guy was sitting with two other dudes. They kept looking over at us every now and then smiling.

"I doubt they let her go just like that," Trina Boo said. "I mean, can you imagine? Them poor kids!"

"How she not goin' know what was goin' on?" I asked, shaking my head. "I don't care what y'all say, she had to know something. I hate when women try to act like they don't know what's goin' on in their own house. Andre used to play tag and Red Light, Green Light out front like he was one of them!"

"Mm-hmm," Trina Boo said. "All along, he touching them little boys."

"Hey, KiKi, this my man Rick," the guy with the sausage-sized dick said, now standing in front of our table.

"How y'all doing, ladies?" Rick said, smiling from ear to ear.

"We good. But we eating," Shakira said, rolling her eyes. "Can we talk to y'all later?"

"What?!" Rick said, angry. "Oh, you tryna carry me, slim?"

I sucked my teeth and shook my head. Trina Boo rolled her eyes. Why it gotta be all about him?

"Fuck y'all, dirty-ass, dick-sucking bitches!" Rick said real loud, so everybody in the whole restaurant could hear.

I saw a few people look at us and then turn back around. Some laughed.

"Nigga, fuck you! Don't be mad, just take ya skinny black ass back to ya fuckin' seat and eat!" I yelled. I had no idea why I was so angry all of sudden. But I was. *Fuck him.*

"Camille?" I heard somebody say. I turned around and sure enough it was somebody I knew. Jayson. I smiled, and then he stood up and rushed over to the table.

"Fuckin' faggies and hoes," Rick said as he and the other guy walked away.

"Negro, please!" Jayson said. "What you wanna do? I bet I can whip ya ass like the grown-ass man that I am. You care to try me?"

Jayson was definitely out of the closet now, but he still looked like he played football. Rick and his boy backed down. Of course, they knew what was best for them. "I ain't think so, now what!"

I couldn't help but laugh.

"So, Miss Lady, get up and give me a hug!" he sang. I did and then I introduced him to Shakira and Trina Boo.

"What you been up to?" Jayson asked. "It's been a long time, ain't it?"

I nodded. He introduced us to the guy he was eating with and then we exchanged numbers. I told him I'd call him later to catch up. A part of me wanted to, but then the other part was like, *Keep the past in the past.*

I was quiet the rest of breakfast listening to Trina Boo and Shakira talking. I couldn't stop thinking about Jayson and the rest of my brothers. I wanted to know if he had heard anything from Danica. I wondered if Mrs. Brinkley still lived in that house on Rhode Island Avenue, since it seemed empty that day. I wondered if he could tell that I had been living a different life.

I couldn't shake the thoughts even later, when Nut came by to see me that night. He was the only man allowed to visit any of us at his apartment building, especially now that he owned it outright. Yes, he showed us the paperwork with his real name, Sean Crawford, printed and autographed on it at one of his Sunday meetings, just to prove our contribution was making a difference. But I knew for a fact Shakira had some guy coming to see her every now and then on the low, ever since I moved in with her. She said it was somebody who used to go to school with us at Tech, but I ain't know who it was.

I climbed on Nut's back to give him a massage. He swore that I was the best person who could do it. Sometimes he complained about Peaches to me or talked about how stressed he was, but I never said anything. I just listened and rubbed the knots out his back. Today was no different.

When I was done, he turned over and slid his dick up inside me like he always did. I let him do what he wanted. He knew I ain't have no feelings for him.

"Can you move your hips or something? Damn."

I rolled my eyes and rocked up and down. I moaned like it felt good and then he came. He was sweating all over the place. I watched him wipe his forehead with my sheets and then get up. Nut had two bullet scars—one on his arm and the other on his leg, from the day Chu was killed.

I reached out to touch the one on his arm, not even thinking. I saw other old scars on his body, too, but I had no clue where they came from.

He smiled. "War wounds, baby girl. I'm a killer!"

I cut my eyes and got up to take a shower. Why would he say something like that? He was such a jerk. I was relieved that he had disappeared by the time I came out the bathroom. I turned my radio up sky high since Raheem DeVaughn was singing "Guess Who Loves You More," and then I sat on the edge of my bed to roll a J. I got the bag of weed from one of my regulars a couple of nights ago, as a cherry on top. After I rolled up, I went back to the bathroom to smoke it before any of those Hoovers smelled it. I knew Shakira's geeking ass would be the first to come running across the hall, sniffing herb in the air like a hound dog. Nah, I wanted this all to myself.

Chu had been creeping in my mind a lot lately. Maybe it was cuz the holidays was right around the corner. But then again, it had only been a few months. I was supposed to be missing him. I inhaled and blew the smoke out. Tears filled my eyes and ran down my cheeks. I let them fall. I cried until I couldn't breathe with all the smoke in the tiny space. I put the J out and opened the bathroom door and then I went to my room and lied across the bed.

I thought about Rob. Peaches had mentioned that after the funeral he went straight back to Greensboro. I knew he had a basketball scholarship and was busy doing his own thing, but I wondered if he ever thought about me. He never tried to call me. Did he care that I was by myself? Or that Chu left me, too? I wondered if Rob knew what Nut was into all this time. As much as I tried to understand it, I just couldn't see it. But how could he not know? They lived together long before I came around. But then again, Rob ain't seem like the type to keep that away from Chu. They had been too tight.

I stared at the ceiling and wondered what would Rob think if he got a phone call or a letter from me? Word must've traveled back to him, some kind of way, probably through Nut's ass. Rob had to know that I was working for him by now.

I shook my head and rolled over. I closed my eyes and tried to go to sleep, but I couldn't. I stayed up listening to the sounds of Trina Boo and Nut coming from her apartment downstairs, until sleep finally took my mind away.

When Wynika was released from jail, she came straight home with two of her brothers and a U-Haul van. She ain't say nothing to none of us. They packed up her stuff and moved her out. Just like that. She ain't even tell us bye. I watched them load the truck up from my window, trying to figure out why she was mad at us.

"She probably mad at herself," Shakira said, leaning beside me. "I know she blame herself for that shit."

I bit my lip and went back to the table to get rid of my ashes in the tray. Peaches told us Wynika's kids was still with Child Protective Services and that her trial date wasn't for a few more months.

"I guess she don't want nothing else to do with us," Trina Boo said, sipping her wine cooler. "Well, anyway, whatever. Two tears in a bucket, muthafuck it."

"Damn, that's cruddy. I hope you don't treat me like that when I leave," Shakira said.

"Bitch, I'm leaving first. I told you I'm getting a modeling contract," she teased.

"Over Nut's dead body," I said.

"I'm fine with that," Shakira said. She finished the rest of her cooler and then said, "I need to do some laundry. Trina Boo, can you run me around the corner?"

"I ain't doing nothing else."

"Let me grab some of my stuff, too," I said.

"All right, y'all be ready in like thirty minutes, okay?" she said, heading out the door.

"Okay." I went to separate my small pile of dirty clothes. Just as I started stuffing my bag, my cell phone rang. "Hello?"

"Camille, you busy?" Peaches whispered.

"Not really, what's up?"

"Tep just called here collect for you."

"Huh?" I asked.

"Tep. Chu's brother? He just called for you, but I ain't accept it. Nut right in the other room."

"Oh, my God." I started pacing the room. I thought about how Chu wanted me to get in touch with him, but I ain't know how, besides going through his mother, which I ain't wanna do. "Shit."

"I think he called a couple of times before, cuz the same number has been on the caller ID, but I was never here when he called, or maybe Nut answered it first."

"Try to give him my number."

"I'll try, but—"

"Please, Peaches, some kind of way."

"I said I'll try."

The phone got quiet for a few seconds, and then I said, "I heard Nut wants you to get rid of the baby. Is it true?"

She ain't say nothing for a long time, and then she said, "Yeah."

"What you wanna do?"

"You know what I wanna do."

The phone was so quiet, I checked to see if I dropped the call, but there was still bars there. "Hello?"

"Yeah, I'm here."

"Oh?"

"Look, Camille, what you doing later?"

"I was about to go with them to the Laundromat, but I'm not in no desperate need. Why?"

"I'm 'bout to come around there. I have to tell you something."

I raised my eyebrows up, puzzled, and then said, "Okay."

The sun was setting by the time Peaches finally showed up. I was getting angry, cuz I had wasted my whole day waiting around for her to show up. She had a big duffle bag on her shoulder when she finally knocked on the door. I guess she was gonna get dressed for the night over here.

"I caught a cab. Nut don't know where I'm at. You know he's gonna kirk out any minute," Peaches said, sounding nervous. She even had a little bit of sweat on her forehead.

"I left when he went meet up with some contractors about something."

"What's wrong? You want something to drink?" I asked, already heading to the kitchen.

She nodded and sat down.

"I'm about to leave his ass," she said.

"Huh? Oh, shit!" I said, spilling fruit punch on the counter.

I wiped it up and then walked over to hand Peaches the glass.

"I'm having this baby!"

"Oh?" I said and then sat down beside her.

"I'm not gonna let him fuck this up for me," she said and then drank the whole glass.

"Where you gonna go?" I asked.

Peaches shook her head and then stood up to walk around the living room. "You was right, Camille. I should've stayed my ass in hair school. At least that would've been something I could do to take care of my baby without his ass."

I nodded, but I thought she wanted the house with Nut. I don't know what she wanted to hear me say. I couldn't believe she was still having sex for money, knowing she was pregnant. I saw other women on the street doing it, but it just ain't seem right. "Do you even know what you're having yet?"

She smiled and sat back down on my couch. "It's a boy."

"Hmmm . . ."

"I thought about getting rid of it for one split second, but when I seen that sonogram, there wasn't no way I could kill my baby. I'm sorry."

"Hmmm . . ."

"I love Nut, and I'd do anything for him, but not this. I just can't do it, and I'm already in my second trimester, too," she said, shaking her head. "No."

"Hmmm . . ." I mumbled again.

"What? Why you keep saying that?"

I shook my head and stared at the floor. How was I gonna tell her that she was making a mistake by keeping it? No child should grow up with a prostitute for a mama and a nut for a father.

"Say what's on your mind, Camille. Shit," Peaches said, rolling her neck like she had a problem.

"It's just, I don't understand why you want to have Nut's baby for. He's crazy! That nigga got a fuckin' dried-up monkey head dangling from his car mirror, for God's sake. Don't you think your son might be born crazy, too?"

Peaches looked at me like I hurt her feelings. She shook her head and said, "You don't understand nothing."

"What you mean?" I asked, truly annoyed.

"Sometimes I swear I forget how old you are," she said, standing up. "It's easy to forget that shit sometimes."

"Huh?" I said, crossing my arms. She was only two years older than me.

"Just cuz you dress like a grown-up and fuck grown-ass men don't mean you know a damn thing about life!"

"And I guess you a genius, huh?"

"No, I ain't say that, but what you don't get is that me and Nut . . . we get each other," she said, jabbing her finger on the palm of her hand. "He understands me, and I understand him. You have no clue what he been through. Life ain't been easy for him."

"But, Peaches, it's been hard for all of us, ain't it? I sure as hell don't think I had it easy!"

Peaches shook her head again and said, "You don't know. You have no idea what he had to see when he was little, Camille."

She paced back and forth, shaking her head, and then she stopped in front of me. "Yeah, you and me, we been fucked and fucked over, but what we been through ain't nothing like him, trust me."

She pulled out some gum, popped it in her mouth, and then sat back down. "I wish I had a fucking cigarette—a blunt or something."

I smirked and rolled my eyes. She must've forgot who she was talking to. *Now* she cared about what she was doing to the baby, even though she was having sex with anybody who had enough paper to hit it. And she was smoking and drinking long after she learned she was pregnant. I shook my head.

"The police found Nut when he was three years old in a house on East Capitol Street. You know *why* the police found him?" Peaches asked, looking me over. "His neighbors had kept complaining that they smelled something rotten coming from his house. When they went to check what it was, Nut was in there sitting on the bed beside his dead mother. She was tied up to the bed, naked."

I covered my mouth with my hand.

"Her throat was slit from one ear to the other, and his

father was dead in the basement. His head blown off cuz his father had pulled the trigger."

"Damn," I said, shaking my head. "That's so fucked up."

"My baby was in that house for nine days, all by hisself. Starving, scared, confused," Peaches said, shaking her head. "He was drinking water from the toilet, eating out the trash can. Living off of ketchup and relish in a house filled with maggots and flies! And on top of all that, they found out his mother was three months pregnant, too."

"That's terrible" was the only thing I could say. I had never heard of anything so unbelievable.

"Nut ended up living with Rob's mother, but she ended up moving in with her mother, Nut's grandmother, for a little while. But it was so crowded over there that Nut ended up moving in with his uncle around Paradise," Peaches said, shaking her head. She wiped a tear that had started running down her cheek. "That's the same place I grew up. And if that neighborhood don't have enough trouble, he was living with a dude who ain't give a fuck about him!"

"Why? What you mean?" I asked, needing to know more.

Peaches shook her head and stayed quiet for a minute. "I shouldn't even be telling his business like this."

"What?" I asked, anxious.

"It's just"—she took a deep breath—"his uncle used to smoke boat and shit."

Boat was just like dippers, except sometimes the weed was laced with PCP instead of embalming fluid. That made people go crazy and get all violent. Sometimes I thought Nut smoked them from the way he acted.

"The shit Nut told me he used to do to him," Peaches said, staring at the floor, "was just so horrible. I don't even want to talk about it."

"He used to beat him?" I asked.

"Sometimes, but it wasn't even just that. It was the mind games. He told me once his uncle tried to make him jump off the roof of their building."

"Huh?"

"Yeah. His uncle told Nut that he knew Nut could fly and that he wanted him to show him how to do it."

"What?" I asked, shaking my head. "What you mean fly?"

"Girl, don't even try to get me to explain what he meant. It's exactly as crazy as the shit sounds."

I frowned and then shook my head.

"Nut told me he was so scared he thought he was gonna die that day. His uncle told him the only way he could come down from the roof was by flying. He ended up breaking his arm and his leg when he went flying off the roof," Peaches said, resting her hand on her small pouch.

"Damn."

"Sometimes, when you see people who you think are monsters, or you hear bad things about them, you really expect them to look like these big, ugly or evil-looking people, but when you really see them, like see them inside, and learn what they're about, you see that they're just like regular people. Just some bad things happened to them somewhere that made them change a little bit. Nut ain't a monster. He just got stuff going on that is hard for him to get over."

I bit my lip and thought about what she said for a minute. "Well, where you gonna go?"

"I found this women's shelter in Northwest, over on D Street. I'ma go there until my son's born and then maybe I'll go back to hair school."

"But what about Nut?"

"I don't know. I can't even think about that right now. I might get in touch with him later, but right now all I can think about is making sure he don't do something to try to hurt me or the baby."

Peaches gained a small bit of respect from me when she walked out of the apartment, her duffle bag on her shoulder and her head slightly up. I was surprised she had the courage to leave Nut after all the other things he did to her. She was even giving up having a house. Maybe she really just couldn't do it and Nut had finally crossed a line. I was glad she thought about me, before she decided to disappear.

19

LATER THAT NIGHT

Nut leaned up against his horn for a long time, even though he was early as hell. I could tell he was pissed. He kept blowing the horn every two seconds. Me, Shakira, and Trina Boo rushed outside. I hadn't even put all my makeup on yet or had a chance to pack my bag. Shakira had her wig and her heels in her hand. Trina Boo was pulling the straps up on her dress.

As soon as we got settled in the truck, he said, "Where the fuck Peaches at?"

We shrugged our shoulders and waited for what was next, since it was clear Nut was livid.

"Nobody know where she at, huh?" he asked, turning his body all the way around and staring at us. He was so hot, I could see the anger in his eyes. "Ain't none of y'all heard from her today?"

I got scared, cuz I thought he knew she had come by, but I wasn't gonna volunteer no information.

"All right," he said, nodding his head. "Bitches wanna play dumb tonight!"

Nut mashed on the gas and went straight to pick Marcha

up. As soon as she got in, he told her she was moving in Wynika's old apartment, starting tomorrow.

"I don't wanna live over there," Marcha whined. "That nasty-ass apartment building, unh-unh."

But she had no idea that Nut was already pissed off, so she ain't even see his fist coming in time to duck. She screamed as he hit her over and over. We was petrified, sitting in the back of the truck. I grabbed Shakira's leg and squeezed it. I could hear his punches punishing Marcha, and I wanted to get the hell out of the truck. She started crying and begging him to stop. We was too scared to say anything. I just looked out the window and tried to block everything out.

Nut calmed down long enough to pull away from the curb and to drive us to Fourteenth Street. As soon as I jumped out the truck, I lit a cigarette and walked as far away from the rest of them as I could. I ain't wanna see Marcha's face or hear her sniffling. I walked to the bus stop and sat down to put on the rest of my makeup and to try and forget about what had happened. I felt so guilty.

I could hear music coming from around the corner. I looked up to see Joe's Denali pulling to a stop in front of me. T.I.'s "Rubberband Man" was coming from his speakers.

"Hey, sexy," he said, smiling.

I tried to smile back and walk over to his truck, but tears came to my eyes just as I was about to say hello.

"You all right? What's wrong?" he asked, looking sexy and worried at the same time. I guess he could tell I was shaken. I shook my head and started crying.

"Hey, don't cry, beautiful," Joe said. "Get in. I'm going to take you away from here."

A real smile spread across my face. That's exactly what I wanted. To disappear. To forget. To start over. I opened the door and climbed in. I let him drive and I ain't even ask him where he was going. I ain't tell him how much it was gonna cost, and I ain't tell Nut that I was leaving.

Joe drove across the Fourteenth Street Bridge into Arlington, Virginia. He passed me the blunt he had been smoking and I hit it a couple of times until I stopped crying. Then I leaned my head back on the headrest to sleep, listening to the music.

When I woke up, I was staring at a beach. I rubbed my eyes and turned around to look at Joe. He was asleep in the driver's seat. I had his suit jacket laid across me like a blanket. I cleared my throat and then nudged him until he woke up.

"Hey," he said and then cleared his throat.

"Where the hell are we?" I asked, getting scared.

"Virginia Beach."

"Where?"

"Virginia Beach. You was asleep and I just kept going," he said, yawning.

"Oh, my God. Are you lunching?" I said, shaking my head and then rubbing my temples. I could feel a headache coming on. "I'm gonna get in some serious trouble."

"What you mean?" he asked.

All I could think about was how Nut was beating on Marcha and the sound of her crying and begging for him to stop. "I can't be all the way out here without even telling

Nut where the hell I'm at. Oh, my God, you have to take me back."

"You said you wanted to get away. I did what I said. That's the kind of person I am. Ain't no in-betweens."

"Listen, Joe, I have to get back to D.C. This is crazy."

"Just relax, Nectar," he said, squeezing my thigh.

But I couldn't relax. I ain't know nothing about this place. I looked around, and we was the only ones out there. I could see the sun slowly coming up in the distance.

"Let's just watch the sun rise, and then we'll go back. I promise nothing's going to happen to you." Joe said it so calmly that I wanted to believe him. But I couldn't help looking at my cell phone. Six missed calls. Three from Nut, two from Shakira, and one from Peaches. I shook my head.

"How far away are we? I need to get back, like ASAP."

"It's going to take us around four hours to get back."

"Four hours! Nigga, are you crazy bringing me all the way down here?!"

He laughed. "Listen to you. It's going to be all right. I promise. Just chill."

"You have no idea!" This nigga was playing with my life, and he really thought this shit was funny.

Joe started rolling another blunt. I watched him picking seeds out and then twisting and licking it up. Soon he was lighting up, and then he changed the music that had been playing real low to another song.

"Listen to this song. It's my favorite. Mos Def. 'Umi Says.'" He turned the volume up until the music filled the truck.

"Umi?" I asked, confused.

"I think it means mother or grandmother," Joe said, and then he hit the blunt and passed it to me.

A voice came over the speakers. It was a slow hip-hop song, with pianos and soft drum beats. Almost like a rap-jazz joint. Mos Def kept saying "Shine your light on the world." I hit the Bob and blew the smoke out.

"I ain't no perfect man," Joe sang along with Mos, closing his eyes. "I be feeling like this all the time."

I closed my eyes and listened to what the rapper was saying. I wondered what my mother and grandmother would think about how I was living now. Would they be mad that I wasn't shining my light on the world? It was a cool song, but it was real long. By the time it was over, I opened my eyes and the sun was just about all the way up.

"It's beautiful, ain't it?" Joe said, looking mesmerized.

I wasn't sure if he was talking about the song or the sunrise, but they both was beautiful, so I nodded. I had never watched the sun rise on the beach before, only from the streets or after leaving a motel room. The sun was about to shine its light on the world.

"All right. Let's get you back," he said, throwing the car in reverse and then pulling onto the street.

"Good," I mumbled, relieved.

"Let me ask you something," he said, merging onto 264 West. It was a lot of people on the road, but it was the middle of the workweek and a little before rush hour.

I rolled my eyes cuz I already knew what he was gonna say.

"How you get into this?"

"Don't even ask that . . . please," I said, throwing my hand up. I ran my fingers through my weave with my other hand and stared at the cars in front of us.

"Well, do you want to get out?"

"Joe," I said, annoyed. Why he keep pushing it?

"I'm just saying. You are a beautiful girl. Ain't there something else you want to do with your life?"

"How you gonna ask me that? I could turn right around and ask you the same thing. Why you paying for pussy?" I covered my mouth, cuz I ain't mean to actually ask the question, but it just fell out.

He rolled his eyes and got quiet. "We ain't never had sex. So don't even try it."

"Oh, so eating pussy not having sex?" I asked, sarcastically. "Since when?"

"There's no penetration."

"Whatever, Joe," I said, rolling my eyes. "What? You wanna save me or something? Is that it?"

The car got quiet. We drove for an hour without saying anything, and then Joe pulled off the highway and stopped at a Cracker Barrel restaurant.

"You hungry, right?"

I started to say no, so we could hurry up and get back, but I was already really late. Nut was gonna be mad, one way or the other. I ain't think it was such a thing as making him madder. "Yeah, I'm hungry."

My cell phone kept vibrating the whole time we ate breakfast. After I went to the bathroom, I decided to call Peaches first. She just wanted to know if Nut was looking for her. Of course he was. But I told her not to worry about it and to just

let me know how everything goes from time to time. After
we got off the phone, I called Shakira.

"Bitch, where the hell are you?" Shakira shouted in the
phone. "You know that nigga is going berserk!"

"I'm on my way home."

"You better hurry the hell up. He talking about holding
me and Trina Boo hostage and shit, since you and Peaches
gone!"

"Where you at?" I asked.

"At the house, but he's downstairs with Trina Boo. That
nigga talking real crazy."

I shook my head and walked a few feet to see what Joe
was doing. "Oh, my God."

"You with a trick?"

"Yeah."

"Girl, just hurry the hell up and get here. I hope that
nigga paying your ass a lot of cash, cuz Nut is going fucking
crazy!"

"Okay, okay. I'm on my way," I said and then hung up.
My heart started racing. I knew Nut was gonna whip my ass
when I came back unless I had enough money that would
make him shut the hell up. I had saved almost two thousand
dollars from charging double. If I couldn't talk Joe into giving me a lot, I ain't know what I was gonna do. I walked
back over to the table, twisting my hands.

"What's wrong, Nectar?"

I shook my head from left to right. "I told you he's gonna
trip."

"Who?"

"Nut! Ain't you listening to anything I've been saying?"

"Listen, how much you need?"

"Two thousand," I said, pouting.

"For real?" he said, rubbing his chin. He looked at his plate and then said, "I'll have to go to the bank, but okay."

Okay? He had it like that? I relaxed. I would give Nut $1,500 and keep the other five for me. That was a lot more than I ever gave him in one night, so he'd definitely be satisfied.

When we was back in the truck and on the road, I couldn't resist asking Joe what he did for money.

He shook his head and said, "I'll tell you, if you tell me what's the one thing you'd do if you wasn't doing this."

I snorted. "You think you so slick."

"What? Just tell me, slim," he said, smiling.

That was something I never even thought about seriously. Hair school was Peaches' dream, not mine. I just said that cuz that's what she said. I did like dancing, but not all like that. I thought about helping kids, but wasn't sure how.

"I don't know, really," I said.

"You have to know. Any ideas?"

"I don't know. Maybe work with kids."

"Teach?"

"Nah, not teaching."

"Maybe a pediatrician?"

"What's that?"

"A doctor for children."

"Nah, I don't think I'm smart enough to be nobody's doctor."

"How can you say that?" Joe asked, looking over at me seriously.

"It's true."

"Please, sweetheart. You are a survivor. If you can do what you do, then you can do anything you want."

I raised my eyebrows, cuz I never thought about it like that. "Well, I guess since I used to be in foster care, I think I wouldn't mind helping other foster care kids."

He looked shocked but said, "There isn't anything wrong with that. Yeah, you should give back. Maybe a social worker or counselor or something."

I nodded. "There was this lady named Ms. Lewis, she was my caseworker. A big lady like Queen Latifah, but she was real fly, though. I used to like her up until she ain't wanna believe something I told her that happened at the house."

"Oh, for real?" Joe said, changing lanes. "What was that?"

"I told her that my foster parents put my sister out for no reason, and she told me to make sure I don't be stealing like my sister was. But my sister wasn't stealing. Me and my sister was getting raped by my foster father and then my sister got pregnant and had his baby," I said, wiping a tear that surprised me by slipping from my eye. "And all of a sudden my foster mother ain't want her at the house no more."

"Damn," Joe said, shaking his head. "You know where she at now?"

I shook my head. "I haven't seen her since that day they sent her away. I liked to think that her and her real family finally got back together," I said, wiping away another tear. "That would be nice. But anyway . . . what about you? What you do?"

"Oh, I work in finance."

"Oh?" I said, trying not to show how impressed I was. He was so young. "How old are you?"

"I just turned twenty-seven last month."

"Oh."

"What happened to your foster father?" he asked. "Did he ever get in trouble for what he was doing?"

I cocked my head, not sure how to answer that question. "It depends on how you look at it."

"What you mean?"

"He got murked this summer."

"For real?" he asked, looking over at me.

"Yeah, robbery or something."

"Damn, son. I guess that's karma," he said, shaking his head.

"Yeah, I guess so."

"I'm sorry you had a life like that," Joe said. "I wish you didn't have to go through any of that. But I guess that sounds strange coming from me."

I looked out the window and watched the cars and trees passing by us blur into one another. Yeah, cuz if I hadn't gone through that I probably wouldn't be sitting with him right now.

"I hope you do go back to school and maybe one day college. You could get a sociology degree, I bet," he said.

My phone vibrated and I looked down to see Nut's picture flashing across the screen.

"You should probably answer that," Joe said.

I took a deep breath and then said, "Hello?"

"Where the fuck your little ass at?" Nut yelled into the

phone. "I been calling you all fucking night and all god-damn morning."

"I'm on my way to the house and I got all of your money, plus some," I said quickly. "I had to do a special for one of my regulars."

Nut grunted in the phone. "Bitch, you just love testing me, don't you?!"

"Nut, I'm sorry. Please, don't be pissed at me, baby," I said before I felt Joe grabbing the phone.

"Dude, stop yelling at her! She said she's going to give you your money. Chill the fuck out!" he yelled before closing the phone.

I was so stunned that I looked at Joe as if he had lost his mind. I stayed quiet the rest of the way home, even when Joe stopped to get gas and he asked me if I wanted anything from inside the store. I kept my mouth shut when he stopped at his bank to take out two thousand dollars in cash. Nut ain't even call me back for the rest of the ride, surprising the hell out of me. He was gonna kill me when I got home. If it wasn't for Shakira and Trina Boo, and even Peaches and her unborn baby, I probably wouldn't have ever come back.

AND IF YOU THINK ABOUT TURNING BACK/

I GOT THE SHOTGUN ON YA BACK.

—ERYKAH BADU, "SOLDIER"/HARRIET TUBMAN

20

JANUARY 2006

He kept calling the new Spanish chick he brought on the strip with us Almond Joy, cuz he thought it pissed us off, but we ain't care. She wanted to just go by Candy, but hell, as long as the bitch pulled her weight I ain't give a damn what she was called. Her dumb ass got Nut's butterfly tattoo on her titty *and* on her back. The bitch had even moved in with Nut. The only person who cared Joy had jumped the line was Marcha, cuz me, Shakira, and Trina Boo wasn't even thinking about replacing Peaches in the first place. While Marcha on the other hand was so used to living by herself across town, she thought she was next in line to be Nut's bottom bitch, if the chance came up. And we could tell she wasn't feeling living on the first floor in our "little dirty-ass" apartment building anyway.

The only time we got to hang around Joy was at Sunday meetings, and when Nut called hisself "treating us." He took us to two shopping trips up to the outlets in Philly and Jersey and he gave us a thousand dollars for each of us to spend. I don't know what came over him cuz he never did that when Peaches was there. The whole time Joy clung on to Nut like he was her purse or something.

He even took us to Kobe's a couple days before New Year's Eve for some Japanese food. We all sat around the U-shaped table as the funny chef chopped, diced, and flipped raw food in the air before he cooked it. I was amazed. The chef made a tiny volcano out of chopped stacked onion rings, vegetable oil, and some soy sauce. When he lit it on fire, I knew I wasn't the only person amazed, cuz the *oohs* and *ahhs* came out. The chef even cracked jokes with us, too. But he ain't have a clue that when he teased Nut, by calling him "a pimp with all the beautiful ladies," that he was really telling the truth.

But Joy wasn't even that cute, that's the thing that got me. I mean, of course she had her own curly honey blond hair down her back, and an okay body, but her face looked like she had been hit in it one too many times. She tried to be nice, but her face just reminded me that Peaches was missing. Even though I knew my girl was trying to do better with her life, I missed the hell out of her.

Me and Joy was walking fast down Fourteenth Street, trying to keep warm and to get one of those niggas to take us to a hotel instead of a quickie in their cars. It was so cold white smoke came out of our mouth when we talked. I kept drinking small bottles of Grey Goose, since it made me feel hot after I drank them.

Joy was telling me about her last pimp, who she said treated her like shit, and nothing like Nut (I had to roll my eyes at that), when this car full of drunk and high white guys stopped in a black Benz truck. One of them shouted, "We got five thousand dollars to let us fuck all night long! Five for both of you!"

Joy started smiling and looking at me to see what was up. But I rolled my eyes. "No, thank you."

"Mami, why not? I need the money bad," she whined. "Let's do it!"

"Hey, you with the red coat!" one of the guys yelled.

I looked at him and smirked.

"I love brownies. Let me see your ass!" he shouted.

I rolled my eyes and turned around to walk the other direction.

"*Qué,* Mami?" Joy said, *click-clacking* behind me. "Let's go. It'll be okay."

"Bitch, are you crazy? That's way too many dudes. Who knows what the fuck they'll do to us. Ain't no muscle gonna be there for us, either. Nah," I said, shaking my head.

"*Mami, pero necesito realmente el dinero!*" Like I really knew what the fuck she said.

"Come on, girls! The party's in here," one of the guys yelled.

"Ay, Papi," she purred and then looked at me like her coochie was itching and only that money they was offering could scratch it.

"That shit is way too dangerous. I'm not cool with it, and you should stop acting so damn pressed, Joy."

She sucked her teeth and started walking over to the truck. A couple seconds later, she turned around and said,

"All right Mami. Tell Nut I'll see him in the morning." She giggled and jumped in the truck.

I shook my head and walked down the street. Dumb bitch. That must be why her face look like that. Shakira was smoking a cigarette when I reached her. "It's cold as shit out here," I groaned, rubbing my palms together.

"Aw shit, don't come over here with that," she said, puffing. "Where your girl go?"

I smirked and reached for her cigarette, then took a puff. "That bitch just as crazy as her boyfriend."

"Oh, shit! Jump Out!" Shakira yelled as she popped up, grabbing my arm and dragging me down the street. We ran inside the hotel and headed straight to the stairwell before the cops had even seen us. We stayed there for a while cuz Nut told us they had blocked the street off. He told us to go ahead and take some of the money to rent a room, but since we ain't have a reservation they wouldn't let us get one. Some rule they had, but I knew it was cuz we looked like prostitutes. We was stuck. Shakira tried to pick up one of the men at the hotel bar, but since the Feds was right out front, everybody was acting like they was above us tonight.

"What the fuck?" I asked, standing in the lobby.

"They kill me with that Jump Out shit," Shakira said, rolling her eyes. "Always trying to round *us* up, like them dudes buying the pussy ain't breaking laws, too!"

We needed to figure something out, cuz I was still underage and I wasn't going back in the system. *Fuck that.* And then I recognized the fat bellboy. I gave him head before, but he was trying to act like he ain't know me.

"Where's the back door?" I whispered as soon as I got up on him.

He tried to ignore me, and then I said, "Freebie next time."

I could tell he was trying not to react, but it was too late. A smile spread across his fat face, and then he told me how to get to the back exit. Me and Shakira hurried up before the front desk clerk decided she needed to get heroic and report us to the cops.

We made it out okay and headed straight home. Nut was there when we got there, doing a head count. He was pissed when he found out Trina Boo, Marcha, and Joy was nowhere to be found. I ain't tell him I knew Joy was with tricks, cuz it wasn't my place. Plus all I kept thinking was at least they wasn't minors and wouldn't get shipped back to foster care like me and Shakira would've.

The next morning when we still ain't hear nothing from Trina Boo and Marcha, Nut called up to the station and found out that's where they was. I was hoping that at least they was with tricks last night, too.

When Nut came back from bailing Marcha and Trina Boo out, he was livid cuz Joy wasn't there. Now I was stuck between another rock and a hard place, cuz if I told what I knew, then he was gonna be mad at me for not stopping the dumb bitch. If I ain't tell, he was still gonna be mad.

"The last time I saw her, she was getting in a black Benz truck just before Jump Out raided." I decided to tell him, so he wouldn't be mad I ain't say nothing when he found out later.

"You sure?" he asked, walking around Marcha's apartment. "I've been calling her all night."

I knew better than to say more than that. I knew Nut, and he was bound to blame me for her stupidness, since Joy was new.

"Why you ain't say that shit last night?!" he snapped.

"Cuz I ain't know if that meant anything then," I said, rolling my eyes. How was I supposed to know that she wasn't gonna show up for morning roll call?

"Stupid bitch," he said as he kept walking around the room.

Was he talking about me or Joy? Shit, at this point, as long as he spelled it right, I was fine with being called a bitch. I was a smart one, unlike Joy. I crossed my arms over my chest.

Hours passed by and still no word from Joy. Nut was growing restless. He had come to each of our apartments to hang out while he waited for her. Marcha called herself cooking for him, and I could smell her fried chicken upstairs. She could've offered us some. *Bitch. Still trying to take Peaches' spot.* Later, him and Shakira smoked J's. The strong herb smoke slipped underneath my door across the hall, clouding my head and making me sleepy. When he came to me, I rubbed knots out of his back again.

"Do you hate your life?" he asked me while I was on top of him.

"Why you ask me that?" I asked, shocked.

"I just wonder sometimes."

"Do you hate yours?"

"Sometimes," he said.

I was surprised he admitted that. "Why?"

He sighed and said, "I like it, more than I hate it."

I wanted to hear him say more than that, but he wouldn't. I kept rubbing my fingers across his back.

"You never answered me," he said, turning his head the other direction.

"I don't know if *hate* is the right word, cuz there's things I like about it, too."

Nut rolled over and stared me in my eyes. "Do you hate me?"

I blinked a few times. He caught me off guard. But then I started thinking about it and I had to shake my head no, cuz I ain't hate him. "You not making me stay, like most pimps do."

"So why you here?"

I thought for a long moment, knowing I had to choose my words right. And then it came to me. "I need you, remember?"

He smiled and then lifted me up off of him. "Good answer."

I thought he was gonna try to fuck, but he ain't do it. He put his shirt back on and went downstairs to see Trina Boo. It was the strangest conversation we had ever had.

A few days later, a Channel 4 Newsflash scrolled across the screen about a senator's son being found dead in Rock Creek Park with three other boys and an unidentified female in a torched car. When they showed the mangled, burned-up Benz truck I wondered if the woman was Joy since we still hadn't heard from her. The reporter said the car had flipped over a couple times before bursting into flames. She pointed out how twisty the roads was and how dark it gets at night, that a lot of people use the roads in the twelve-mile park that cut through the city to Maryland and to Virginia. But if it was the same truck that stopped that night on Fourteenth Street, I bet the car accident had something to do more with the drugs and alcohol, cuz it was written all over their faces that night.

I had a hard time sleeping after I saw that on TV. The only person I told what I thought had happened to Joy was Shakira. She let me sleep in her bed until the nightmares stopped and I felt better.

Nut found out a couple days later when Joy's mother came by looking for money from him to help bury her daughter. I couldn't tell if he was sad when he found out or not. He just stopped talking about her. None of us talked about her again. It was almost like she never even existed.

21

APRIL 2006

In April, the Tradewinds was so jam-packed I couldn't even stop niggas from squeezing my butt when I tried to go to the bathroom. It was pointless. Marcha said she had cramps, so she stayed home. Shakira and Trina Boo kept dragging me all around the club. As much as I loved Go Go music, I never really liked going to Go Go clubs. Outside events, yeah, maybe, since hearing it live was tight, but it was always so goddamn crowded, hot, and sweaty inside the clubs. Plus bitches was always trying to fight over some ignorant shit and niggas always started shooting for even stupider shit. That's why security was all over the club and the reason they wasn't even letting us bring lipstick, eyeliner, or mascara inside. Stupid. Like I'm really gonna try and stab a bitch in her eye with some lipstick.

Big G was shouting out different hoods—CRT, Lincoln Park, KDY, LDP, Simple City, Choppa City, Third World, 640, Trinidad, Sursum Cordas, and 21st, which was near where we lived, so we threw our hoods up. Two fingers on one hand and one finger on the other as we rocked to the beat. Big G even called out Trina Boo and KiKi's names over the mic. I'm not gonna front, I was jive jealous, but I tried not to show it. The crowd was getting hyped, rocking to the congos and Back's version of John Legend's "I Can Change."

Jayson and his friends met us up there, but we was on opposite sides of the club. He and I had talked about a lot over the past few months. Mrs. Brinkley moved down to South Carolina to live with her sister. Jamal was in Dover working as an accountant, and Ja'qui was in Phoenix playing arena football for a team called the Arizona Rattlers. Jayson was an assistant manager at BCBG in Georgetown, talking about come in and get the hookup whenever I wanted. No doubt. We was still cool, but we never really had the same relationship we had back in the day.

Me, Shakira, and Trina Boo was getting twisted off of all the shots of Patrón that different niggas kept buying us. Some dude with dreads asked me if we could dance, and I nodded. He led me to the overcrowded dance floor, where everybody was lined up trying to see the band better, their arms extended in the air, flashing their hoods, beating their feet. Some dudes was busy grinding on apple bottoms, rocking to the bass drum, rollatons, cow bell, and Sauce on the congas, until sweat ran down their faces, making the hot room funkier.

Nut ain't know we went to the club tonight. He thought we went heavy-duty grocery shopping at Shopper's Food Warehouse and then to the Laundromat. That was all Shakira's idea. The dude I was dancing with was all right looking, and I could feel his dick growing hard as he pressed up against me. He thought he was slick trying to raise my miniskirt up higher, but there was no such thing as *free pussy,* so I kept moving his hand away even though we was still grooving. When Backyard started another song, I leaned in and shouted into the guy's ear, "Thanks, cutie, but I'm about to get a drink."

He nodded and let my waist go. *Cheap-ass muthafucka. Why he ain't offer to buy me one?* I walked over to Jayson, who was standing near the bar, as usual.

"Buy me a drink, big brother," I said, smiling and fluttering my eyelashes.

"Now, bitch, you should know by now that flirting shit don't work for me," he teased. "But I'll get you one anyway. What you want?"

"Grey Goose and cranberry juice."

He ordered it and got him a Midori sour. "Ain't that dude fine as shit," he said, staring at a light-skin guy with curly hair. "I just love me some Puerto Ricans and Dominicans."

"He *is* cute," I said, admiring the guy wearing a colorful embroidered Coogi T-shirt. "I hope he straight."

"Why you hating, Camille? I'm calling dibs."

I laughed and sipped my drink.

"Camille! Oh, my God. Guess who up here?" Trina Boo squealed and grabbed my arm.

"You goin' knock my drink over, though?" I asked, wiping the spill off my arm. "Damn."

"Guess who? Guess who?" She was looking too excited, like a child on opening day at Six Flags.

"Who Trina Boo, damn?"

"Walt Wilson."

"Who the hell is that?"

"For real? Where?" Jayson asked, looking around.

"Right there with the white hoodie and the aviator shades," Trina Boo said, nodding in his direction.

"Oh shit," Jayson said. "I ain't know he was that short."

"Who the fuck is Walt Wilson?" I asked, taking another sip.

"Girl, he be producing all those songs that got the Go Go beats mixed in it. You know who we talking about," Jayson said. "I think he did a song with Beyoncé and Mary J."

"Amerie, Eve, and Gwen Stefani, too," Trina Boo shouted.

"Oh, okay," I said, still not sure.

"Bitch, you don't know who we talking about," Trina Boo said, salty.

"Why you geeking, though?" I asked.

"I'm about to go over there and talk to him. Shit, I told your ass I'm going to New York," she said, fixing her silver top and grinning from ear to ear. "See y'all later."

"That girl," I said, shaking my head and taking another sip. I watched Shakira hugged up on the dance floor with some tall dude. The way they was all bunned up, I knew she knew him before tonight and she wasn't treating him like a trick. As soon as she came up for air, I was going to snatch her up and get in her business.

Just as Back started singing "Last Call for Alcohol," Shakira came over with the tall guy she was dancing with, smiling from ear to ear.

"You remember Kareem?" she asked, cheesing.

I shook my head.

"He used to go to Tech with us. He was a couple years older, though."

I shook my head. "Nah, I don't remember. But hi, Kareem."

"What's up?" he said.

"Umm . . . I'm about to go home. You goin' be all right with Trina Boo?"

I tried not to look surprised and nodded. "Yeah, have fun, but be careful."

She winked and led Kareem away.

I shook my head and sipped my drink. "Wow. That girl is playing with fire."

"All right, girl, we about to dip, too. Where Trina Boo at?" Jayson asked.

"I don't know. She in here somewhere. Call me later," I said.

"You sure she ain't leave with Walt?" he said, teasing.

"You never know with her trick ass. You right, let me call her cell phone." I dialed her up, and of course the phone just kept ringing. "All right, I'm riding home with you. I'll leave her a message, in case she decides to look for me."

"All right, I'll meet you at the car," Jayson said. Two of his guy friends followed him.

I looked around the club one more time, since the crowd was dwindling. But I ain't see her, so I left.

The next morning, I woke up to Trina Boo bouncing on my bed and shaking me and screaming, "Camille!"

"What the . . . how you get in here?" I asked, wiping my face.

"I got a key. You don't have one to my apartment?" she asked, confused.

"No."

"Oh? Nut gave it to me."

I shook my head and sat up. "Well, why you using it?"

"Guess what?"

"What?"

"Walt Wilson told me about a model casting call for his next video with Young P! He said all I had to do was show up and I'm in it!"

"For real?"

"Yeah, girl! Oh, my God. Help me pack."

"Pack?"

"Where the casting call at?"

"New York!"

"For real?"

"Yeah. He told me I could ride up there with him. He leaving tonight."

"Tonight? Leaving?" I asked, sitting all the way up. "Bitch, what you gonna tell Nut?"

She rolled her eyes and headed for the door. "Not a damn thing."

"What you mean, not a damn thing? He gonna go crazy on us! He still mad about Peaches and Wynika leaving . . . then Joy, and now you?"

"I'm saying, I can't pass this up. I'm sorry, Camille," she said, looking convinced.

"So you basically saying fuck us?"

"Listen, y'all my girls, but this is my dream," she said, disappearing behind the door.

I got up and put my slippers on and then went downstairs. Trina Boo turned up her radio and started trying on different outfits, some she had bought from this cute boutique in Baltimore called the Dollhouse. A lot of celebrities shopped there. It was some real fly shit, too, nothing she would wear working the streets, but something she was saving for a special occasion.

I sat on the edge of her bed and watched her pack. I still talked to Peaches, every now and then. She told me how Nut had begged her to come back, but she told him not until after she had their son. But for some reason, I knew that she still wouldn't get back with him. Things had changed since she left the streets. I knew she wasn't going to want his crazy ass around her baby.

Wynika was in jail, cuz she got three years. The judge wanted to make an example out of her. Ra-Ra and Meko was still in foster care. Neither one of her brothers wanted to take them. Andre was in jail for child molestation. They tried him as an adult, and he got eight years.

"Don't forget about us when your ass blow up," I said, picking up one of the dresses she tossed on the bed.

"Girl, please. How the hell am I gonna forget about any of y'all? Shit, I'm your muthafuckin' wife-in-law. Till death do us part, bitch."

I smiled.

"Okay," she said, holding up a dress and pressing it against her in front of the mirror. "What about this one?"

"Promise me something else," I said, standing in front of her.

"What? Why you so serious all of a sudden?"

"Just promise me, when you roll out, you don't ever come back here."

Her smile disappeared.

"Not to this building, not with Nut. You got a chance to do something different, take it."

Her smile came back and lit up her face. She reached over and gave me a hug. She squeezed tight and said, "Girl, I'ma be all right. You will, too, watch."

I heard a lot of footsteps coming down the stairs and turned in the direction of the noise. Shakira was pushing it. Her ass was just now walking Kareem to the door.

"Who is that with her?" Trina Boo asked, peeking out the window.

"Bitch, get ya ass in here!" I said, opening Trina Boo's door and yanking Shakira's arm to snatch her inside the apartment. "Are you losing your mind?"

"What?" she asked, grinning.

I rolled my eyes and sat on the couch. Marcha must've heard all the noise cuz she was tapping on the door and opening it at the same time.

"Y'all up early as hell," she said as she plopped down on the couch. "I'm so glad we ain't have to work last night."

"Me, too," Trina Boo said.

"You packing?" Shakira asked.

"Yep."

"Why?"

Trina Boo flashed a sinister smile and started dropping her booty like it was hot.

"Uggh, freak!" Shakira squealed.

We all laughed.

Nut ain't get as irate as I thought he was going to get when Trina Boo disappeared. I mean, he bitched about it for a while, but I guess he thought he could replace her easily or something, cuz he ain't pop off on nobody like he did when Peaches disappeared. Lately, he had been staying to hisself and not causing that much trouble. I had a feeling something was up his sleeve.

I was standing on Fourteenth Street smoking a jack when a gold Camry pulled up. It was a pale-face white dude, missing two teeth on the side of his mouth.

"Hey, baby," I said, walking over to the car.

"Hey, um . . . Can I get a date?"

"What kind of date?"

"Half and half."

"Are you a cop?"

"No," he said, shaking his head.

"Okay," I said, tossing the cigarette and then climbing in his car.

"How much?"

"Two hundred."

"Two hundred? Sheesh. Inflation for the recession, huh?" he said, digging in his pocket.

I nodded. Something about the dude seemed mighty suspect. I put my hand on the latch to open the door.

"Where you goin' honey?" he asked, handing me the money.

I stared at the money but then decided to climb back out the car.

"Where you goin', honey? Here's your money!" he shouted behind me. "Here's your money!"

"I don't know what you talking about!" I shouted and walked down the block and flagged down a cab. I text Nut as soon as I was inside: *Block hot. Cop in gold Camry.* I rode around the block and waited for a while before paying the cab driver.

My phone rang a few minutes later. It was Peaches.

"Hey, girl!" I said. "What's up?"

"Camille, I think I'm going into labor," she groaned.

"Ain't you early?"

"Yeah, but this baby coming. Can you meet me at Howard Hospital?"

She wanted me to be there? I felt important and special. I ain't get to go when Danica went into labor. I begged to, but just Mrs. Brinkley and Mr. Big went. I wanted to be there for her.

"Okay," I said, smiling. "I'll be there in like twenty minutes. Oh, my God, Peaches! Are you excited?"

Peaches groaned and took a few quick breaths. "Hurry up, Camille."

I quickly flagged down another cab and rushed over to Georgia Avenue. Peaches was in a wheelchair in the lobby when I got there. She was all bloated and tired looking, but I kissed her on her sweaty forehead and said, "It's gonna be okay."

"I called Nut up here, too," she said. "I hope he act decent."

I blinked back my surprise. After all she was saying about wanting better for her and her baby, she gave in to him anyway. "You did?"

"I know what you're thinking, but"—she groaned and held her belly—"I wanna give him a chance to prove hisself now that the baby almost here."

Peaches needed support right now, not my opinion, no matter how on point it was. So I said, "That man gonna wanna see his son. Trust."

"I hope so. You know, I ain't seen him since that day I left," she said, looking worried. "I hope he stays cool."

I felt for her. This was her first child and labor, and on top of everything else, she had to be concerned if Nut would show up as Lucifer or if he would be Sean Crawford. I wanted to ease her fear and keep her as calm as possible. "Don't be scared. It'll be okay."

"Look at you," she said, smiling. "I should've brought your ass a change of clothes."

I looked down at my black outfit and smiled. "Hell, maybe I can get a date while I'm in here, too. Doctors got cake!"

She cracked up laughing until her stomach hurt and she had to rub it.

After Peaches was given a room, the nurse said she wasn't dilated enough yet and that she should start walking around the hospital. I helped her big butt out of her wheelchair and walked with her. She looked so happy, even though I could tell she was in pain.

"You nervous?" I asked. "You about to be somebody's mother, girl!"

"A little, but it's like a good nervous," she said, smiling. She was dragging her swollen feet as we shuffled down the hall.

"Have you ever worried that it might not be Nut's baby, Peaches?" I just had to ask her, since she never mentioned it.

"No. Not once," she said, and then she stopped. "Okay, I lie. Maybe once or twice."

I smiled.

"But I know in my heart it's his. This baby was made out of love, even if Nut wants to forget."

"No, that nigga loves you. Just a weird kind of love. You should've seen how pissed off he was after you left," I said, rolling my eyes. "Girl."

I told her how he went off on Marcha that night and how he started getting all strict on us. I ain't tell her about Ms. Joy's arrival and departure. For a minute, I forgot I was supposed to be keeping her calm, I was so busy catching her up on all the drama. I thought I made Peaches get fully dilated since I ended up making her nerves worse, cuz by the time we got back to her room, she clutched her stomach real tight and moaned. But when I turned around to see what she was looking at, Nut was sitting in a chair reading a baby magazine. His cane leaned up against the wall.

"Hey," he said.

"Hey," she said, still holding her belly. I could tell she was jumpy, cuz her eyes darted around.

"You fat as shit, girl," Nut said, standing up.

"I know that, *and?*" she said with an attitude. She was the only person he let talk to him like that, without going off.

"And . . . you look good," he said, and he smiled. "Real good."

She smiled and Nut walked over to hug her. I knew then that she felt better.

I left to give them some privacy. Nut ain't seem angry and I wasn't worried that he'd kirk out in a hospital. I went to the snack room to get some Doritos and a fruit punch soda. By the time I came back to the room, the nurse had already scrubbed up and was rushing me. Peaches was about to have her baby, and she told the nurse she wanted me in the delivery room, too.

"Goodness," I whispered as I went to wash my hands. When I walked in the room, Nut looked weird and out of place. No cane anywhere. Maybe it was cuz he looked like he was a normal guy for a change.

Peaches was in labor for a long time, screaming, hollering, pissing, shitting, sweating, and pushing. By the time the baby came, I felt like I had been working out. Nut was grinning so wide when the doctor passed him the baby that I thought he wasn't even gonna give Peaches her son.

"What we goin' name my son?" Nut asked.

"Sean Jr.?" Peaches asked, smiling.

"Nah, I don't want him to be nothing like me," he said, shaking his head. Nut looked mesmerized, and I saw a look in his eyes I had never seen. "He's gonna be a great man one day. Let's name him something else."

"What?" Peaches asked, staring up at her two men.

"Chu?" I said, not sure why. "Chukwuemeka means—"

"God has done something great," Nut said, looking at the baby. "I know, but no. I don't think it's right. Let's call him Amir."

"Amir," she said, reaching for her son. "I like it. Hey, cutie."

"He look just like me, Peaches," he said, and he kissed her on her forehead. "I'm gonna try my best to be a good father. You hear me?"

Peaches nodded and rubbed Amir's cheek. I hoped for Amir's sake Nut was telling the truth for once in his life.

22

FEBRUARY 2007

It was so cold outside, me and Shakira was practically walking up the street arm in arm. She had on a black fur and I had on a brown one, but we was both ass-naked underneath, except our thigh-high leather boots.

"If somebody don't come buy this pussy soon, I'm gonna rent my own self a hotel room," she said, holding on tight. "Hey, I got an idea."

"Your ass always got ideas."

"Why don't you call that nigga Joe and I call Kareem?"

"No, I'm not trying to fool myself about Joe. You, on the other hand, in love with that nigga."

"No, I'm not," she said with a giggle.

"See."

After Peaches had Amir, Nut dropped off the scene. He started charging me, Shakira, and Marcha rent for the apartments. He ain't charge that much, but we still had to work the streets to pay for it since we ain't know how to do nothing else. I had money saved up, but I knew it wasn't really enough to do what I wanted to do. Or maybe I just was scared to try to do something else. I'm not gonna lie—

Shakira was right, this kind of work was easy. We ain't
have to clock in or answer to nobody, and we could work
whenever we wanted to. Marcha had started stripping at
the Skylark on New York Avenue. She said it was too hard
and dangerous working the streets. If I was old enough, I'd
probably do the same thing.

Now that it was just me and Shakira, we ain't have rides
to Fourteenth Street or protection from Nut no more. If
one of us got locked up or harassed by the cops, we had
to deal with it ourselves. We paid for our own condoms,
weed, liquor, and even vaginal exams. Everything. A couple
of other pimps tried to step up, but we wasn't trying to jump
into another situation like that so soon. One day became
one week, then one whole month, and next thing we knew,
it was almost one whole year that passed without us having
a pimp.

It was scary doing it without knowing Nut was in our
corner. But at the same time, we ain't have to worry about
him beating nobody at the drop of a dime. We had a rough
night once when one of Shakira's regulars tried to get three
of his friends to run a train on her on a sneak tip. The niggas was hiding in the back of his truck when he first pulled
up. Shakira ain't know until after she finished sucking him
off. She heard some dudes' voices in the back. They was
coming to the front, talking about how they was gonna fuck
her, naming all the positions they wanted her in. But when
she said the price she wanted, they started lunching out and
they tried to rape her, but Shakira's regular finally talked his
buddies off of her, feeling guilty probably from hearing my
girl screaming like crazy. If he wouldn't have stopped them,

Shakira would've been got, cuz no one was there to help her. It was the first time we had really thought about getting another pimp. Niggas knew not to try that shit when we had one. We both started carrying blades on us, just in case some shit popped off again.

Nut had become strictly legit. He got a loan to start rehabbing houses by using the apartment building for clout. After he fixed the rundown houses back up, he sold them for twice the money he first paid for them. It was strange to know that he got his start from the money we was giving him, but hell, Peaches said he was a hustler. I guess he hustled the hell out of us, cuz we ain't never see no houses in our names.

Joe had taught me how to open up a bank account and I had nine thousand dollars in something he called a money market account that no one knew about but me. Deep down inside I knew what I wanted to do with the money, but I ain't wanna jinx myself by saying it out loud.

"Call him, Camille," Shakira begged.

I did like Joe, but it was hard to forget that he was a person willing to pay money just to spend time with me. He ain't never try to fuck me, but he did eat me and lick me all over, even my ass. A few times, he stuck his finger inside me, but he never tried to stick his dick in me. I thought that was strange. Every time I asked him about it, he just said he just wanted to please me, and then he asked, "What's so wrong with that?" Of course, I liked that kind of attitude, so I stopped asking.

But he also spent a lot of time talking to me. He ain't want me to be out on the streets, and he even said he'd put me up in one of those new condos on U Street. But I was too scared to turn my life back over to another man like that.

"Oh, my God. Hold up," Shakira said. "Would you look at this shit?"

She was pointing at a men's magazine stocked on the newsstand. We both screamed at the same time and jumped up and down in the middle of the sidewalk.

"Trina Boo!" I yelled.

"How much?" Shakira asked the man behind the counter. She snatched the magazine up and flipped through the pages.

"Three ninety-nine," the man said.

Shakira gave him five dollars. "Oh, my God. It says she's the new 'it' girl for hip-hop videos!"

"Oh, my God. That bitch did it!" I said, reading with her. "Look at all the videos she's about to be in—Kanye, Young Jeezy, Jay Z!"

We started screaming again and running in place. I was proud of the girl. She had a dream and she followed it. Seeing Trina Boo posed up in all different kinds of positions, in her slinky clothes, looking like a black Jessica Rabbit or something, made me want to chase the dream I had.

I decided to call Joe up right then and there. He seemed happy to hear my voice and then he said he was on his way to scoop me.

He took me to another hotel, this time at the Ritz Carlton, out in Virginia. This was top-of-the-line luxury like I had never experienced before. The sheets was so soft and the bed was so plush. Room service was crazy. Food made to order. There was a jetted tub in the bathroom, and my God, the showerhead rotated and pulsated like a vibrator. "A treat," he called it.

"I been seeing you for what, like almost two years?" he asked, lying on his back under the sheets.

I nodded.

"And you never told me when your birthday was."

I smiled. "Well, you never asked."

"Well, I'm asking now."

"It's in January."

"Shit, so I missed it again?"

"It was just last month."

"Hmmm . . ."

"When's yours?"

"October."

"Oh, what's that, a Virgo?"

"A Scorpio."

"Freak."

"Yep," he said, smiling and then flipping me over. He started kissing me down my neck and then down my back.

"Man, you make me feel so good all the time," I said.

"I'm supposed to," he said, planting kisses all over my back.

"Why?"

"Cuz, you deserve it."

"You still want me to stop working the streets?"

"Mm-hmm . . . ," he moaned, kissing my butt cheeks.

"So what if I told you I wasn't going back out there no more, what would you say?"

"I'd say that's good. I'd say that's great. I'd say about time."

"Would you help me still?"

"What you mean?"

I turned around and looked him in his eyes. Joe was still real sexy to me. His thick eyebrows and chiseled jaw line looked so damn good. He was the only guy I kissed on the lips, who paid to be with me.

"I'm just saying, if I stopped, would you help take care of me until I could figure out what I was going to do?"

Joe sighed and then sat up. "There's too many empty variables in that statement."

"Huh? The fuck you talking about?"

"I mean, first of all, you don't have a plan, and secondly, you're talking about an infinite timeline. What are the parameters for this proposition?"

I sat up and started looking for my stuff. Clearly, all this time, Joe was just talking shit.

"What, Nectar?"

"Nothing. I need to go back."

"Why? You mad at me?" he said, sitting up on one arm.

"You know what I just realized, Joe?" I said with one hand on my hip. "The minute I started playing with the idea that everything you been saying all this time was sincere, you just let me know in one sentence that you are full of shit, just like the rest of them!"

"Come on, Nectar, don't do me like that. What am I supposed to do, treat you like a trophy wife? Pay all your bills and chauffeur you around town?"

I put my boots on and zipped them up as he rambled.

"Nectar? Are you really going to leave? I want to see you do better and everything, but . . ."

I put on my fur and grabbed my bag. It was crystal clear he never cared about me. I was kidding myself.

"Come on, don't be mad. Let's talk about this like two adults."

"My point exactly. I'm still a minor, remember? And my muthafuckin' name ain't Nectar!" I said, opening and closing the door before walking out.

I could hear him walking down the hall behind me.

"Okay, okay. Let me at least drive you back."

"Back where?" I asked, stopping to look him up and down. "Back to the street? No fuckin' thank you!"

A few weeks later, I was walking to the corner store on Benning Road to buy a pack of Newports and a grape Dutch when a skinny short woman who looked like my mama walked to the bus stop at the corner. I had to do a double take, cuz I knew it was her. She just looked a whole lot older than she was supposed to look. Gray short hair combed straight back, wrinkled skin, missing teeth. She had glazed-looking eyes.

I told myself if she was still at the bus stop when I came out the store, that I would call my mother's name out and see what happened. When I walked out, the woman was still sitting there under the glass shelter with the big Heineken beer ad on the back. I took a jack out the pack and lit it. I needed the smoke to calm my nerves before I tried to talk to this woman.

I inhaled and walked over to the bus stop. "Shelly?"

The woman looked up and smiled. Just then, I knew it was her. I could see the face I remembered hiding behind her eyes, but I asked again just to make sure she heard what I said. "Are you Shelly?" I asked.

"Yes, why? I know you?"

I could tell she ain't recognize me, and I ain't feel nothing about that. I just asked, "Do you have a daughter named Camille Logan?"

Her smile faded and then she started rocking back and forth, real slow. I sat down beside her.

"She hate me," she said, staring at the ground. "I know she do. And I can't blame her. I left my baby. I left her, and it's nobody's fault but mine."

I glared at Mama, though she looked like a messed-up version of the woman I remembered. Her hands looked ashy and scarred up, like they belonged to a woman twice her age. She looked hard, like she'd seen things only her and God knew. But behind her eyes, I could tell she was the same woman who used to braid my hair and tell me stories about when she was little and living in North Carolina with Nana.

"My baby girl hate me," Mama said, nodding.

She looked like a person who ain't need me to hate her. But I couldn't offer her my love, though, either. I just knew I ain't hate her. That was for sure.

"You seen her?" she asked, looking me in my eyes.

I shook my head. How could I tell her who I was? I knew it would break her heart that she ain't recognize me.

"When the last time you seen her?"

"A while ago," I mumbled.

"She doing okay?"

I nodded.

Mama smiled and stared back at the ground. I puffed the cigarette and stared at the ground, too.

"Next time you see her, can you tell her I'm sorry. I ain't mean to leave her," she said, letting tears fall. "Tell her I'm sorry. I swear to God, I ain't mean to leave my chile. I was gonna come back. I was gonna come back."

I nodded and fought back the tears creeping up. I took another puff of my cigarette and stood up.

"You got another Lucy, honey?"

I passed her the cigarette and walked away. I couldn't take any more. The tears poured out as I rushed back to my apartment. I bought a dime bag from one of the dudes around the way and rolled up as soon as I got in the house. I started blazing until Shakira tapped on the door, asking if she could hit it, too. I opened the door and let her inside.

"You okay?" she asked, squatting on the floor and sitting down in front of the couch.

I nodded.

"You look like shit, though. You sure?"

I nodded again and blew smoke out.

"But you look like you been crying."

As soon as she said it, the tears started falling and then I started wailing. I cried hard, until I could feel snot mixing with my tears.

"What's wrong?" Shakira asked, jumping up and rubbing my back. "Talk to me, man."

I shook my head, and then the words poured out. "I have to stop doing this."

Shakira sighed. "Where did that come from?"

"I can't believe I'm really living like this!" I said, shaking my head.

"Camille, did something happen today?"

"I saw my mama for the first time in like seven or eight years."

"You did?" Shakira leaned in, surprised.

"She ain't even recognize me." I shook my head. "Her only child, and she ain't know who the hell I was."

Shakira looked away. I could tell she ain't know what to say, but then she said, "Did you recognize her right away?"

I started laughing, cuz I didn't. I shook my head.

"See?" Shakira said with a slight smile.

"But still." And I took another hit from the J.

We sat in a quiet room for a while, and then Shakira said she was going outside to buy another bag. When she came back, I had opened up some wine coolers. She rolled up two fat-ass J's and then we both smoked one.

I lied with my back flat on the floor, staring at the ceiling, smoking until my head felt lighter and I felt giddy.

"Guess who I saw today?" Shakira asked, lying next to me, but upside down.

"Who?"

"Rob."

"Rob, Chu Rob?" I said, sitting up.

"Yeah."

"Where?"

"He was at a light on Bladensburg Road, just when I was about to cross the street."

"Did he see you?"

"Yeah, he saw me. But he ain't say nothing."

"You ain't, either?"

"What was I supposed to say? The last time I saw him, he was acting like he was better than me. Fuck him!"

"Shakira, don't say that," I said. "How he look?"

She sat up and said, "What? You trying to holla?"

I shook my head. "Girl, no."

"Oh," she said, lying back down. "But he did look good. Real good. I ain't even gonna lie. His skin look all smooth and shit now."

"What kind of car was he in?"

"A green Yukon."

"Oh, he done moved up from the old Explorer, huh?"

"Evidently."

23

APRIL 2007

Nut and Peaches was throwing a party for Amir's first birthday at their brand-new house in Mitchell-ville, Maryland. He stayed true to one part of his word, cuz Peaches finally got that house he promised her and he had even bought her a little salon with some of the money he made flipping houses.

He even married her. I couldn't believe it. They had went to the courthouse in Virginia and she ain't tell nobody until after it was over, flashing her wedding ring around and shit, all proud.

Me and Shakira pulled up in her 2002 Acura. Her boyfriend, Kareem, had bought it for her since she registered for GED classes. Yes, her *boyfriend*. He promised her he'd do it if she went back to school. Shakira begged me to go with her and I did, but not cuz she begged me to. I was already thinking it was time to shine my light on the world. It was just cool that I ain't have to be by myself when I did.

Trina Boo's white Range Rover pulled up in front of the house and she jumped out in an all-white Fendi pants outfit. She was covered in designer labels from her Dolce & Gabbana sunglasses sitting on top of her head, all the way down to her Prada stiletto sandals. "Hey, y'all!" she squealed, running over to us, carrying a cute little black Yorkie and a banging-ass Gucci handbag I seen in a window up Georgetown.

We gave her a big hug and quickly started talking about New York and all the celebrities she had been hanging out with.

Peaches waddled over with a gift someone had given Amir and the baby on her hip. She was pregnant again and glowing like it was her first pregnancy. "Wait, I want to hear about it, too!" she yelled.

"Girl, give me the baby!" Trina Boo squealed. "He's so cute."

I took the box from her and sat it down. "He look like his father," I said, rolling my eyes playfully.

"He look like me, too," Peaches whined.

Trina Boo told us the music business scene wasn't all she thought it was cracked up to be. Of course, the parties was live, but she said a lot of the rappers was still spitting the same corny-ass lines as the dudes in the streets.

"The only real difference is they willing to spend more money, faster," she said, smiling. Her diamond tennis bracelet slid up and down her arm as she played with her dog.

Nut was grilling meat on the barbeque and talking to some of his friends, who was drinking beer. I couldn't help but shake my head at him. This dude was living the life, while I was still working the streets. But Peaches was my girl, and at least she was benefiting. I never really saw him much anymore since we mailed him our rent. He still was an animal in my book, but I ain't want him dead like I had secretly wanted Mr. Big to be. Nut never even looked at me or in my direction the whole time. I guess that was his way of taking the high road.

We stayed for a while, but Shakira wanted to go out to Love with Trina Boo later, so we left a little early to get dressed. It was International Night, and I ain't wanna go, but since Trina Boo was in from out of town, we had to party.

Peaches left a message on my cell phone while we was at the club. I was checking my missed calls, when her voice popped on:

"Hey, girl. Rob showed up a little bit after y'all left. You know I ain't seen that boy since Chu's funeral? Well, anyway, he asked me if I kept in touch with you. I told him, no duh? But anyway, he told me he bumped into Shakira the other day. I told him y'all live together. Of course, he was shocked"—she laughed—*"But anyway, it's a lot that boy don't know. He looks good, though. You should call him. He gave me his number to give to you. It's 240 . . ."*

I closed my mouth and then replayed the message twice while Trina Boo zipped through the city heading toward Denny's. My heart skipped a beat. Maybe it was cuz he reminded me of Chu. I saved Rob's number in my phone, but I wasn't ready to call him. I ain't even mention it to Shakira or Trina Boo. I knew they would try to syce it up, hyping the situation. All Rob probably wanted to do was check on me. Though I *was* kinda mad he was just now doing it. I lit a cigarette and thought about what he had been up to all this time.

* * *

Spingarn High School sat on a hill, a few blocks down the street from our apartment building and right across from the old Redskins stadium. The first day of night school began in the middle of May. It was cool, since mostly all the people in our classes was right around our age or a whole lot older. I ain't feel like I missed that much, but only time would tell if that was true when they started giving us tests. Neither one of us felt out of place or like we was stupid, thank God. But on the third day, this guy stopped me in the hallway.

"Don't they call you Nectar?" he asked, grinning.

I rolled my eyes and said, "Nope."

"You sure?" he asked, like he ain't believe me.

"Positive," I said and then kept walking down the hall.

"I swear you look just like her," the guy said behind my back.

Every time somebody did that to me, it burned me up. It was like I could never get away from that part of my life. I went into the bathroom on the first floor. After I finished washing my hands, I walked out and bumped into a big woman with long auburn dreads pulled away from her face.

"Oh, excuse me," she said, straightening out her jacket.

"Excuse me," I said, adjusting my bag and the books I was carrying.

We locked eyes, but neither one of us said anything. It had been a long time, and I ain't know what to say to my first love's mother. He had her eyes. She smiled knowingly, and I smiled back.

"You work here?" I asked.

"Yes, I do. I am the curriculum coordinator."

"Oh, okay," I said, and I shifted my bag to my other shoulder.

"I still teach courses at American, but I like this. It's different," she said, before frowning. "Wait, are you a student?"

I nodded. "I take GED classes."

"Oh." I could tell she was shocked and maybe even a little disappointed.

"Yeah, I stopped going a while back. But I'm here now," I said proudly.

"And that's wonderful," she said, staring into my eyes. She rested her hand on my arm and then said, "Please let me know if you ever need any help. I really mean it."

"I will," I said, and I smiled at her. Ms. Abani was reaching out to me cuz of her son, and I appreciated it, but I knew school was gonna have to be *all* me this time. I had to focus. Being around her would just make me think of her son.

"You ready, girl?" Shakira asked, walking up the hall.

I nodded. "I'm ready."

Ms. Abani smiled. Something made me think she was still judging me as I watched her walk down the hall.

"I think I'm ready," I mumbled.

A few weeks later, I was trying to clean my pussy under my miniskirt with the last baby wipe I could find in my beat-up knockoff Prada bag, when a familiar voice said, "Camille?"

I dropped the used wipe on the ground and turned to see who it was, hoping it wasn't somebody who remembered me from middle school. Rob's face sitting in the green truck brought back memories of a different time and of a different place and of a person who I had been trying to forget. I lit a cigarette and walked over to his truck.

"Camille?" he asked, confused.

"Hey, stranger," I said. "You wanna date?"

"A date?" he asked. "Nah, shawty. Peaches told me you might be down here."

I could beat Peaches' ass. I crossed my arms over my chest. "Why you looking for me, Rob? Why now? It's been two years since Chu died. Why'd you forget about me?" I cried.

"I've been trying to get Nut to tell me where you was all this time. Tep used to call the house for you and everything. I gave Peaches my number to give you. After she told me you and Shakira lived together, I went back to the last place I seen her, just about every day at that same time, hoping I'd see her again. I asked Peaches to tell me where you lived, but she ain't want to do that. So I begged her to tell me where you might be."

I shifted my weight and leaned on my other leg.

"Can you get in? Please? I don't want to talk to you like this."

I rolled my eyes and snatched the door open. After I climbed in his truck, I started smelling Chu's Bvlgari Aqua. I inhaled the sweet muscular scent and exhaled like I had hit a J. It wasn't right that he smelled like him. Rob drove up to Fourteenth and U Streets before making a right. He parked on Eleventh Street, near Ben's Chili Bowl, but then he took me across the street to this Ethiopian restaurant. I pressed my lips tight together and then sucked my teeth. "What's this?" I asked.

"You'll like it. Watch."

I rolled my eyes.

Once inside the dark, crowded restaurant lighted by candles, I excused myself to the bathroom so I could at least wash my hands and get my makeup straight. When I came back, the hostess escorted us to a table where Rob pulled the chair out for me to sit down. I was shocked, cuz I certainly wasn't expecting that kind of treatment after he just seen me wiping myself on the street. I felt a little uncomfortable in my zebra-print tank top and jean stretch miniskirt. My four-inch stilettos was drawing just as much attention. But Rob did look good, like Shakira said. I could tell he was working out. His shoulders was all broad and his chest looked thicker. I couldn't believe he would even bring me to a place like this. It just ain't seem like his style. He used to be eating Yum's carryout right along with me and Chu back in the day. Maybe college was teaching him something.

"What you looking at me like that for?" Rob asked, sitting down across from me.

"I can't lie. I'm surprised," I said, looking at the menu, not even sure what to get.

"About what?"

I shook my head and looked over the menu. *Here we go again with this crazy-ass language,* I said to myself, squinting.

"Have you ever eaten Ethiopian food before?"

"Nope."

Rob smiled. "I'll order something we'll both like, then.

So what's been up with you, man? You disappeared off the
face of the planet and shit."

"Me?! I was looking for you at Chu's funeral. I tried to
call you and I left messages. No, *you* disappeared."

Rob shook his head and then started cracking his knuckles. He looked away and then back at the menu.

The waitress came over to see if we wanted something to
drink. He ordered a beer and I got a ginger ale.

"So?" I asked, still waiting to hear what he had to say
about his vanishing act.

"Man, after Chu got killed, like that . . . that shit fucked
with me," he said, shaking his head. "It happened so
quick."

He sat quiet for a moment like he was trying not to let
me see him cry. I looked at the menu again, even though
I wasn't really looking for nothing. I tried to focus on the
soft music playing in the background, instead of looking at
Rob.

"I blamed myself for leaving D.C. and for not being
there that day. It was hard, man. I almost just stopped going
to school altogether. You know, I just said, 'Fuck it!' But
then . . ." He paused as the slender waitress with wide eyes
brought over our drinks.

"Ready to order?"

He cleared his throat and said, "Yeah, let me get that
doro wot fit-fit."

The waitress nodded and disappeared.

"What the heck was that you just got us?" I asked, confused. "Because I don't eat nothing crazy like diced rat
knuckles."

He laughed. "I promise, you'll love it. Trust me."

"Hmmm . . ." I sighed before clasping my fingers in front of me on the table.

"What?" Rob asked. He seemed relieved to change the subject. "What are you thinking right at this very moment?"

"How you even know about this place? Is this where you take all the girls when you come to town?"

Rob shook his head and laughed.

"Are you back for good or what?" I asked. "You still play basketball for A&T?"

He shook his head. "Nah, I ended up transferring to Wake Forest."

"You still play basketball, right?"

"Yeah," he said, nodding. "After Chu died, I just stepped it up and started pushing myself. I cut back smoking and then I was working out like crazy. Lifting weights, running ten miles every other day. I just started getting even better at ball," he said, animated. And then his mood changed. "Me and Chu, we was doing a lot of shit we wasn't supposed to be doing. Shit was starting to get hot down there. As soon as Wake came up A&T talking about recruiting me for the second team, I jumped at it. Shit. I wanted to leave Greensboro and jive like start over anyway."

"Hmmm . . ." I sighed.

"My bad, I ain't call you back. I ain't know what to say. I wasn't ready. I'm just now starting to feel like I can handle anything else," he said, staring at the candlelight.

"Here's your order," the waitress said while placing a big

dish in the center of the table. The spicy smell was so rich it made my mouth start watering.

"It's like a chicken stew," Rob explained.

"Miss, we need some silverware," I said, signaling the waitress, who had already walked away.

"No, she don't," Rob said over his shoulder. Then he leaned forward and said, "Ethiopians eat with their fingers. Here, let me show you."

I frowned, confused, and then I watched him pick up the thin flour wraps that looked like tortillas and break off pieces to dip into the stew that was filled with different beans, herbs, spices, and bits of flavorful chicken.

"And we're both supposed to eat out of the same bowl?" I asked, totally mixed up, cuz I ain't never heard of no stuff like this.

"Mm-hmm," Rob said, smiling.

"You are getting too much of a kick out of this," I said, copying what he did. I dipped a piece inside the bowl, careful not to get any of the stew on my fingers, and then took a bite. "Mmmm . . ."

Rob winked at me from across the table. "Good, ain't it?"

I was so surprised at how good it tasted. I could taste everything—the chickpeas, onions, and peppers. Different flavors exploded inside my mouth. Before I knew it, I was scooping up some more and sucking it off my fingers. A couple of times Rob's fingers grazed mine when they was both in the bowl. I tried not to look at him whenever it happened.

"How you find out about this place?" I asked as I dipped the thing he called a fit-fit.

"Man, I'm not scared to try things. New, old. It builds character."

"Is that what they teach you in college?" I asked sarcastically.

"Yup, and other stuff, too. You want the rest?" Rob asked, as the food had dwindled to the last drops.

"I don't wanna look too greedy, but . . ."

He smiled, too, and scooped the last of the dora wot onto his last piece of bread. I couldn't believe my body's impulse to lean forward and eat from out of his hand. I blushed and chewed at the same time before wiping my mouth with a napkin. I could feel Rob's eyes staring through me, so I cleared my throat and looked away.

"So tell me what you been up to," he said as he dipped his fingers in the lemon water dish on the table.

Where was I supposed to start? "I just been out here trying to survive, that's all." I copied him, then wiped my fingers dry with my napkin.

Rob ran his hand over his head and sighed deep. I knew he was uncomfortable, but what I was saying was true. I chose to leave details out to make it easier.

"You want to go somewhere else to get dessert?" he asked.

I shrugged. "Okay."

He left money on the table before the waitress had even come back.

In his truck, Rob was quiet and didn't start up the engine right away. I turned toward him and said, "You know I don't blame you, Rob, if that's what you thinking. But I do wanna know if you knew what Nut was into all this time?"

"What you mean? Him being burnt out off those dippers?" He smirked. "Yeah, I knew. That crazy muthafucka, my cousin."

"Hmmm . . ." I groaned and looked out the window. If that's all Rob was talking about, then I ain't wanna bring up shit else. But there was so many unanswered questions and things I wanted to know. "He told me about Mr. Brinkley."

Rob gripped the steering wheel and bit down on his bottom lip. "To be honest, Camille, that nigga made Chu give him fifty thousand dollars so he wouldn't snitch to the cops about that shit."

My eyes almost popped out of my head.

"If I knew Nut was gonna try some shit like that, he wouldn't have rolled with us out there in the first place. Don't get me wrong, I ain't even want the dude to get got, for real. I was like maybe we should just fuck with him, scare him and shit . . . but Chu was fuckin' heated for what that man had did to you. Chu just let off. *Bap! bap! bap!*" Rob said, imitating the gunshots. "He shot that nigga cold in his chest, his neck, and his head. And then Nut took a piss on him, just because he could. But that's Nut for you."

I stared out the window as Rob took a deep breath. That nigga lied to me about killing Mr. Big. It was Chu all along. I was itching for a cigarette, but I ain't have a single one on me.

"The next day, man, Nut was talking all kind of shit about how he was gonna snitch and shit, unless we came up off some of that work for Smurf," Rob said, shaking his head. "It was crazy. I ain't know my cousin was foul like that."

"You have no idea." I smirked.

"I had to talk Chu into doing it, too. He ain't wanna give Nut shit. I couldn't blame him, but I knew Nut was just greedy and wanted to get put on. So Chu gave him some," Rob said and then sighed. "But then the very next day, he said he ain't want the coke. He said he wanted the money instead. Chu was pissed, but he gave it to him and Nut gave the coke back."

"Was y'all sure it was the same package you got back?" I asked, frowning.

"Yeah, why?" Rob asked, like a light had just come on.

"What y'all do with it after that?"

"Ummm . . . ," Rob said, and then started thinking on it. "That dirty muthafucka!"

"What?"

"That muthafucka gave us back some bullshit!" Rob yelled.

"Huh?" I asked, confused. "What you mean?"

"Man, we took that shit to Greensboro and sold it to one of our regular connects down there. We was just starting to build a little something, you know?"

I shook my head as all the pieces came together. Nut was one dirty dude.

"Them North Carolina niggas thought we sold them some garbage on purpose!" Rob said angrily. "Them niggas must've followed Chu back up here and shit. They just waited for his ass."

He pounded his dashboard and stared out the window in

front of him. I shook my head, cuz it was all Nut's fault that my man had walked straight into a trap.

"That dirty muthafucka. And this nigga fuckin' flipping money, buying and selling houses and shit. He played us like some muthafuckin' bamas, young."

And not to mention what the fuck else he was doing. But I decided not to add fuel to Rob's already burning fire.

24

THE NEXT DAY

Rob fell asleep on my old love seat, which was entirely too short for his long legs, but he did his best to get comfortable. He was so angry about everything he had found out that I had to calm him down with a little bit of herb when we first got home. Rob was only in town for just a few weeks in between the end of spring semester and the start of summer school and training camp. He even calculated how much weed he could smoke between now and the time his system had to be clean for when he went back to school.

I went to the kitchen to make breakfast—spinach and cheese omelets and turkey sausages. He woke up as soon as the sausages started sizzling in the pan.

"Mmm, hell yeah," he said, smiling and stretching at the same time. He stood up and stretched even more.

"Your body fucked up right now, ain't it?" I said, giggling.

He laughed. "It's all good. I just want whatever the hell it is you cooking. That shit smells good as a mug."

I smiled and made our plates, while he went to the bathroom.

"You don't mind if I grab one of these washcloths, do you?" he yelled.

"Nope." And then there was a knock at the door.

Knock! Knock! Knock!

That chick was right on time. I knew she was gonna be sniffing over here. She knocked some more.

Knock! Knock! Knock!

"Now, a bitch ain't come over here when she smelled the weed last night, but this, yeah, this I have to come over for," Shakira shouted as soon as I opened the door.

"Hey." I stepped aside and rolled my eyes.

"Oh? You got company," she said, looking Rob over. "What's up, negro? You can't speak."

"Hey, KiKi, what's up?" he said, before going back in the bathroom.

"Bitch, what the hell he doing over here?" Shakira whispered.

I shrugged and tried to play innocent.

"No, you better start talking, heifer. Don't give me that shit."

"It's a long story. Can I tell you later?" I asked, smirking.

"Mm-hmm," she said, rolling her eyes. "If you make me a plate."

"I only made two omelets. Here, take some sausage, and here," I said handing her two eggs from the carton. "Help yourself and go."

"Uh, no, you didn't," she said with her mouth wide

open. She took the food, though, and headed to the door. "See how bitches do you when sexy men in the house."

"You know I love you, girl," I said, smiling and closing the door behind her.

Rob came out the bathroom a few minutes later. "So, I ain't know you and her was still tight like that. How that happen?" he said, sitting down at the table.

"That's a long story." I went to the fridge and poured both of us some orange juice.

"I got time," he said and bit into the food.

I sat down and started telling him what life was like for me since Chu's murder. I felt like I was confessing to a priest or something. My heart poured out. He reminded me of Chu, when he used to listen to me. The words and the stories flowed out like a river. By the time I finished telling him everything, I had cried, he had wrapped his arms around me, and I had kissed him on his lips.

Even though telling Rob about everything made me feel better, I could tell that he was way more pissed off now than when he came over the night before. He sat on the couch rubbing my back in the quiet room. We listened to Shakira shuffling around across the hall and the noise from the other tenants who lived downstairs. Marcha had been moved out, and Nut had two young couples renting now.

"That nigga goin' get what's coming to his bitch-ass," Rob said. "Believe it."

I took a deep, painful breath and thought about what he said.

"You not going back out there, you hear me?" Rob said,

looking down at me. "Not while I'm here. I don't care what I gotta do. You not doing that shit any fuckin' more!"

More tears slid down my face. That's all I wanted to hear since the day I started.

"You don't have to. You know why?"

"Why?" I whispered, with my hoarse voice.

"Chu left something for you with Tep."

I sat up and wiped my face. "What's that?"

Rob pulled out his phone and started dialing. "I got in touch with his mother when I first came home, and she gave me his number."

I watched Rob waiting for Tep to answer the phone.

"Guess who I finally caught up with?" Rob said into the phone. "Yes, sir. She right here."

"Hello?" I said and then cleared my throat. "Tep?"

"Hey, baby girl, how you doing?"

"I'm all right."

"Man, I've been trying to get up with you for a minute."

"How long you been out?"

"It's been like thirteen months. I didn't get released right when I was supposed to, though. Shit, after Chu died, man, I kirked out a little bit, and they added some time for some trouble I got into."

"Oh?"

"But what about you? You been taking care of yourself?"

I smiled and wiped away more tears that fell. "Yeah, I've been trying."

"Well, listen, I moved to Miami after I got out. Shit, D.C. still got too many memories for me, Joe."

"Un-huh."

"But hey, I got something Chu wanted me to make sure you had if anything ever happened to him. He kept it in a safe place over my mother's and I made sure I got it as soon as I got out. But anyway, I wanna make sure I get you some ends first. Then maybe you and Rob can make a trip down here."

I smiled. "For real? That sounds good."

"Yeah, beaches for days down this bitch. So y'all make sure you bring your swimsuits."

"Okay," I said, laughing and looking at Rob, who was confused.

"All right, let me speak back to my man."

I passed the phone back to Rob and then listened as he rushed to tell Tep what he had suspected happened between Rob's cousin and Tep's brother. I went to the kitchen to clean up, cuz I ain't wanna hear nothing they planned to do about Nut. But I did hear Smurf's name mentioned a couple times.

After a while Rob hung up. He walked up behind me while I washed the dishes. "Tep is gonna wire you some money today. He said he was gonna call me later to let us know everything. How you feel?"

I shook my head. "It's all so overwhelming. I don't know."

He squeezed my shoulders and said, "Camille, everything is going to be okay. Believe me."

I looked up at him and smiled.

He bent down and gave me a kiss on my forehead. "I got you, you hear me?"

For once, I felt optimistic. Like real change was just around the corner. There was no looking back to the past, only looking forward.

25

A COUPLE DAYS LATER . . .

We drove from D.C. to Miami just so we could spend more time talking and catching up about the two years since Chu died. It was a long, humid ride that was taking us forever. Rob took 95 South, cutting through Virginia, fighting traffic with all the tourists on their family vacations just so we could visit his college in North Carolina. We was in Emporia, Virginia, when the air conditioner had the nerve to conk out. But we got it fixed the same day with some of the money Tep sent me. We was just outside of Durham when we got a flat tire. It was way too hot for all that sitting on the side of the highway waiting for him to change it, but I managed.

By the time we got to his campus, I really ain't even care no more. But it was stunning, all the grass, trees, and old buildings mixed with newer ones. The campus was pretty quiet when we got there since school was out, but Rob walked me around, pointing out the dorms and the buildings where he had classes. It was beautiful. Peaceful, mostly.

"You don't get bored all the way down here? It seems way too quiet and country looking for me."

Rob shook his head. "When school is in, it's always a lot of people around and always something to do. Man, you'd be surprised. Most of the people from D.C. hang together, so it's cool. We don't hang together all the time, I mean, you know, my closest friends are my roommate, Paul from Florida, and this dude from Chicago named Mike."

After we finished walking around, we grabbed something to eat at a sandwich shop.

"Let's get a hotel room," I said stirring my straw in circles, mixing my lemonade. "I'm tired and it's getting all late."

Rob rubbed the back of his head and dragged his hand down his neck. "You sure you don't wanna just hit the road? We got a long way to go."

"Ain't you tired of driving? It's not like I'm helping or nothing."

He chewed his lip and then tapped his knuckles on the table. I could tell he wasn't sure what I meant by me wanting the room, but I was really just tired. I took a sip of my drink and stared out the window until he made his mind up.

"All right, but let's just get two different rooms."

I frowned, cuz that seemed odd. "Okay. Whatever."

"Nah, not like that, Camille. I mean, I just don't want you to feel no pressure about anything. One room is just gonna complicate shit, you feel me?"

I shrugged my shoulders and looked back out the window. I guess he really thought low of me. All I was thinking about was saving money, not screwing him.

"No, Camille, not like that. It's just . . . you been through a lot, and I don't want you to feel like I'm trying to pressure you or trick you or like I'm running game. I just wanna get to know you, like from scratch. You feel me?"

I rolled my eyes and stayed quiet, since no, I wasn't *feeling* him.

"Listen," he said, reaching across the table for my hands. "Every time I think about all that shit you went through, that shit hurts me to my heart, young."

I could tell Rob had created in his mind all the little details I purposely left out of the stories I told him. He was probably seeing them replayed over and over again in his head every time he looked at me.

"I don't want you to feel strange about nothing that happens with me and you," Rob said. "I mean that kiss the other day was—"

"You don't have to say nothing else, Rob, I understand. It's cool."

"Nah, it was what's up. I liked it . . . a lot," he said, squeezing my hands. "But I mean, don't get me wrong . . . you was Chu's girl and shit, Camille. That part's still fucking with me hard." He shook his head and looked away, and then he turned back around and said, "I don't know how that man would feel—"

I nodded and then put my finger to his lips. He ain't have to say no more. I understood what he meant. I wasn't really sure how I was feeling about Rob, and he was right—Chu was still in my heart, and it was clear he was heavy on Rob's mind. One thing I knew for sure, with Rob I could breathe and relax in a way I hadn't done in a long time. That felt good. I just wanted to keep that feeling around me as long as I could. Plus, I needed to wipe my slate clean anyway and take a break so I could focus on what was ahead of me. "Believe me, I understand, Rob."

When we checked into the hotel, and headed in opposite directions after we got off the elevator, I wondered if Rob was having second thoughts, so I turned around to see if he was looking at me. But he had already hit the corner at the end of the hall and I could hear him going into his room.

The next morning we picked over the dried-up muffins and stale cornflakes they was calling a continental breakfast before we jumped back in his truck.

"You sleep okay?" he asked.

"Yeah, you?" I said, buckling my seat belt.

"Nah," he said, smiling. "I couldn't sleep at all."

I smiled, too.

"Hey, I was thinking we should get some real breakfast. I know this spot that got the best cheese grits and salmon cakes I ever had. You like that, right?"

"Not salmon. They got fried fish?"

"Do they," he said, smiling. "It's banging, too."

He whipped the truck around and drove a few miles until he got to this little diner with a huge porch wrapped around the front. It was screened in, to keep the bugs out, and looked real homely, but the parking lot was jam-packed with cars. And before I got outta the truck, I could smell the food. There was even a line to get inside.

"Are you serious?" I asked, staring at the people who looked like they was giving something away for free inside.

Rob nodded. "It's just that good."

"You love eating, don't you?"

He nodded again and smiled.

After breakfast, we got back on the road and crawled through the rest of North Carolina, but before cruising through South Carolina, Rob wanted to show me the South of the Border. It looked like a Mexican carnival plopped down in the middle of nowhere, on the borderline between North Carolina and South Carolina. We bought a lot of useless stuff like maracas and taffy candy, and we even played a couple games where Rob tried to show me how good he was (he won me a stuffed flamingo on his first try, but lost every game after that) before we jumped back in the truck.

"Hey, I called Paul and told him we was gonna stop by his house when we got to Florida. You cool with that?"

I shrugged. "Cool with me."

"He lives in Jacksonville. I want you to meet him. He's cool as shit."

I smiled and then unwrapped a piece of taffy. It took us a while to hit Florida, but I wasn't complaining since Rob was telling me about all the trouble him and Chu used to get in with Tep, and how him and Paul clashed the first few weeks after he moved in with him.

"Man, I was not feeling that white boy at first. He had such a big-ass mouth, man. Always bragging and shit, but then I found out he was all right, just too fucking hyper. I got his little ass loving Go Go music now," he said, laughing.

My cell rang for the first time in a long while. I could hear the muffled sound coming from deep in my overnight bag. I crawled to the backseat and opened the phone when I saw Shakira's face on the screen. "Hey, girl, what's up? Don't tell me you miss me already?" I teased.

"Camille, Peaches called me."

"Oh, yeah? How she doing?"

"She lost the baby last night."

"Nooo," I said. Rob looked over at me, anxious to know what was the matter.

"I got Amir while she in the hospital."

"Hospital?" I asked. "She's still there?"

"What's wrong?" Rob asked.

Shakira took a deep breath and I knew she was smoking. "That nigga went crazy and tried to kill her last night."

I shook my head. I could hear Shakira inhale her cigarette and then blow the smoke out. "You should've seen her, Camille. Her face was all swollen and purple and shit. That dirty muthafucka even knocked one of her front teeth out. That nigga is fucking sick!"

With Shakira yelling, Amir's cries rose up and echoed through the phone. The last time I spoke to Peaches was about a month ago. She had seemed so happy. Like everything she ever wanted, she finally had. I felt for her, though, cuz I knew Nut couldn't have changed all that much. He was still a wolf, just fronting in sheep's clothing. Wasn't no way in hell he was a family man now.

"Is she gonna be all right?" I asked.

"Girl, I hope so. I thought I was done dealing with this nigga's bullshit. Now I'm sitting here babysitting his damn son."

"Hmmmph." I sighed. "Girl."

"What's going on?" Rob asked again.

"Your cousin beat the shit outta my girl again," I said. "She lost the baby."

"Damn."

"Camille, I'ma talk to you later," Shakira said before tak-ing a puff. "Have a safe trip, and call me when you get some time."

"All right, girl. Kiss Amir for me."

Me and Rob rode for a while without saying anything. We both knew what fucked-up shit Nut was capable of doing. I think we just ain't know he was still that damn stupid.

"My cousin is one fucked-up individual," Rob said, squeezing the steering wheel tight.

I felt a little guilty since I played along with Nut's "new-found" self. I never tried to talk Peaches out of their new relationship, and I acted like everything was all cool with him, too. Now my friend was laid up in a hospital, probably fighting for her life, knowing him.

By the time we got to Jacksonsville, me and Rob was both worn out from the ride. As soon as we pulled up in the driveway of Paul's big yellow house with the huge yard that wrapped around the sides, I could feel Rob getting his energy back. He must've really liked this white boy.

"What up, cuz?" Paul said, running off the porch to dap Rob up. He had short red hair and a beer in his hand.

I couldn't help but smile when he looked me over like he was giving Rob his thumbs-up.

"Okay, okay," Paul said, nodding. "I know y'all hungry. Follow me."

There was a small house in the back of the main house that Paul kept calling a pool house cuz it was beside a pool. He had some hot dogs and hamburgers on the grill. After we ate, we went in the pool house to smoke some weed Paul said his parents bought him from some Jamaican cat that lived two houses down. I had no idea if he was lying or not, but it was a lot of weed and I knew they smelled us smoking since all the windows was open.

Paul had tiny freckles under his eyes that twinkled every time he laughed from telling stories about Rob and the basketball team. They joked for hours about people I ain't know, teachers they couldn't stand, parties they went to, and games they played. I was glad to get Peaches and Nut outta my mind for a minute. Rob looked just as relieved, and the herb looked like it was working its magic on all of us.

Hearing their stories made me really wanna go to college now. Paul said his freshman year was just like if there was a thirteenth grade in high school. It wasn't any harder, just more people from across the country with different backgrounds.

Paul left us in the pool house after me and Rob had yawned a couple times. We ended up falling asleep on the same bed in our clothes. I woke up in the middle of the night, after I heard water splashing. The bed was empty and Rob was gone. I looked at my cell phone to check the time. It was only one in the morning, but it felt much later.

I walked over to the pool, sat on a chair, and watched him do a couple smooth laps before he noticed me. He swam over with those tight, toned arms and smiled.

"My bad. I ain't mean to wake you up. Just couldn't sleep."

I nodded and then rubbed the back of my arms.

"You know, if you get in, you won't feel so cold," he said.

He was definitely flirting, regardless of whatever he said earlier, and I was ready to take him up on his offer.

"You're probably right," I said, peeling my tank top and jeans off. Now, I can't swim, but I know how to look cute in the pool, especially in my matching white bra and panties.

Rob's smile got even brighter. "Oh, okay. I see you."

I sat on the edge of the pool and tested the water with my feet. He was right—the water wasn't so bad. Rob inched closer before grabbing me by my waist and throwing me over his shoulder.

"Oh, my God, Rob, don't get my hair wet, for real!" I screeched.

"Sheeiit," Rob sang before dipping my whole body in the water.

As soon as I popped back up, and coughed water out of my lungs, I whispered, "I can't swim."

"Oh, shit, Camille. Why you ain't tell me?" Rob rushed me to the poolside and waited for me to catch my breath before he went back to the pool house to grab both of us towels.

"Girl, you're crazy," he said, smiling. "You came out your clothes all gangsta and shit. I thought you knew what you was doing."

"I thought so, too." I laughed a little bit and wrapped the towel around my shoulders.

"Hold up. Let me see your tattoo again."

He caught me off guard with that. I always forget about that dumb-ass tattoo Nut made us get. I wished the shit just disappeared.

I flashed the towel up real quick.

"Hold up. Not so fast," he said, lifting the towel off of my lower back. "Damn. Six, six, six?"

I felt ashamed. That tattoo told a story I wished I never had to remember. "Your sick-ass cousin."

Rob looked me over like he wanted to say something, but he ain't know what to say or how to say it. And I understood. "Let's go back inside before we wake up everybody."

In the middle of the night, I felt Rob's arms wrap around me. I smiled and snuggled closer. I still couldn't believe he was the same guy who used to hug the block with Chu, selling drugs and doing whatever else. He had become this whole *other* person even though he was the same, still cracking jokes and teasing me, but he seemed different.

I lied there and thought about my plan to take the money I had been saving to go to UDC when I finished with my GED classes. After I told Rob my plan about me wanting to look into social work, he told me about a law that he heard about for D.C. residents. About us being able to go to any public state college in Virginia or Maryland for in-state tuition since D.C. only had one public college, UDC, and it wasn't an actual state. Rob said I should think about going somewhere else. I told him I'd look into it, since I had never thought that far ahead. *Going to college outta town might not be such a bad idea.* Maybe I could be normal again.

26

THE NEXT AFTERNOON

When we got to beautiful Miami, Tep met me and Rob outside with his albino-looking dog with a bright red choke collar. Tep was grinning from ear to ear, like he was so happy to see us. He kept giving out hugs and squeezing Rob's shoulder. Maybe seeing us made him feel like he was with family again. He looked more like his mother than Chu to me now, but I could definitely see Chu in his face.

"I'm glad y'all finally made it," he said, dapping Rob up before hugging me again. "It's so good to see y'all, man."

Tep had picked up a little weight since the funeral, but I could tell from his plushed-out crib he was living the life down here. He had tropical-colored paintings hanging from the walls and a strange-looking fish tank that stretched from the floor to the ceiling. Three jellyfish glowed and floated up and down like bubbles in a lava lamp. I was mesmerized.

After Tep gave us a little tour, him and Rob disappeared for a few minutes. I knew they was talking about Nut and Smurf, but again, I was glad they spared me the details.

I wondered if Rob told him what Nut did to Peaches last night. Sick bastard deserved whatever they was planning.

I tried to take my mind off of what they was doing and decided to look around the living room. There was a chef cooking something delicious smelling in the stainless steel and dark wood kitchen. Tep had a picture of Chu made into a painting. I couldn't break away from his eyes until I heard Tep standing behind me.

"I miss him, too," he said.

We talked and had drinks over broiled lobster, scallops, and asparagus out on Tep's big patio. A view of a sea-blue bay stretched from one house to the next. Tep was really doing good for himself. The chef had just placed some dessert on the table when Tep dug in his pocket and slid a set of keys across the table.

"What's this?" I asked, confused. "What these go to?"

"My brother had sent me pictures of the condo he bought when I was in jail. That boy was so proud of hisself. He wanted to surprise you," Tep said, leaning back in his chair. "It's a one bedroom in Southeast, over there off of Stanton Road."

"A condo?" I asked, smiling, not just cuz of what Chu bought, but cuz he had remembered that Stanton Road was near the neighborhood I grew up.

"You can do whatever you want with it. Here's the papers, cuz it's already paid for. I pay the taxes on it. If you want to sell it, that's up to you," Tep said. "He left this for you, too."

He handed me a band of white gold on a necklace. The tears started falling before I could even blink them back.

"Chu was a great brother with a huge heart, Camille. I miss him like shit . . . and I know he wouldn't want nothing else but for you to be happy. That's all he ever wanted. He always said you deserved it."

I wiped the tears away and nodded. "I'm happy now."

"Good," Tep said. He passed me and Rob a glass of champagne. "Here, drink up. We got a lot to celebrate today."

Rob and I both raised our glasses and smiled at each other.

And then Tep said, "Here's to life, happiness, and to my nigga Smurf, for wanting muthafuckin' payback."

I knew just what Tep meant. Nut had to be dealt with for all the shit he put everybody through. He was the reason Smurf almost died. Those North Carolina dudes came up there busting off for some shit Chu ain't have nothing to do with. Nut had Chu and Rob selling some bullshit to them dudes without them even knowing it. He basically stole money outta Smurf's pocket when he blackmailed Chu and Rob.

But that was just it: Nut was Lucifer all around. Peaches' face popped in my head, then Almond Joy's and Marcha's. Shakira's and then Chu's. I felt my eyes fill up with tears. "You think he might need my help?" I heard myself say. I knew I could help set Nut up easily, if they wanted me to. I bet if I called Nut and told him to meet me somewhere, he would come if he thought some pussy or some money was in it for him. He was just that dirty.

Tep looked at me so hard it seemed like he was looking

through me. I could feel hair standing on the back of my arms. I glanced over at Rob, who was staring at his dessert.

"Nah, Camille. Chu would never forgive me," Tep said. "This life ain't for you. You been through enough."

I went back to playing with my dessert, cuz I knew he was right.

About a week after Rob and I got back to D.C., Shakira and Peaches, who was feeling much better, though she was no-where near 100 percent, was helping me unpack some of the stuff I decided to take with me to my condo. Her and Amir was staying with me until they could get their own place. She had left everything behind, even her precious salon. I think she really had enough of Nut this time.

Shakira had moved in with Kareem, cuz she ain't want Nut coming around asking about Peaches. He would spazz out the minute he realized she was lying.

I was hanging clothes in my closet when my cell phone rang. It was Rob.

"Hey, you," I said.

"Hey, you home?"

"Yeah, why?"

"Turn to channel four real quick."

I hesitated for a second and then grabbed the remote to flip the channel.

Nut's face was on the screen. Peaches gasped behind me. I cut the volume up, but all I could hear the police say was they was looking for leads on last night's homicide.

"He dead, ain't he?" Peaches asked. Shakira wrapped her arms around Peaches.

I turned to channel 7 to see if they had it on, but they didn't.

"Rob, what happened?" I asked before sitting down on the bed.

"Karma, Camille."

"Nut's dead," I said. The details, I ain't even need for real. I exhaled a deep breath that I ain't even know I was holding in. A gentle peace fell over me. I looked at Shakira and then Amir and Peaches. I think we was all thinking the same thing. *Good.*

READING GROUP GUIDE

1. Why does Mrs. Brinkley keep her thoughts to herself regarding what she feels she knows about Danica, Camille, and Mr. Big? How does she live with what she thinks she knows?
2. The bond between Jayson and Camille evolves deeply over the years for many reasons. Why does Camille decide never to share her dark secret with her foster brother? Should she have? Why or why not?
3. Camille and Danica seemed to be best friends when they lived with the Brinkleys. Should Camille have tried to reconnect with Danica? Why or why not? Why does she not reach out to her?
4. Many physically and verbally abused women find it difficult to leave their abusers behind. What is it about Nut that keeps so many women locked in his grasp despite it all?
5. What does Trina Boo mean when she calls Camille her *wife-in-law*?
6. Chu's mother, Ms. Abani, was given the ultimatum of marrying into a polygamous family with Chu's father.

Although she decided not to, many women today decide to continue in relationships fully aware that their partners are also involved with other people. What do you think contributes to this growing trend? Will sharing partners ever subside, or is this a solution to today's new dating scene?

7. How does Almond Joy fill a void after Peaches leaves Nut? How does Joy's disappearance affect Nut and the other women?

8. Was there a clear way out of Camille's desperate situation? If so, what was it?

9. Do you see Rob and Camille ever having a romantic relationship?

10. Should Camille feel guilty about dating her first love's best friend, if she does decide to pursue a relationship?

ABOUT THE AUTHOR

Kia DuPree, a former assistant editor at St. Martin's Press, received the Fiction Honor Book Award from the Black Caucus of the American Library Association for her debut, self-published novel, *Robbing Peter*, in 2005. Kia's short story, "Lost One," was recently included in number one *Essence* best-selling author Shannon Holmes's anthology *Hood 2 Hood*, which was released in March 2008.

Kia holds a BA in mass media arts from Hampton University, as well as an MA in English from Old Dominion University. Kia currently resides in Washington, D.C., with her husband and son.